THE MYSTERY OF
THE BOGUS BLOOMS

Sally Handley

Cover design by:Carol Monahan Design (https://
www.carolmonahandesign.com)
Library of Congress Control Number:
Printed in the United States of America

Dedicated to

Gardeners Everywhere

1 THE ECO-FAIR

"You're going to love the planetarium!" Holly Donnelly grabbed her sister Ivy's arm the moment the stoplight turned red, rushing her across Memorial Drive.

"Slow down," Ivy said as she struggled to keep up. "Do we really need to run?"

Holly giggled as they reached the opposite side of the street and stopped directly in front of the entrance to the new Pineland Park Community College Planetarium.

"Sorry. You know me. I'm just so excited about this Eco-Fair." Holly grasped the handle and pulled open the gleaming glass doors of the new building.

"I get that," Ivy said, "but it's only set-up day. We may have to get you a sedative tomorrow when you do your presentation."

"Oh, c'mon. I'm not that bad. But I really am thrilled they asked me–an English professor–to be a speaker!"

"Doesn't surprise me. I don't know anyone who knows more about home-composting than you," Ivy said as her sister pressed the elevator button.

"Seriously? There are about a million people who know

more than I do–people who could address the scientific aspects of composting better than I can."

"Yes," Ivy nodded as the elevator doors opened, and the sisters stepped inside. "But you've been composting since you bought your house and started gardening more than twenty years ago. Didn't you say home gardeners are one of the targets of this fair? I know I'd rather hear from a fellow gardener than from a scientist."

"I suppose so," Holly said as the elevator started its ascent. Suddenly she grasped her sister's forearm, her mouth widened in a huge grin. "I forgot to tell you. I got the Garden Club of New Jersey at Rutgers University to advertise the fair on their website. Can you believe it?"

Ivy smirked. "Can I believe it? Please. You can talk anyone into anything when you're really excited about it."

Holly gave her head a slight shake. "Not always, but I have to say, this was an easy sell. A few Rutgers professors are invited speakers on some of the panels. Ah, here we are."

The sisters stepped out onto the new building's second level mezzanine. A hum of activity filled the space as students and faculty moved about, arranging tables, mounting posters on exhibit display boards and easels, and installing computers and video monitors in preparation for tomorrow's big event.

In spite of the many visuals competing for her attention, Ivy's gaze swept upward, as she admired the two-story glass walls that arced in a semicircle to form the outer wall of the mezzanine and the building's façade. "This is really impressive."

"I know," Holly smiled, her head bobbing like a dashboard doll's.

"Professor Donnelly," a voice called from behind.

Holly recognized the rich baritone before she even turned around. "Doctor Miller, how good to see you." She extended her hand, and the tall man pulled her in for a hug instead of a handshake.

"Isn't this wonderful?" he asked, unable to conceal the pride he felt as he surveyed the beehive of activity around them. His white lab coat contrasted with his sun-tanned complexion. At least 6'2" tall, the doctor towered over the two sisters.

"Yes, it is quite wonderful," Holly agreed, "and we owe it all to you."

"Now, now," he said, waving an index finger at her, "you know we have many, many people to thank for this fabulous facility—yourself included. Don't think I don't know about all of your work in getting publicity and sponsors for this event."

"Oh, that was nothing." Holly gave her hand a dismissive wave. "The program sold itself. You, on the other hand ..."

Doctor Miller held up his hand, stopping Holly mid-sentence. He smoothly turned to Ivy. "I didn't know you were a twin," he said, looking from one sister to the other.

Holly laughed. "We're not twins. Just sisters. Ivy, meet Doctor Miller, head of the Physical Sciences Department."

"A pleasure to meet you," Ivy said, shaking the doctor's hand.

"The pleasure is all mine." The doctor once again looked from Ivy to Holly and back again. "Really, the resemblance is remarkable." Turning back to Ivy, he asked, "Are you a professor also?"

"No." Ivy shook her head. "I was a nurse. Retired now."

"Is that right? You know we have a shortage of experienced nurses to teach in our Nursing Program."

"No offense, Doctor, but teaching is Holly's thing, not mine. Besides I am very happily retired." Before the doctor could continue his recruitment pitch, she quickly changed the subject. "This facility is awesome. Congratulations!"

"Thank you. Yes, everyone is so proud of this building. It's the first new construction on campus in twenty–five years."

"And this two-day fair is our first opportunity to showcase it," Holly added.

"Exactly." The scientist nodded, a satisfied smile on his face as he again surveyed the exhibit space.

A young man carrying a clipboard approached. His ice-blue eyes peered through black, nerdy glass frames that were all the rage, a trend Holly couldn't understand.

"Doctor Miller. Sorry to interrupt, sir." The young man's brow wrinkled with concern.

"What is it, Rodney?" Dr. Miller asked.

"One of the Astronomy panelists had a death in the family. We need to find a replacement quickly. The committee would like your input."

The doctor shrugged and let out a sigh. "Ladies, duty calls. I'll see you both tomorrow morn ..."

An ear-piercing scream from the other side of the exhibit hall cut him off.

"What now?" the doctor asked, turning to the empty space beside him. Holly and Ivy had already headed in the direction of the scream.

2 VANDALISM

When Holly and Ivy reached the far end of the exhibit space, they had to weave their way through a crowd that started to form in front of the last exhibit booth. Ivy gasped when they were finally able to see the reason for the scream.

"Oh no," Holly said as she viewed the totally trashed display.

Red spray paint obscured the words and images on the posters. A laptop sat on the floor, its screen shattered. Torn papers lay everywhere.

A boy sat on the floor, his back against the display booth, shaking his head in disbelief. Two girls were locked in an embrace, crying inconsolably.

"Who would do this?" Ivy whispered.

"I don't know," Holly replied. "I can't imagine ..." She stopped as the girls pulled apart. She recognized Ariana Alvarez, her landscaper's daughter.

"Ariana," Holly said walking over to where the girls stood, seemingly unable to move.

When Ariana saw Holly, she rushed into her arms. "Oh, Ms. Donnelly. We worked so, so ..." She broke down and began to sob, unable to complete her thought.

"What in the world ..." Dr. Miller exclaimed as he arrived on the scene and observed the damages. Sighing, he turned to the students milling about and said, "Please get back to work now, so we can take care of this."

Only a few students peeled off from the crowd.

"Go on now." The doctor made a shooing motion and the rest of the group finally disbursed. He turned to Rodney. "Go get a security guard."

"But Dr. Miller, you need to ..."

"I *need* to talk to these students, Rodney."

"But, sir, the Astronomy panel ..."

The doctor's expression hardened. "I can take care of that later. Now go get security over here."

Rodney's face reddened. He grasped his clipboard, pivoted, and rushed off.

Dr. Miller walked over to Holly and Ariana. "This is your exhibit?" he asked.

"Yes," Ariana sniffled. "All three of us worked on it." She pointed to the other weeping girl who sank down beside the boy. "We have one other team member. She couldn't be here today."

"Come on over here," Dr. Miller motioned to them and turned back to Ariana. "What are your names?" he asked.

"I'm Ariana Alvarez. This is Debby Lewandowski and Luis Navarro. Brittany Holzman is the other team member.

Dr. Miller glanced over at the destroyed computer, then up at the vandalized posters. "It looks like your project involved GMOs. Is that right?"

Ariana stifled a sob. "Yes. We worked on this over two summers." Tears again filled her eyes.

"Do you have all of your work backed up?" Dr. Miller asked.

"Yes. At home."

Dr. Miller smiled. "Okay, then. You three go home and get your back-up. I'm going to assign a Teaching Assistant from the Studio Arts Department to work with you to reprint all your materials. And we'll get you a laptop from the computer department to replace this one."

"For real?" Ariana said, her face brightening just a bit.

Dr. Miller laughed a deep belly laugh. "For real."

"Thank you so much," Ariana said as Debby came up beside her. "Yes, thank you," she echoed.

Luis extended his hand to Dr. Miller. "We can't tell you how much we appreciate this."

As Luis shook Dr. Miller's hand, Rodney returned with two security guards.

"Rodney," the doctor said, "get Tanisha Jefferson and tell her I have a special assignment she needs to work on today."

A frustrated Rodney frowned. "But, sir ..."

"ASAP, Rodney. And I also want a new booth set up nearer the entrance for this display."

"Sir!" Rodney appeared absolutely flabbergasted at this last request.

"Just do it, Rodney." Dr. Miller turned to the two security guards, but then paused and looked back at Ariana, Debby and Luis who appeared dumbfounded by what they just heard him say. "What are you three still doing here? Go get your back-up and return here as fast as you can."

"Yes sir," Ariana said. She and Debby quickly grabbed their bags as Luis looped his arms through his backpack. The trio scurried off.

As Dr. Miller began talking to the security guards, Holly looked at Ivy and shrugged. "Well, that's that, I guess. Come on. Let's go turn in the flash drive with my presentation on it and see the auditorium where I'll be presenting tomorrow. Then we can go home."

As they headed to the auditorium, Ivy glanced at her watch. "It's already three o'clock. Isn't Kate arriving around four?"

"Oh, gosh I almost forgot that. We better get a move on."

As they rounded the exhibit mezzanine, they spotted Ariana and her friends waiting for the elevator. Luis appeared angry and rather animated as he spoke to the two girls. As they drew nearer, the elevator door opened and the three students got inside. Before the door closed, they heard Luis say, "You know who did this, Ariana."

3 CATCHING UP

Nick refilled Kate's wine glass with the last of the Prosecco, then got up and got Holly another beer from the refrigerator.

"Thank you, Nick," Kate said. She shot Holly a teasing grin as he sat down and poured the beer into her pilsner glass. "You're a lucky woman, my friend."

Holly aimed a contented smile at her husband. "To borrow one of his favorite phrases, tell me something I don't know."

"Okay, okay. Enough of that," Nick said, though he looked quite pleased at the exchange. "So, you all set for tomorrow?" he asked Holly.

"Yes. All set."

"Have you seen the new planetarium, Nick?" Ivy asked.

"Not yet. I'm going to try to sneak out and catch Holly's presentation tomorrow, but it all depends on what's going on at the precinct."

"I thought you were going to retire," Kate said.

"Yeah, I'm thinkin' about it," he replied.

"Really?" Ivy said, her tone skeptical. "I remember you said that when you got married a few years ago."

"Did I?" Nick stood up. "Come on, Lucky. Time for a walk."

Holly laughed as their border collie jumped up from where she was lying by the door and followed Nick out of the kitchen to the entrance hall. "Excellent evasive skills, don't you think?"

"I heard that," Nick said as he closed the front door.

Kate took a sip of Prosecco. "Seriously though–isn't he getting a little old for detective work? Don't you worry something will happen to him?"

Clearly annoyed at the question, Holly glared at her friend. "How could you even ask me that question? You know me better than that." She stood up, grabbed the dessert plates and silverware, and dropped them in the sink with a loud clatter. Yanking the dishwasher door open, she said, "You're lucky we've been friends for thirty years or I'd send you back home to the Catskills right now."

Kate's eyes widened in alarm at her friend's uncharacteristic reaction. "Holly, I'm sorry. I didn't mean ..."

"I know." Holly's shoulders sagged as she gripped the edge of the counter. "Sorry I snapped at you." She turned to face her friend. "It's just that I do worry about him–all the time, but ..." She paused and let out a loud sigh.

"A man's gotta do what a man's gotta do, right?" Ivy filled in the blank.

"Right," Holly replied as she gave the dishwasher on-button a punch. "Let's just go sit in the living room and talk about something pleasant."

"Sounds good to me." Kate stood up, looking relieved. She grabbed her wine glass and led the way. Selecting the wing chair nearest the fireplace, she asked, "Want me to add another log?"

"I'll do it," Ivy volunteered.

Holly sat on the couch. "So, what's new in Reddington Manor?"

Kate shrugged. "Not much." After a moment, she smiled and moved to the edge of the chair. "Oh yeah, I almost forgot. Benny and Razor send their regards."

"Benny and Razor!" Ivy chuckled." How are those guys?"

"Well, they said life has never again been as exciting as when you two were last up to visit. I mean, a murder, a kidnapping and a wedding. Not everyday occurrences up by us. They want to know when you're coming back for another visit."

"I suppose we could come up to see the foliage in October," Holly said. "But I hope they don't think that murders and kidnappings occur wherever I go."

Kate nearly spit out her Prosecco. "Sorry, but they kinda do."

"Yeah," Ivy agreed. "You know, when I heard that scream this morning, I actually was terrified we were going to find a body."

"What?" Kate sputtered. "What happened this morning?"

"Oh, it really wasn't anything," Holly gave her head a slight shake.

Ivy ignored her and looked over at Kate. "So here's what happened."

Kate smiled as Ivy began to recount the vandalized student display, but midway through the telling, her face turned deadly serious.

"So, this project was about GMOs? Was this project for or against them?" she asked.

"We don't know. We'll find out tomorrow when the students take the stage and present their project to the audience."

"Well, I'll tell you this," Kate said, "if their project found any supporting evidence to show the harmfulness of GMOs, I guarantee you a company like Sanmarto was behind the sabotage."

"Sabotage! Seriously, Kate," Holly scoffed, "you really think a Fortune 500 company would vandalize a community college student science fair project?"

"Absolutely! Those corporations are capable of

anything–especially destroying the environment."

"I've only read a few articles about GMOs," Ivy interjected. "Genetically Modified Organisms, right?"

"Right," Holly replied.

Ivy looked at Kate apologetically. "Well, from what I read, they're not all completely bad."

"Oh, that's what they'd like you to believe, but they haven't done enough research on the effect on the surrounding ecosystems where GMO plants are being grown. And just like the pharmaceutical companies that swear new drugs they put out are not addictive, then years later–like with the opioids ..."

"Oh, stop!" Holly held up her arms, forming a time-out signal. "Don't start with the pharmaceutical companies." She scowled at her sister. "You see what you started?"

It was Kate's turn to glare at Holly. "Well, you can stick your head in the sand, Pollyanna, but I'm telling you now, if those kids conducted an experiment that did find evidence proving something negative about GMOs, you can bet a big GMO company like Sanmarto would want to silence them." Kate pounded the arm of the wing chair with her fist.

"Kate," Holly said, "those kids haven't presented their findings yet. How would Sanmarto, not even a New Jersey firm, find out about it?"

"They have spies." Kate jutted her chin out combatively.

"That's it," Holly said jokingly. "I'm cutting you off. No more Prosecco for you."

"Laugh if you want." Kate sat back and crossed her arms. "I can't wait to hear the presentation tomorrow. We'll see who's laughing then."

****

"So, what was all the shouting about?" Nick asked as he got into bed. "I could hear you half-way down the street."

"Oh, just Kate on one of her alarmist rants about GMOs," Holly replied as she turned out the light on her night table.

"Correct me if I'm wrong, but haven't I heard you

complain about GMOs?" Nick asked.

"No, you're not mistaken," Holly admitted, nestling back into her pillow. "I do think that GMOs are harmful to the environment, but Kate was in full-on conspiracy theory mode."

"What brought that on?"

"Ivy told her about one of the student projects that got vandalized this morning, and you know Kate. She claimed a Fortune 500 company was probably behind it. She actually said they had spies."

Nick let out a small, throaty laugh. "Yeah, that does sound a tad unlikely."

"Exactly," Holly replied, but then she remembered the ominous expression on Luis' face when he said, "*You know who did this.*" She began to wonder if Kate might possibly be onto something, but then Nick shut off his bedside light and reached for her.

4 COMPOSTING

The next morning Holly smiled at the audience as she wrapped up her presentation on the benefits of home composting. "Yes, absolutely, you can toss used paper towels and napkins into your compost bin. Remember, paper is made from wood, a totally biodegradable item. I'm sorry that we don't have time for more questions, but feel free to email me. Don't forget to go to the on-line library of handouts for a list of all the items you can safely compost. Thank you for attending this session, and good luck with all of your home gardening projects."

The audience applauded as the moderator stepped up to the podium. "That was great, Professor Donnelly. I think you may have persuaded many here today that home composting is easy, and the results are so beneficial to the environment. You've convinced me to give it a try in my own small backyard. Let's hear it again for Professor Donnelly."

Holly grinned, waved and headed off stage as the moderator reminded everyone to fill out their session evaluation sheets. As she walked down the short flight of steps from the stage, she was greeted by Nick, Ivy and Kate.

"Pitch perfect," Kate said, tapping her friend on the shoulder.

"Yes," Ivy agreed. "I heard one woman behind me say she got more out of this session than the last three garden shows she went to."

"Yep, great job, honey," Nick said, kissing her on the cheek.

Thanks," Holly glowed at the praise. "I'm so glad you were able to get away from work."

"Slow crime day." Nick frowned as his phone vibrated. "I spoke too soon." He glanced at the cell screen. Giving her another kiss on the cheek, he said, "Sorry, I gotta run. See you tonight."

As he headed to the exit doors, Holly made eye contact with Kate. Wordlessly, her expression made clear that she did not want to hear any remarks about his retiring.

"Let's go see Ariana's display," Ivy said. "I only caught a glimpse as we got off the elevator."

"Great idea," Kate replied. "I'd like to see it too."

"I have to say, they ended up with a much better location than where they originally were, way back in the corner," Holly said.

"For sure." Ivy nodded as they headed out of the auditorium. "Do you think Dr. Miller did that on purpose?"

"What do you mean?" Holly asked.

Ivy lowered her voice. "I've been thinking about what Kate said yesterday."

"Glad someone's listening to me," Kate muttered under her breath.

"Well," Ivy continued, "do you think maybe there is something controversial about their project, and Dr. Miller was aware of that and that's why he moved them to a more visible spot?"

"Or maybe he's just aware of some student rivalry, and

he didn't want to risk their project being vandalized again," Holly said.

"Hmpf," was Kate's only comment.

"Ms. Donnelly!" A joyful Ariana ran up to Holly and hugged her.

"Congratulations!" Holly hugged her back. "The display looks great."

"Did you guys have to work all night to get this done?" Ivy asked as she surveyed the posters on DNA and genetic modification.

"No," Debby replied, her smile as broad as Ariana's. "Just until midnight."

"Oh, to be young again!" Kate grinned. "I'm very much looking forward to your presentation this afternoon."

"This is my friend, Kate," Holly said. "She's an herbalist and very interested in this topic. Kate, this is Ariana, Debby, Luis, and—I'm sorry—we didn't meet you yesterday."

"I'm Brittany," the fourth team member replied without a trace of a smile. Dressed in black cargo pants, a black sweatshirt and combat boots, she sported dark-framed glasses similar to Rodney's. Her pitch-black bangs were cut short, reaching only the middle of her forehead, another style trend Holly disliked.

"So where do you stand on the GMO debate?" Brittany eyed Kate with a somber, borderline menacing, expression.

"Oh, I'm totally against GMOs," Kate replied. "I think they're the worst thing that's happened to agriculture since locusts."

Though it couldn't be characterized as a smile, a slight flicker crossed Brittany's lips. "We'll have to talk later," she said, never taking her eyes off Kate.

"I'd love that," Kate replied.

"Well, we better get going before the lunch line gets too long," Holly said. "Again, congratulations to you all and good luck with the presentation."

"Thank you," Ariana said. "We'll look for you in the audience."

Once they were out of earshot, Ivy asked, "That girl, Brittany—is she what they call 'Goth'?"

"Yes," Holly said. "Was it just me, or was there something odd about that girl?"

"Oh, I don't know," Kate said. "You can't judge a book by its cover. I know some really nice Goths."

"I'm not talking about her being a Goth," Holly said. "She just didn't seem a good fit with those other three kids."

"Yeah," Ivy nodded. "I don't really see her as part of that group."

"Well, it doesn't matter what we think," Kate said. "In life, lots of people who aren't alike have to work together. After all, isn't that what the college experience is all about?"

"You're right," Holly conceded as they got on the box lunch line, but as she reached for a box labeled 'Veggie Wrap', she couldn't help wondering why Brittany was absent from the set-up yesterday.

5 AN ANONYMOUS CALLER

"Do we have enough time to view some more of the exhibits before the student presentations begin?" Ivy asked, then took another bite out of her chocolate chip cookie.

Kate glanced at her watch. "We have about fifteen minutes."

"That's not much time." Holly placed her crumpled napkin inside her lunch box and stood. "The auditorium will start to fill up early, and I don't want to get stuck standing for the presentations. Let's go."

As they rounded the mezzanine, Ivy stopped to view a display on organic gardening. Holly followed her. As they picked up a handout on companion plants, Kate took Holly by the arm.

"Something's up over at Ariana's booth," she said, "and it doesn't look good."

Holly and Ivy quickly turned and followed Kate over to where Dr. Miller and two other men, one in a lab coat, stood talking to Ariana and her teammates. No one was smiling.

From where they'd stopped to observe, they couldn't hear what was being said until Brittany stomped her foot and yelled, "This is bullshit!"

"Uh-oh," Ivy whispered. "What do you think this is about?"

"I have no idea," Holly replied.

"Well, I want to know what's going on," Kate said and headed over to the booth.

"Oh, boy," Ivy said to her sister. "We better follow her, or she may end up in the middle of a brawl."

"Or start one." Holly grimaced.

Before they caught up with Kate, Dr. Miller, the two men and Ariana headed off in the opposite direction. Debby and Luis appeared crestfallen. Brittany, however, was pacing back and forth in front of their booth cursing.

"What happened?" Kate asked her.

"Somebody hacked Ariana's computer and viewed our presentation. That's what happened," she shouted.

"You need to calm down," Holly said, looking around at the faces of people staring at the angry student.

"Just start at the beginning." Kate said in a matter-of-fact tone of voice. Holly was relieved that her friend adopted a soothing tone. The girl didn't need anything that might further stoke her agitation.

Brittany's ordinarily pale complexion flushed scarlet as she clenched and unclenched her fists.

Again, in a gentle tone, Kate said, "If you tell us, maybe we can help."

A subdued Luis stepped forward. "An anonymous caller contacted the college's Legal Department."

Debby appeared on the verge of tears. "The caller said the college could face a lawsuit if we revealed our findings."

Kate's left eyebrow shot skyward as she turned to Holly. "You see?"

Before Holly could respond, Brittany snarled, "Well, if

Gree ...

"No," Debby said loudly, holding up both hands palms outward. "Don't say it, Brittany. You'll only get us disqualified."

"Yeah," Luis nodded. "Dr. Miller said he had a solution to propose. Let's see what that is before we do anything to jeopardize our entry completely."

Brittany glared at the pair for a moment, then turned and walked over to the glass wall of the mezzanine where she stared out at the street. Kate followed her.

Holly turned to Luis and Debby. "I'm so sorry this is happening to you." When they did not reply, she asked, "The man in the lab coat was Professor McNair, right? Who was the other man?"

"Yes. Professor McNair is our project advisor," Luis replied. "Dr. Miller introduced the other man as legal counsel for the college."

"Well, I know one thing for sure," Holly gave Luis' shoulder a reassuring squeeze. "Dr. Miller is very supportive of your project. I'm sure he'll come up with a solution."

"Yes, he came through for you yesterday," Ivy said. "Just try to stay calm until you hear what he's proposing. I'm sure it will all work out."

"Yeah, if Brittany doesn't blow it for us," Luis said, casting a look of disgust in her direction.

"I wish Ariana had never agreed to let her join our team." Debby appeared more sorrowful than disgusted.

"Why do you think she did that?" Holly asked. "We only just met her, but I have to admit she doesn't seem to be a good fit with the rest of your team."

Debby was about to reply, but then she exchanged a glance with Luis. "I don't know," she said, turning her gaze to the auditorium doors as they began to close. "Oh, no!" Her expression grew even more mournful. "The presentations are about to begin."

6 A CONFRONTATION

Kate walked over to where Brittany stood looking through the glass façade onto Memorial Drive below.

"I know we just met, and you have no reason to trust us, but my friends and I are on your side," she said.

Continuing to stare at the street, Brittany gave her head a slight shake. "Your friend is a professor here. She has to toe the party line."

"Maybe." Kate hesitated. "Maybe she doesn't feel quite as strongly as I do about the negative effects of GMOs, but she is committed to environmental issues. And I can tell you this. Holly is the most loyal friend anyone could ask for. If she's convinced you kids are being treated unfairly, she'll go to bat for you."

Brittany turned and faced Kate. "Look, our experiment proves a company –a well-known, highly regarded company– is lying. They claim their products have no GMOs, but we have proof they do."

Kate breathed in deeply and blew the air back out through her lips. "That's huge. And you were going to name the company in your presentation?"

"Yep."

It was Kate's turn to stare out the window.

"See," Brittany sneered. "You're all anti-GMOs, but even you're afraid of the companies that produce them."

Kate pursed her lips. "I'm not afraid of anyone," she said. "But I understand the college's concern about a lawsuit. Particularly if the results of your experiment are uncorroborated. Surely you can understand their concern."

"Oh, so let me get this straight." Brittany jeered. "You're not afraid, but you accept that the college, a purported bastion of academic inquiry, is afraid to go up against a corporation."

Kate sighed. "Be realistic. There are libel laws. If you defame a company, they're not going to sue you. They're going to sue the college. That doesn't mean there aren't other ways to handle a situation like ..."

The sound of shouting interrupted Kate. Brittany immediately took off at a run in the direction of their booth. Kate followed, arriving just in time to see Debby and Ivy helping Luis to his feet.

"What the hell?" Brittany huffed. Her gaze shifted from them to two students moving quickly in the direction of the auditorium. The backs of their T-shirts read 'GMOs Rock'. "Oh, hell no," she said and started to move in their direction. Kate stepped in front of her, blocking her path.

"Don't do this," Kate said, her tone pleading. "You'll only make matters worse."

Brittany tried to get around her but stopped when she saw the auditorium door close behind the pro-GMO pair. She turned around to face Luis. "What did the 'geek squad' want? Did they attack you?" Before he could answer she glowered at Holly. "Why aren't you calling for security?"

Holly grimaced. "Those two students said they saw your presentation time had been changed. They wanted to find out why."

"So, they knocked Luis on the floor?" Brittany's cheeks

flushed with color.

"No," Ivy replied, her expression apologetic. "That was my fault. The boy made a disparaging remark and Luis was about to–um–engage in physical contact. I grabbed his arm, and he slipped and fell. They had nothing to do with it."

"That's why we're not calling for security," Holly added.

Brittany's scowl grew more intense. "Why don't the three of you just leave us alone? You can't help us. All you want is to shut us up–calm us down and let those creeps win. I'll bet they were the ones who trashed our booth yesterday. And they'll get away with it, while we're being told to just behave and take the high road." She pounded her right fist into the palm of her left hand. "Well, I'm not going to let them get away with it."

"Brittany! Debby! Luis!" Ariana called from the hallway adjacent to the auditorium. "I need you to come with me. Hurry," she said, motioning for them to join her.

Luis and Debby immediately took off in her direction. Brittany cast a scornful glance back at Kate. "I just bet whatever they've come up with, it won't include telling the truth."

7 PRESENTATIONS

"What do you think she means by that?" Ivy asked as she, Holly and Kate stood watching the quartet disappear into the hallway.

Holly sighed. "I don't know, but while Ariana wasn't exactly exuding joy, she certainly didn't appear to have bad news. I'm sure Dr. Miller has come up with a way to resolve the problem."

"Based on what Brittany just told me, I'm not sure even King Solomon could come up with a solution that would please everyone." Kate shook her head.

"Why?" Ivy asked. "What did she tell you?"

"The experiment these kids conducted proves that a well-known company claiming to sell non-GMO products is lying."

"Oh wow," Holly said, her voice flat. "So that's what this is all about."

"Yes." Kate nodded.

"What company is it?" Ivy asked.

"She wouldn't tell me."

Holly let out a heavy sigh. "That's good. She may be a

loose cannon, but I guess it stuck when Luis warned her not to say anything that would get them completely disqualified."

Kate shook her head. "I don't know. She's pretty angry. If the school tries to whitewash their findings, she may just go rogue."

"She does seem a bit radical," Ivy said. "But really, what could she do?"

"She could go to the press," Kate replied.

"That would not be good." Holly gave her head a slight shake.

"Well, there's nothing we can do about it." Ivy looped her arm through her sister's. "Let's go grab some seats and catch the other student presentations."

****

After the applause subsided, Kate turned to Holly. "What a load of crap that was. That presentation endorsed GMOs without addressing any of the environmental concerns. I wouldn't be surprised if they didn't get help from Sanmarto's marketing department," she said with disgust.

Holly shrugged. "I admit the presentation was a bit slick for college students. But they did make some valid points about the potential for GMOs to increase crop production and reduce world hunger."

"Yeah, while poisoning the earth and killing off dozens of species ..."

"Shh!" Holly cautioned as Professor Platnick, a bio-chemistry professor, stepped up to the podium to announce the next speakers.

"Our next presentation is entitled "The Growth Rate of Poa pratensis in Pure Humus," the professor announced.

At the conclusion of the presentation, Holly leaned

toward Kate and whispered, "I know why I majored in English and not one of the sciences. I didn't understand most of what they were talking about."

Kate replied with a quiet chuckle. "Too bad. It really was a brilliant presentation."

Professor Platnick again stepped to the podium. "Our next presenters will talk to us about their work on combining recycled objects with more durable material for use in the production of 3-dimensional printing."

"Ugh!" Holly uttered under her breath.

Ivy poked her in the ribs. "Really, you're worse than a six-year-old."

Kate nodded in agreement. Holly waggled her head, slid down in her seat and yawned as the next presentation began. Twenty minutes later, she awoke, startled by thunderous applause.

Professor Platnick returned to the podium. "Okay, we're going to take a short break before our final presentation. Everyone please be back in your seats in ten minutes."

"Holly, did you really sleep through that entire presentation?" Ivy frowned at her sister and shook her head in disgust. "You really are pathetic."

"Sorry," Holly apologized, appearing genuinely chagrined.

"Well, I suppose we can cut you some slack," Kate grinned. "You did do a presentation this morning."

"That's right," Holly sat up and rolled her shoulders. "I worked today."

"Really?" Ivy's voice dripped skepticism. "Or are you tired because last night you and Nick ..."

"Ivy!" Holly cut her off and jumped to her feet. "I'm going to the ladies' room." As she made her way across the row to the aisle, she could hear Kate and Ivy giggling.

Out on the mezzanine, Holly headed to the restrooms located in the hallway adjacent to the auditorium. She grimaced when she saw the line spilling out of the ladies' room door. No choice but to get behind the last person. Within seconds, an older woman got behind her, quickly followed by a pair of chattering female students.

As the line edged forward, Holly's ears perked up when she heard one of the girls directly behind the older woman say, "I can't believe they're getting to present after all."

The 'they' could only be Ariana's team. Holly mustered all the self-control she could not to turn around.

"Yeah," another girl's voice replied. "And how'd they manage to get that display back up so fast?"

"And score the prime booth location up front!" the first girl's voice added.

Holly reached the ladies' room door. As she turned to step over the threshold, she cast a casual glance at the line behind her. The two chattering girls wore 'GMOs Rock' T-shirts.

8 DNA

The lights in the auditorium dimmed as Holly shimmied down the row, dodging the knees of people already in their seats. As she took her seat between Kate and Ivy, Professor Platnick tapped the microphone.

"Okay. Now for the last presentation of the day. This team of four students conducted a two-year long study of GMOs and they are eager to present their findings," he said. Ariana, Luis and Debby took their seats and smiled as their names were announced. "A fourth member of the team, Brittany Holzman, is unable to participate in today's presentation, but has been a vital part of the project."

Kate elbowed Holly and whispered. "Didn't I tell you even Solomon couldn't come up with a solution to please everyone?"

"Probably best she's not up there." Holly frowned.

Ivy leaned closer to her sister. "I hope she's not outside calling *The New York Times*," she said as Ariana approached the podium.

Adjusting the microphone, Ariana began. "Today, when you go to the supermarket you may see "No GMOs" on the labels of many products. But did you know that there are only eleven commercially available genetically modified crops in the United States?" Ariana paused as the audience audibly reacted and the list of crops appeared on the screen.

"I didn't know that," Ivy whispered to Holly.

"Yeah." Holly nodded. "I figured corn and soybeans, but alfalfa and sugar beets?"

Kate leaned over. "Even I didn't realize it was just eleven crops." She looked back at the screen. "Apples and potatoes I would expect, but alfalfa, papaya and summer squash?"

"What really surprises me are canola and cotton," Ivy added.

Ariana smiled as she gave the audience time to digest the information on the slide. After a few moments, she continued, "In spite of the limited number of GMO products authorized for commercial use, over 50,000 products are advertised as non-GMO products." She pointed a remote control at the screen in back of her and a new slide appeared showing numerous ads and product labels claiming "No GMOs" for items ranging from vitamins to freeze-dried meat.

Again, Ariana gave the audience a few seconds to peruse the slide before she continued. "While the claim is certainly true, it is at best misleading. However, consumers purchasing those products are not harmed because they are, in fact, purchasing non-GMO products."

Ariana turned over the first page of her notes. "Our initial project did not set out to deal with this aspect of the GMO debate. We instead set out to determine the effects of genetically modified corn on a bee colony. In our presentation today, my partner Luis Navarro will describe the genetic modification process. Debby Lewandowski will discuss our initial hypothesis and describe our methodology. I will conclude by discussing the anomalies we found, and the unexpected discovery we made in the course of our experiment."

Ariana returned to her seat as Luis stepped up to the podium. "So what is genetic modification?"

"Uh-oh," Holly muttered. "Hope I don't' fall asleep again." Ivy poked her in the side.

"Let's begin with a description of deoxyribonucleic acid, better known as DNA," Luis continued. "Everyone in this audience has probably heard the term because of the many police TV shows and movies that rely on DNA to help identify criminals."

Photos of actors from the various CSI spinoffs appeared on the screen.

"Or you may have learned about DNA from all the companies that use it to help individuals trace their ancestry. But did you know that DNA is the molecule that carries genetic information for the development and functioning of an organism?"

Luis aimed the remote at the screen and a colorful diagram appeared. "Here you can see that DNA is made of two linked strands that wind around each other— a shape known as a double helix."

As Luis continued his part of the presentation, Holly was pleased she was able to follow his explanation of how new DNA is transferred into plant cells to produce a genetically modified plant.

"While there is much debate and controversy over the ethics of genetic modification, it was not the focus of our experiment. We simply set out to observe and report on the effects of genetically modified corn on an existing bee colony. Debby will now describe for you exactly how we did that."

As Luis returned to his seat, Ivy tapped her sister's arm. "Did you get all that?"

"Yes," Holly replied, clearly annoyed. "I'm not totally stupid."

"These kids are really good presenters," Kate whispered as Debby arrived at the podium.

Before Debby began, she clicked on the remote and a photo of a screened-in garden plot with a wood-framed beehive appeared.

"This is one of three screened-in garden areas we created for our project." She went on to explain how over two summers, the team planted corn seeds from three different companies, two with non-GMO seeds and one with GMO seeds. She described their careful efforts to maintain the separate environments in each of the screened-in plots, as well as their observation schedule and their record-keeping methodology.

"And now, Ariana will present our findings," the young scientist concluded.

Ariana returned to the podium. "So, here's what we learned." As she pointed the remote at the screen and clicked, the audience joined in a group moan as the screen went blank, and the lights went out.

9 THE RESULTS

The groan was followed by a hush that lasted only moments. A nervous buzz followed.

"Everyone, please remain in your seats."

Holly recognized Dr. Miller's voice, both calming and commanding. After a brief pause, his face appeared in the glow of his cell phone light. "We'll have this glitch corrected momentarily."

"What bad luck," Holly said.

"Hmpf." Kate clicked on her cell phone light, her expression of disbelief apparent. "You can't possibly believe this was bad luck. You honestly don't see this as just another attempt to stop the results of this experiment from being revealed?"

Ivy nodded. "Really, Holly. I'm with Kate. There's been a pattern of sabotage starting with the vandalizing of the booth yesterday."

"Ugh." Holly sank back in her seat. "I don't want to believe it, but I know you're both right." After a moment she sat up straight and pulled Kate and Ivy closer. In just above a whisper, she said, "I almost forgot. Listen to this."

She recounted the conversation between the "GMOs

Rock" girls that she overheard while standing in the ladies' room line.

"Sure sounds like they knew an awful lot about what happened," Kate said.

"Do you think they were responsible for trashing the booth?" Ivy asked.

Holly shrugged, "Maybe ..."

Suddenly the lights went on. Dr. Miller stood at the podium. "Thank you all for your cooperation in remaining seated during that–uh–unscheduled intermission."

A polite titter rewarded the scientist's attempt to lighten the mood and re-assure the audience.

"I have a few remarks I was saving for after this presentation, but I feel it may be more important for me to deliver them before Ms. Alvarez resumes her report."

Dr. Miller paused for effect and the auditorium grew silent. "This team made some surprising discoveries in their work–the often-serendipitous result of true scientific inquiry. Their findings have the potential to seriously impact some of the companies involved."

Again, Dr. Miller paused and gazed pointedly at the audience before continuing. "The team has agreed to keep the names of the companies confidential as they reveal those findings. With the advice of legal counsel and the consent of Ms. Alvarez's team, the college will turn over the team's carefully documented data for further study to the three government agencies responsible for regulating the safe use of genetically modified organisms–the U.S. Department of Agriculture's Animal and Plant Health Inspection Service, better known as APHIS, the EPA, and the Food and Drug Administration."

Turning back to where Ariana, Luis and Debby sat, he smiled. "Now, Ms. Alvarez. It's your moment."

Even from where they sat near the back of the auditorium, Holly could see Ariana take a deep breath before she stood and returned to the podium.

"As Debby explained earlier, we established three separate screened-in plots for our experiment. In only one, we used GMO seeds. Each plot contained a wooden beehive. Weekly during the growing season we checked the beehive for observable behavioral changes including: locomotion, reproduction, and feeding behavior or foraging." Ariana pointed the remote at the screen. "Here are the results."

Ariana paused, giving the audience a moment to take in the data on the screen.

"Oh wow!" Ivy whispered. "Do you see that?"

"See what?" Holly said. "It's all Greek to me."

"Don't you see ..." Kate began to explain, but Ariana resumed speaking.

"In accordance with legal counsel, we've identified the three companies whose seeds we used as Companies A, B and C. Companies A and B produce non-GMO seeds, while Company C produces genetically modified seeds."

Using a laser pointer, Ariana highlighted the results for Companies B and C. "Like us, you may be surprised to notice that the results for Company B's non-GMO seeds and Company C's genetically modified seeds are very nearly the same."

A student in the front row, wearing a GMOs Rock T-shirt raised his hand. Without waiting to be called on he shouted, "How do you know you didn't make a mistake?"

Ariana turned off the laser pointer and calmly addressed the questioner. "We actually worried that we made a serious error in our process. So, we re-examined every aspect of our experiment, including a thorough examination of the screening of the plots to ensure they had not been damaged and contaminated."

"So, you self-checked your own work?" the questioner scoffed.

"Yes," Ariana replied," but then we consulted with Professor McNair, our advisor for the project. In our meeting with him, Debby had an insight and asked the Professor if it was possible that Company B's seeds actually were genetically modified."

Once again, an agitated buzz swept across the auditorium as the audience reacted to the question.

After a moment, Ariana continued. "Professor McNair then assisted us in testing Company B's seeds." She explained in detail the methodology used. When she finished, she once again aimed the remote at the screen. "The result showed conclusively that Company B's seeds contained recombinant DNA. In other words, they were genetically modified."

At this point the auditorium erupted into applause. Ariana returned to her seat. Dr. Miller once again stepped up to the microphone. As the applause continued, he extended his arm in a gracious sweep to the three students who were smiling, appearing quite pleased by the audience reaction.

"Okay now," Dr. Miller said in an attempt to quiet the auditorium. "I'd like to introduce Professor McNair, the bio-chemistry professor who acted as advisor to this team."

To another wave of applause, a short, balding, bespectacled man, wearing a lab coat appeared from the wings and made his way across the stage. Dr. Miller stepped aside as Professor McNair got behind the podium."

"Thank you. Thank you," he began. "I just want to say that it was my privilege to advise this team of future scientists. They did all of the hard work associated with scientific inquiry–work that is painstaking and frequently boring, but oh so necessary to the advancement of science."

McNair cast an appreciative smile back at the team.

"What I found remarkable about this team is that when they did not get the results they anticipated, they didn't stop. They wanted to know why and that is what makes them exemplary scientists. This is a proud day for Pineland Park Community College."

10 CONGRATULATIONS

"I think they have to take first place in the competition," Ivy said as she, Holly and Kate slowly made their way toward the aisle to join the crowd spilling out of the auditorium.

"I'm just relieved they got to present their results," Holly said.

Kate huffed. "I'm grateful they finished their presentation without someone blowing up the auditorium."

Holly took a deep breath. "Really, Kate? Must you always think of the worst possible scenario?"

Kate glared back. "Come on. You still think those lights went out accidentally and had nothing to do with the fact that Ariana was just about to reveal the results of their project? Don't be naïve."

"I wasn't worried about anything as extreme as a bombing," Ivy said, "but you have to admit, all of the things that happened yesterday and today could not have been coincidental."

"Well, it's over," Holly said. "Ariana and her team can relax. It's now in the hands of the government agencies."

"Oh goody!" Kate said in a sarcastic tone. "I'm sure they'll take care of everything."

"I didn't realize you were such a cynic, Kate," Ivy remarked.

"When it comes to our food supply, I do not trust the government to make the right decisions–especially not if large corporations are involved and there's money to be made," Kate replied, scowling.

When they finally passed through the exit doors out onto the mezzanine, Holly spotted Brittany leaning against the glass wall, her expression sullen. "Look who's over there."

"I'm going to go talk to her. I'll meet you at the booth," Kate said.

Holly sighed as her friend separated from them. "I don't know if that's such a good idea."

"Well, wouldn't you like to hear her side of the story?" Ivy asked. "I know I'm curious."

"You know her side of the story," Holly replied. "I'm sure she refused to participate in the presentation when they weren't allowed to announce the name of the company fraudulently claiming their corn seeds do not contain GMOs when they do."

"Yes, but I want to know what she's planning to do about it. Don't you?" Ivy asked.

"To be honest, no, I don't," Holly replied. "Because if I did know, I'd feel obligated to report it to someone, and right now I just want to congratulate Ariana and go home."

"I get that," Ivy said as they got on the line of people waiting to speak to Ariana, Luis and Debby. "I can see Ariana. She looks ecstatic."

Holly peeked around the shoulder of the person in front of her. "Luis and Debby look pretty happy too."

After a five-minute wait, they finally reached the front of the line. They both hugged Ariana.

"Congratulations," Holly said. "You were great."

"Yes, I'm sure you'll take first place," Ivy added.

"I honestly don't care about that," Ariana replied. "I'm just happy we got to present. Honestly, I'm glad it's over." She leaned in close to Holly. "Can I maybe talk to you tomorrow?"

"Certainly," Holly said. "I have a class in the morning at ten, but I plan to attend the final ceremony for the presentation of the awards at noon."

Ariana nodded. "I'll meet you at your classroom–before the presentation."

Holly glanced back at the line of people waiting to speak to Ariana. "Well, don't let us keep you from your fans," she said as two students edged closer. Looping her arm through Ivy's, they moved away from the booth to an empty spot near the elevators.

"What did she say to you?" Ivy asked.

"She asked if she could talk to me tomorrow."

"She looked a little concerned. What do you think it's about?"

Holly frowned. "I don't know. Hey, do you see Kate?"

Ivy raised herself up on tiptoe and peered back to where they last saw her. "Yes, here she comes."

"Well?" Holly said when her friend reached them.

Kate looked around at the people standing nearby. "Let's get outside first."

When the elevator doors opened, the trio managed to squeeze in. Out on the street, Ivy said, "Okay, so what did you find out?"

Again, Kate looked over her shoulder. "Let's head to the parking garage." After they'd walked a block, and no one was within earshot, Kate said, "So, when Dr. Miller suggested they make their presentation without revealing the name of the company making the false claims, Brittany objected and refused to participate."

"Exactly what you said, Holly." Ivy tapped her sister's shoulder.

"Did she see the presentation?" Holly asked.

"No." Kate's eyes widened. "When she tried to enter the auditorium, she wasn't allowed in."

"Oh boy!" Ivy's eyes matched Kate's. "I'm sure that made her mad."

"Is she threatening to do anything rash–like call a reporter?" Holly asked. "Because , like I said, before that would not be good."

"Actually, she seemed uncharacteristically calm," Kate replied. "She claims she's over it, and she doesn't care what the college does."

"You believe her?" Holly appeared unconvinced.

"Yes. She says she's going to put her energy into an anti-GMO group she belongs to." Kate shrugged. "I told her I thought that was a great idea."

"That is a good idea," Ivy said as they reached the car. "She needs to channel that anger into something she can feel good about."

Holly clicked on her keychain fob and the car locks popped up. "I just hope she means it."

"Oh darn," said Kate as she got in the back seat and pulled out her cell phone. "My phone is dead. I forgot to charge it last night. Holly, can I borrow yours? I need to send a text."

"Sure." Holly handed Kate the phone over her shoulder. She started the car and as she drove to the exit she heard a ping. "Was that mine?"

"Yep. It's from Nick," Kate replied. "He says, 'What do you say I take you all out to dinner tonight, *amore, mio*?'" Kate snickered. "Isn't that adorable?"

Holly stopped the car and turned around. "Give me back my phone or you're staying home eating leftovers."

11 CAMPUS SECURITY

"So, what do you think, Nick?" Kate asked as the waitress walked away from the table.

"Do I think all the things that happened are a coincidence?" Nick hesitated, then gave his head a small shake. "No."

"But you don't think they're all part of some sabotage scheme orchestrated by the company that's lying about GMOs, do you?" Holly asked.

"No," he repeated, popping a forkful of creamy tiramisu into his mouth.

"What?" Kate exclaimed. "Who else would go to all that trouble to stop those kids from presenting their evidence?"

"There's the keyword–evidence. You don't have any." Nick frowned. "All you've got is your extreme bias against the company involved."

Holly aimed a satisfied smile at her friend. Kate glared back.

"You know he's right, Kate," Ivy interjected, her expression apologetic. "I mean, that's what you were complaining about the other day–the politicians who make all sorts of claims and lose their cases when they get to court because they don't have any evidence for the wild accusations they make."

Kate scowled, grabbed her wine flute and took a sip of Prosecco.

"Why don't we just eat and try to forget about all this–at least until we're through with dessert," Holly said.

Ivy picked up her dessert fork. "How's the tiramisu, Nick?"

"*Delizioso*," he replied.

"But not as good as *Zia* Maria's, I'll bet." Holly grinned as she plunged her fork into her slice.

Even Kate smiled. "Nobody's could be as good as your aunt's, Nick. Have you heard from your family lately?"

Nick nodded. "Yeah, Matteo called. When was that, Holly? Two, three weeks ago. Everybody's doing well. They want to know when we're coming back to Italy for another visit."

"That reminds me," Ivy said, "we haven't heard from Daniella about the intern program she was planning."

"You mean the one you and Kate were planning," Holly said.

"You have to admit it's a great idea." Kate finally dug into her dessert. "I mean, they could make a fortune offering internships for senior citizens at the vineyard."

"Right," Ivy nodded. "Who else has the money and time to spend a month or two in Tuscany just learning how to cook all things Italian?"

"And grow grapes and olives," Kate paused, "without GMOs."

Holly groaned. "Nick, get the check and let's go."

"Wait a minute," Kate held up her hand, palm outward. "I'm not finished. Besides, I have a question for Nick. If you were investigating the sabotage, or whatever you want to call it, where would you start?"

Nick shot her a penetrating stare.

Shifting uncomfortably under his gaze, she continued. "No, I'm serious now. I know this isn't a homicide, but if you were in charge of security at the College, what would you do? Would you talk to the company referred to as Company B?"

Nick sighed. "Look, I don't want to answer your question and tomorrow get an urgent phone call from Holly saying you're being held by the campus police, could I come and get you out."

"No, no." Kate shook her head. "I'm not going to do anything. Really. I'm just asking."

"Okay. I can tell you this. The fact that the students' work has been turned over to the federal agencies means it's totally out of the hands of campus security. It's now up to the Feds to investigate."

"But won't they focus only on the experiment's results? What about the vandalism? Isn't that up to campus security to investigate?" Kate asked, clearly frustrated by Nick's answer.

Nick shrugged, and once again let out a weary sigh. "Technically, yes, but honestly–I think it's highly unlikely they'll do that."

"So, whoever vandalized the presentation booth just gets away with it?" Kate asked. "That's it. It's over?"

"Well ..." Ivy put her dessert fork across her empty plate. "Maybe Holly will find out something from Ariana when she talks to her tomorrow. It did seem like she was worried about something when she asked if she could talk to you."

Nick faced Holly, whose turn it was to squirm under his laser gaze. She held her arms up in surrender. "The girl asked to talk to me. I have no idea what about. I am an English professor, you know. Maybe she needs advice on a paper she's writing. Whatever she wants to talk to me about may have nothing to do with this."

"And if it does ..." Nick prompted.

"I'll tell her to discuss it with campus security or go see Dr. Miller."

Nick leaned over and kissed her on the cheek. "Good answer."

12 CLOSING CEREMONIES

"Essays due on Tuesday," Holly said to her first period English Composition class. "Make sure you do a final proofread. And don't forget to use spellcheck and grammar check, because if you don't find your errors ..."

"You will," the class said in unison.

Holly laughed. "Have a great weekend."

As the students began to exit the room, Holly retrieved her thumb drive from the computer console, slipped her bag over her shoulder and followed. Out in the hall, she stopped and searched the faces of students passing by on their way to their next classes. No Ariana. Should she wait?

Reaching in her bag, she pulled out her phone. No texts or emails. Maybe Ariana forgot she'd asked to talk to her. Holly noted the time. The closing ceremonies would begin in less than half an hour. Maybe Ariana just got a late start and decided to go straight to the planetarium.

Taking one more glance around, Holly decided to do the same. She'd told Ivy and Kate she'd meet them outside the auditorium. She could always talk to Ariana after the ceremony.

When she reached the corridor on the ground floor, she spotted Ariana near the main entrance talking to a young man. With his back to her, Holly couldn't see who it was. She decided it was best to wait until they finished their discussion before she approached.

From where she stood, Holly could see that Ariana wasn't smiling. In fact, she appeared on the verge of tears. When the young man put his hand on her arm, she pulled away. As she did, he turned, his profile now visible. Rodney.

What could Dr. Miller's assistant be saying that would upset Ariana? Holly headed over, but before she reached the couple Rodney moved off in the opposite direction.

"Is everything all right?" Holly asked.

Ariana appeared confused, seeming almost surprised to see Holly. After a brief hesitation, she struggled to smile and said, "Yes. Yes, everything is all right."

"Did you forget you asked to come speak to me after my class today?"

Again, a look of uncertainty clouded Ariana's face. "No— um ..." She glanced at her watch. "I'm sorry. There was traffic ..."

"It's okay," Holly said in a calming voice. "You probably need to get to the auditorium. We can talk later if you like."

"That would be great. I better go."

Before Holly could say more, Ariana bolted out the door.

****

Ivy was standing alone in front of the auditorium doors when Holly arrived.

"Where's Kate?"

"She went inside to save us some seats," Ivy replied. "Did you talk to Ariana? I saw her get off the elevator, and she looked upset."

"I did see her, but we didn't get to talk. I got the impression something is definitely wrong. I offered to speak with her after the ceremony."

"Well, c'mon then. Let's go find Kate."

Inside the auditorium, they paused to scan the crowd.

"There she is," Ivy said, pointing to a row in the middle of the auditorium, where Kate stood waving to them.

As soon as they took their seats, Professor Platnick spoke from the podium. "Good morning, everyone. Please take your seats so we can begin."

"What did Ariana have to say?" Kate asked.

"Later," Holly whispered as the scientist waited for the audience to settle down. She looked past the Professor where the finalists were seated in two rows in the center of the stage.

"I don't see Ariana," she said in a low voice.

"Luis and Debby aren't up there either," Ivy added.

Professor Platnick tapped the microphone and began. "Since yesterday there have been some developments that I need to tell you about before we announce the winners of the Eco-Fair. Due to reasons I cannot disclose at this time, the project involving the effect of GMOs on bees has been withdrawn from the competition."

As an angry groan swept across the audience, Holly said, "Let's go."

13 JEOPARDY

Holly placed her Kindle on the coffee table and reached for her cell phone. Still no return text or email from Ariana. She had hoped to get some reading done while Ivy and Kate visited the garden center but found it impossible to concentrate. Try as she might, she couldn't come up with a good reason for Ariana's project being withdrawn from the competition.

Was that what Rodney had been talking to her about? Ariana said everything was all right. Clearly it wasn't. Did Ariana know her project was withdrawn when Holly talked to her? Why wouldn't she say so? Or was she upset about something else? But what else could Rodney have said to upset her?

Holly looked up at the ceiling and sighed. Was Kate right? Did the company lying about the GMOs somehow find out about the experiment and manage to discredit the project?

And what about Brittany? Where was she? In spite of what the girl told Kate–that she was going to focus her energies on an anti-GMO effort–had she done something to get the team project disqualified?

Holly shifted her gaze from the ceiling to the mantel clock. Only three. Too early to start dinner. But she had to do something to get her mind off the questions she couldn't answer. She got up, stuffed her phone in her back pocket and headed to the kitchen.

Grabbing a basket from the counter, she said, "C'mon, Lucky. Let's go pick some lettuce for tonight's salad."

Outside she cut enough leaves from the lettuce patch to fill the basket. On the way back to the kitchen, she heard her phone ping. She quickly retrieved the cell phone from her back pocket. A text from Ariana. "Can Luis, Debby & I come CU?"

She immediately responded. "Yes. When?"

"Now ok?"

"Yes."

Holly hurried back inside, Lucky on her heels. She pulled a colander out of the cupboard and dumped the lettuce into it. As she ran the water over the green leaves, she heard the front door open.

"I got you some tulip bulbs." Ivy held up a paper bag as she entered the kitchen. "I can plant them for you before I leave."

"Great," Holly said.

"Hear from Ariana?" Kate asked as she followed Ivy into the kitchen.

"Yes. She, Luis and Debby are on their way over."

"Oh good," Kate said. "We haven't been able to talk about anything else since we left."

"Well, we did discuss what we're planning to grow in our gardens next Spring." Ivy smiled.

"And I'm totally jealous of how much earlier Ivy can plant things in South Carolina," Kate said. "Do you realize their frost date is more than a month earlier than mine up in the Catskills?"

Lucky interrupted the conversation with a sharp bark a

split second before the doorbell rang.

"That was fast. Ariana only texted me a few minutes ago," Holly said heading to the entrance hall.

When she opened the front door, three somber faces greeted her. Both Ariana and Debby were red-eyed.

"Come in," Holly said, extending her arm in the direction of the living room.

Wordlessly, the subdued trio walked through the archway.

"Come sit down." Ivy pointed to the couch. "We're so sorry about what's happened to you."

When everyone was seated, Holly said, "So, tell us what happened."

Ariana inhaled deeply and began. "We had to get a signed release from each of the companies to use their seeds in our experiment. Professor McNair said he got a call this morning saying the signature on the form for Company B was forged and that's why we got disqualified."

"Another anonymous phone call?" Kate scoffed.

"He didn't say," Ariana replied.

Holly sat quietly as she processed the information. After a moment, she said, "I have to ask. Was it forged?"

Ariana just stared back, her chin trembling.

"We don't know," Debby answered for her.

"But it probably was," Luis said, his face registering annoyance.

"Don't say that, Luis," Debby chided. "We don't know for sure."

"Sorry, Debby," Holly said, "but I'd like to hear why he thinks that."

"Because it was Brittany who volunteered to get the

THE MYSTERY OF THE BOGUS BLOOMS

seeds and the signature," Luis said. "I was against having her on our team from the start."

Debby shot him an angry glance, putting an arm around Ariana who dabbed at her eyes with a tissue.

"How did she come to be on your team?" Ivy asked.

"She approached me about joining us for the project," Ariana said. "Since she never really spoke to any of us in class, I was surprised. But when she told me she had a relative who worked for Company B and she could get their seeds for us, I thought she was bringing something critical to the project, and so I said yes."

"So what did Brittany say about the forgery?" Kate asked.

"That's just it," Luis said, unable to conceal his anger. "Nobody can reach her."

"We tried calling," Debby added. "Ariana and I even went to her apartment, but she's gone. Her roommate said she hadn't seen her since Wednesday."

"The day of the presentations," Holly noted.

"Not that I'm defending her," Kate began, "but why would she jeopardize your entire project by submitting a forged document? She seemed genuinely anti-GMO, which means she'd want your project to succeed."

"Who knows what that freak was thinking?" Luis replied. "She probably just wanted to get the story in the newspapers and didn't care what happened after that." Here he turned to his teammates. "How many times did she say, 'This will make headlines'?"

"Still, she's not stupid," Kate countered. "She had to know that a forged document would get the project discredited sooner or later."

"Yes," Ivy agreed. "Not only would a forged signature mean you didn't have permission to use the seeds you had, you also couldn't prove the seeds were Company B's."

"Have you talked to Dr. Miller?" Holly asked.

"No," Ariana replied. "Professor McNair was the one who told us we were disqualified."

"Did you tell him about Brittany?" Holly asked.

"Yes. He said he was sorry, but there was nothing he could do. When we asked to talk to Dr. Miller, he said he 'wasn't available'." Luis put air quotes around the words.

Ariana sobbed, "I'm so sorry. It's all my fault. And now our scholarships to attend Rutgers next year may be withdrawn."

"Oh wow," Holly said barely above a whisper.

"That would be so unfair." Ivy looked at Holly. "Is there anything you can do?"

Holly looked from her sister to the three distraught students. "I don't know." After a few moments, she said, "I suppose I could talk to Dr. Miller."

"Do you think that would help?" Debby asked, just a trace of hope in her voice.

"Well, it can't hurt," Holly replied. "But I probably won't be able to reach him until Monday. Why don't you all go home and try to have a good weekend?"

"Yeah, like that's possible," Luis muttered.

"I know it won't be easy," Holly said as she got to her feet.

"Thank you," Ariana sniffled.

"Yes, thank you." Debby added.

Luis just nodded and frowned as they got up to leave.

"I'll let you know if I find out anything on Monday," Holly said as she walked them to the door.

"What a horrible mess!" Ivy said when Holly returned to the living room. "Do you honestly think Dr. Miller can help them?"

Holly shrugged. "I have no idea. Their credibility is shot. Unless they can find Brittany, I don't know how they can prove they didn't do anything wrong."

"Well here's what I want to know." Kate pursed her lips. "Who's behind these phone calls?"

14 MONDAY, MONDAY

As Holly drove to campus Monday morning, she reviewed the list of questions she, Ivy and Kate had prepared for her to ask Dr. Miller. For the first time ever, she was happy when Kate packed up her car and headed back to the Catskills Sunday morning. Her friend seemed unable to talk or even think about anything other than GMOs all weekend. When she wasn't discussing the topic, she was researching on the internet, looking for anti-GMO groups she could join. Like the proverbial dog with a bone, she just couldn't let go.

While Holly agreed with Kate about the harmful effects of GMOs on the environment, she didn't want to join a group or become an activist. The closer she got to campus, the less sure she was that she even wanted to insert herself into Ariana's problem.

After she parked and crossed the pedestrian bridge linking the parking deck to Pineland Hall, her courage faltered. She wondered if she was overstepping by going to Dr. Miller. Yes, they had a good relationship, but this situation really was none of her business. Was she jeopardizing that relationship by simply asking questions?

But how could she not try to help when these students' scholarships were on the line? Would they be able to afford the next two years at Rutgers University without that scholarship money? A bad outcome could affect their entire future. No, she had to try.

"Good morning, Rodney," Holly said when she reached Dr. Miller's outer office. She smiled at his nameplate prominently displayed at the front of his desk: Rodney M. Blakely III. She was certain he had it made for himself because none of the other administrative assistants had one.

Rodney stared at his laptop screen several moments before he looked up and said, "Good morning, Professor." His voice lacked warmth, his expression unwelcoming. Holly realized he had the perfect demeanor for a receptionist whose job it was to act as gatekeeper for his employer.

"Is Dr. Miller in? I just need a few minutes of his time."

"No." Rodney shook his head. "He's out of town at a conference this week."

"All week?" Holly's voice reflected her disappointment.

"Yes." Rodney's eyes returned to his screen.

"Can you give me a number where I can reach him?"

"No, I'm afraid I can't do that." Rodney peered at her through the black-rimmed eyeglasses she so disliked.

He really didn't know who he was talking to if he thought this officious attitude was going to intimidate her. In fact, it spurred her on.

"A shame what happened to Ariana Alvarez and her team, wasn't it?" she asked.

Rodney simply shrugged in reply.

"I saw you talking to Ariana in the hall Friday morning," she continued. "You know, before the closing ceremonies. She seemed pretty upset. Is that what you were talking about? Did you tell her they'd been disqualified?"

"No." Rodney failed to make eye contact.

"You know you seem to be a real insider here. I understand the release document from one of the companies they used in their experiment was forged. Do you know how they discovered that the document wasn't legitimate?"

"Look, Professor, if I were to reveal what I know and don't know to everyone who asked, I wouldn't have this job for very long. Now, I really have a lot of work to do, so if you don't mind ..."

"Of course, of course," Holly said in as obsequious a tone as she could muster. "I'm sure Dr. Miller will call in while he's away. You will talk to him, won't you?" she asked as she reached into her bag and pulled out her business card.

"Why don't you just email him?" he huffed, unable to hide his growing annoyance.

"Oh gosh," Holly smiled, tapping her forehead. "Now why didn't I think of that?"

She had thought of emailing Dr. Miller, but unlike this younger generation, she preferred to handle important matters in person. A telephone call was a poor substitute, but still better than an impersonal email.

"Well, I'll send an email, but when you do speak to Dr. Miller, would you please let him know that I stopped by and that it's really important I talk to him?" She gave him a pleading look. "My cell number is on this card."

As Rodney reached for the card, his cell phone signaled. Holly had to stifle a laugh as his ringtone played *We Are the Champions*. She waited as he answered.

"Hello. Yes. Hold on a second." He looked up at Holly. "I'll give Dr. Miller the message," he said through gritted teeth.

Not giving her a chance to say more, Rodney swiveled in his chair and bent to pull open a drawer in the file cabinet behind him. As he did, Holly scanned his desk. She spotted a National Science Teaching Association conference brochure.

Squinting, she was able to make out the location. Atlanta, Georgia. She left before Rodney closed the file drawer.

15 PROFESSOR MCNAIR

Out in the corridor, Holly stood still a moment, wondering what to do next. She really hadn't thought past talking to Dr. Miller. She could go to the office shared by the English Department adjunct faculty and do an internet search to find out the Atlanta hotel where the NSTA conference was being held. And then what? Call Dr. Miller? Interrupt him at his conference? No. She'd received work-related calls when she was out of town, and she never liked it. If Dr. Miller was annoyed with the interruption, she might do more harm than good.

No, she'd follow Rodney's advice and send an email as soon as she got to the adjunct faculty office. On the way, she laughed to herself as she considered calling and telling Dr. Miller that Rodney gave her the hotel location where he could be reached. It might be worth it just to get that little creep in trouble. She smiled to herself as she imagined his indignant denials when confronted by Dr. Miller.

But no. While she didn't score any points with Rodney just now, she clearly didn't want to make an enemy out of him. He was, after all, Dr. Miller's gatekeeper. He could prove useful sometime in the future.

Why did she dislike him so, she wondered as she entered the empty adjunct faculty office. She thought about their first encounter as she sat down at one of the computer stations. It was the morning of the Eco-Fair set-up. He was all in a tizzy about a panelist who cancelled at the last minute. Even after they discovered the vandalism to Ariana's display booth, he was still more interested in finding a replacement panelist than in helping to get the display posters reprinted.

Wait a minute!

Suddenly, Holly remembered that Ariana, who'd been crying in her arms, seemed to tense up when Rodney appeared on the scene. She hadn't given it much thought at the time, but now she wondered if something more was going on between the two of them. She had to ask Ariana next time they spoke.

When she reached her destination, she was happy to see one of the computer workstations was unoccupied. She turned on the computer and instead of logging into her email, she searched the NSTA site. The conference was being held at the Omni Hotel in Atlanta. She checked the time. Only 10:00 am. Dr. Miller would probably be at a conference session. She could call and leave a message. No, not yet. She needed to think about exactly what to say before she did that.

Instead, she entered the hotel number in her cell phone and headed to the cafeteria. She needed to think. And coffee. She really needed coffee.

In the cafeteria, she found an empty table near a window. Other than calling Dr. Miller, was there nothing else she could do? No one else she could talk to? As she sipped her coffee, she suddenly remembered Professor McNair. Of course. Why hadn't she thought of him earlier?

Gulping down what was left of her coffee, she got up and headed to the Science Department wing of the building, hoping the Professor was in this morning. She'd start with the department's administrative assistant, Barbara Gillis. If he was in, she'd know where to find him.

"Good morning, Barb," Holly said.

"Good morning, Professor." The secretary smiled. "I heard you were a big hit at the Eco-Fair. Are you here requesting a transfer to the Physical Sciences Department?"

"Definitely not," Holly laughed. "But I am happy to hear the reactions to my humble home composting presentation were favorable."

"So, what does bring you here?" Barbara asked.

"Is Professor McNair in?"

"He's teaching right now." The admin glanced at her computer screen. "But class is out in a few minutes. He usually comes back to his office right after that."

"You think he'll have some time to talk to me?"

Again, Barbara glanced at the screen. "Well, he doesn't' have another class for two hours. What's this about?"

Holly wasn't sure how to answer. Should she make something up? Say she had a science-related question? She didn't know Barbara well. But if there was one thing Holly had learned after she started teaching at Pineland Park Community College, it was that the administrative staff knew more about what went on than most of the faculty.

"I wanted to talk to him about the project that was disqualified from the Eco-Fair Competition."

Barbara's artfully shaped eyebrows arched upward. "Oh."

"Touchy subject?"

"You could say that." The admin nodded.

Unsure whether or not to probe further, Holly frowned. After a moment she decided to go for it.

"I'm friends with Ariana Alvarez's father. I've known her since she was a little girl. She's in danger of losing her scholarship. I just want to know if there's anything I can do to help her and her teammates."

Barbara let out a loud sigh. "I'm sorry for those kids, but it doesn't look good for them."

The expression "in for a penny, in for a pound" popped into Holly's head. Why not?

"Barbara, I know those kids didn't forge that signature. By any chance do you know who made the calls to Professor McNair?"

Barbara stared blankly at Holly for a moment, then her eyes dropped down to her desk. When she looked back up, she said, "Professor McNair's office is down the corridor, fourth door on the left. I'll let him know you're waiting for him."

Holly gave a slight nod. "Thanks."

As she walked down the hall, Holly was filled with regret. As she feared, she had pushed Barbara one step too far. Asking her to reveal something as confidential as information about the phone calls that she handled for the members of her department was a breach of trust.

Fortunately, she only had to wait outside Professor McNair's office a few minutes before she saw him approaching.

"Good morning, Professor McNair," she said when he arrived at the door. "Would you have a few minutes to talk to me?"

"Well, I have quite a lot to do this morning," he said as he inserted his key and opened the door, "but I suppose I can give you a few minutes. Have a seat," he said as he entered the office and sat down at his desk. "What's this about?"

"The GMO project that got disqualified."

"Yes. Such a pity," he said, opening his briefcase and rifling through some papers.

"Professor, you do know that the student who obtained the seeds and the form in question is missing?"

"So they say," he replied rather absently as he neatened the stack of papers on his desk.

"Professor, you worked with these students for two years. You praised their work and called them real scientists. You know them."

At this McNair finally made eye contact with Holly. "I thought I did, but it seems I was wrong."

Holly stared at him, unable to believe what she was hearing. If this Professor, the students' advisor on the project, just accepted the false accusations as true and wasn't going to fight for them, what hope was there?

"Will there be an investigation into the matter?" Holly asked.

"That's not up to me," McNair replied, again looking down at the papers on his desk.

As an adjunct, Holly knew challenging full-time faculty was not a smart thing to do. She fought back the urge to say what she was really thinking, and instead asked, "Professor, who called you to alert you to the forgery?"

McNair looked up at her, a momentary flash of anger crossing his face. "I'm not at liberty to discuss that with you, Professor Donnelly." The preoccupied expression returned to his face as he again glanced down at his papers. "Now if you'll excuse me."

Holly got up. "One last question. As faculty advisor to the team that worked on this project, wasn't it your responsibility to ensure that the students' paperwork was in order?"

This time McNair's expression of anger was no momentary flash. "Professor Donnelly, are you accusing me of negligence?"

"I didn't say that." Holly locked eyes with McNair. After a moment, she shrugged, and said, "Thanks for your time."

As she walked out the door, adrenaline pumped through her veins. Heading down the corridor, she was relieved to see that Barbara was not at her desk. She didn't think she could face her.

When Holly reached the main corridor, she dropped onto a bench along the wall. She pulled out her cell phone and saw the number for the Omni Hotel was still on the screen.

Nope.

She shook her head and tapped on the "recent calls" icon instead.

"Hello, Nick. Are you free for lunch? I really need to talk to you."

16 MISSING PERSON

"Yes, Ivy," Holly said into her cell phone as she sat in the Pineland Park Police Station parking lot. "I'll come home right after I talk to Nick. Bye."

Holly ended the call and checked the time. Five to twelve. Nick said he should be back in his office at noon. She dropped the phone into her handbag and got out of the car. As she approached the entrance to the police station, she remembered the first time she and Ivy set foot inside this building.

Ironic, that it was another Alvarez she was trying to help back then–Juan, Ariana's father. A lot more was at stake then. Juan had been accused of murder. Holly took some comfort in knowing Ariana's situation, difficult as it seemed, was not a case of life or death.

When she stepped inside the lobby, Holly had to smile as another memory came to mind–her unpleasant encounter with Nick when she and Ivy first came to visit Leonelle Gomez. From the start, she absolutely hated Nick. Hard to believe she had been so wrong about the man who was now her husband.

She headed across the lobby and down the corridor to Nick's office.

"*Hola!*" Nick's assistant, Officer Yolanda Rivera, jumped

up and came around the front of her desk to give Holly a hug. "It's so good to see you. What brings you here?"

"Oh, I just need to talk to your boss," Holly said.

"Not investigating a murder, are you?" Yolanda teased.

"No, no. Nothing like that," Holly replied. "Is Nick here?"

"He just called in. Should be here in just a few minutes."

"So, what's new with you, Yolanda?" Holly shot her a sly grin. "Still seeing that young man we saw you with at the restaurant a few months ago?"

"No," Yolanda sighed. Her face wore a sad expression, but then suddenly broke into a smile. "Not him."

"Someone new then?"

Yolanda nodded.

"A cop?" Holly asked.

"Oh yeah," Yolanda nodded again. "I hate to say it, but men who are not cops just don't get me. They don't understand the hours you sometimes have to put in when you're on a case. Sooner or later they suggest I should find another line of work."

Holly grimaced. "Well I have to admit, I get that. I'd be happy if Nick would retire."

"Bite your tongue," Yolanda scolded. "He still has a lot to teach me before he can do that." She looked past Holly down the corridor. "Speak of the devil ..."

Holly turned, glad to see Nick headed in their direction. He carried a large brown paper bag that had some oil stains on it.

"Is that what I think it is?" Yolanda asked as he placed the bag on her desk.

"Yep." He reached inside and pulled out a submarine sandwich and soda and handed them to her.

"Mmm! Mmm!" Yolanda muttered as she accepted the food. "A Philly Cheesesteak! My favorite."

"Did you bring me something?" Holly asked.

"Yep," he replied again as he picked up the bag and headed into his office. "A hot Italian."

Holly shook her head and followed him as Yolanda chuckled.

"So, to what do I owe the honor of this visit?" Nick asked as he made room on his desk for the bag and pulled out the drinks and sandwiches.

"So," Holly said as she sat down across from him. "Remember Friday night when I told you about Ariana's visit and how she told us their project got disqualified?"

"Uh-huh. You said there was a mix-up with the paperwork, but that it probably was a mistake and would get straightened out." He began to unwrap his sandwich. "I also remember Thursday night when you said if she came to you, you'd refer her to campus security or Dr. Miller." Cheese oozed over his fingers as he bit into his cheese steak.

Holly gave him a lame grin. "I meant that when I said it, but c'mon. You know me. Besides what could it hurt if I talked to Dr. Miller on their behalf?"

Nick did not smile back. "Did they straighten out the paperwork snafu?" he asked, then took another enormous bite out of his sandwich.

"Yeah, well, about that–I may have mischaracterized what actually happened."

Nick swallowed, grabbed a napkin and yelled in the direction of the door. "Rivera!" He still never used the intercom. "Come in here and bring your sandwich."

"Really, Nick. Is it necessary to bother her?" Holly asked, a tad annoyed.

Yolanda appeared at the door, sandwich and soda in hand.

"Take a seat." Nick raised his chin in the direction of the chair beside Holly. "My wife here is about to tell me something she's been hiding from me, and I want an objective third party to weigh in on it."

"Whoa!" Yolanda stopped short. "I don't think I should ..."

"Cut the crap and sit down," Nick said. "You know you were going to eavesdrop anyway."

"Nick!" Holly chided.

Unabashed, he picked up what was left of his sandwich and looked at his wife. "Okay out with it," he said and took another bite.

Neither he nor Yolanda said a word as Holly recounted everything that happened from the Friday afternoon revelation about the forged documents to her meeting with Professor McNair this morning. By the time she was finished, so were their sandwiches.

"So what should I do?" Holly asked.

Nick turned to Yolanda. "Officer Rivera, what do you have to say?"

"Boss, I'm not sure what you ..."

"Uh-uh," Nick cut her off. "What's your advice to this woman?"

Yolanda shrugged. "Okay then. This missing Brittany person–you gotta find her."

17 MISSING PERSON CONTINUED

"That's your advice to a civilian?" Nick said, clearly not happy with Yolanda's answer.

Yolanda lowered her head. "I knew it was a bad idea to come in here."

Nick placed his palms flat on the desk and stared at her. "Okay, Officer Rivera. Considering that the person asking is my wife, whom you know only too well, would you like to reconsider your answer?"

"Yes, sir," Yolanda replied. "What I meant to say was that someone who knows Brittany should file a missing person report with the police."

Nick nodded. "Much better, Rivera. Now get outta here."

Yolanda scooped up her sandwich wrappings and soda can, shot Holly an apologetic glance and swiftly exited the office.

Holly crossed her arms and stared at her husband. "Was that really necessary?"

"Yes," he said. "Because I know you too well, *amore mio*. If you couldn't get me to help you, your next stop would be Yolanda's desk. I wanted to make sure she knew the whole story and where I stand on any extra-curricular activities you might want to recruit her for."

"Oh c'mon, Nick. You know darn well that the police are too busy to really follow-up on a missing person report."

"You want me to do it?"

"Would you?" Holly asked excitedly.

"No! I'm a homicide detective. You know I can't get involved."

Deflated, Holly sank back in her chair. "Seriously, Nick. It just kills me that these kids may lose their scholarships. I know they didn't have anything to do with the forgery. Are you telling me there's nothing I can do to help them?"

Nick placed his elbows on the desk. "Seriously. No crime has been committed, so there's nothing more the police can do. Someone has to file a missing person report."

"Oh." Holly nodded. "I can do that, right?"

"Yes, but despite what I said to Kate the other night, I want to know what the college is doing. It's been a long time since I was in school, but we had a student government association that dealt with violations of the school's code of conduct. Can't these kids start there?"

Holly sighed and sat quietly for a moment as she considered the question. "But these kids are the ones being accused of wrongdoing."

"Ever hear the word countersuit?"

Holly's eyes narrowed. "So you're suggesting they accuse Brittany of forgery and sabotaging their project?"

"It's worth a shot," Nick said. "But I find it hard to believe that the college isn't looking into this."

"That's just it," Holly said. "When I asked McNair if they were investigating what happened, he claimed he didn't know. I mean if they were looking into it, wouldn't he know

SALLY HANDLEY

something?"

Nick shrugged. "You seemed to have hit a sore spot when you asked if he wasn't partly responsible, as the advisor to check on the release forms. No surprise he's not talking. Besides, he may have orders not to discuss this with anyone. The way things are today, the college may not want to do anything that would result in bad publicity."

"Publicity." Holly's eyes widened.

"Holly ..." Nick said, his tone cautionary.

She sighed. "No, you're right. I'd probably get fired if I did anything like that."

"Rivera!" Nick shouted. When Yolanda appeared at the door, he said, "Call out front and find out who's available to take a missing person report."

She nodded and quickly disappeared.

"But, Nick," Holly said. "I just realized. I don't know anything about this girl. How can I file this report. I don't even know her address."

"Text Ariana."

Holly's shoulders sagged. "Oh right. What's wrong with me today? Why didn't I think of that?"

Nick smiled. "Just do it."

As she pulled out her phone and started tapping in the message, Nick's phone rang. After listening for a minute, he said, "Perfect. I want you to escort my wife down there."

As Holly tapped "send", Yolanda reappeared in the doorway. "Ready?"

"Yes." Holly dropped her phone into her handbag and got to her feet. "Should I come back here after I'm done?" she asked Nick.

"No. You should go straight home and spend the rest of the day with your sister," he replied. "She's only here a few more days."

Holly frowned. "You're right." She walked behind his desk, bent down and kissed him. "I hate it when you're right." She kissed him again. "But you know I love you."

"Love you back," he said, then glanced at Yolanda grinning in the doorway. "Show's over. Get going and hurry back here. I have another job for you."

"Yes, sir," Yolanda replied, struggling unsuccessfully to stifle her grin.

As they walked down the corridor, back to the main lobby, Holly asked, "Do you think this filing a missing person report will really help?"

"Yes and no," Yolanda replied. "The police may not be able to mount the same type of search they would for someone accused of a felony, but I think it's important that you go on the record as having made an effort to locate this girl. The fact that she disappeared, and the other three students haven't, should make anyone suspicious that she's behind the forgery."

As they headed down the corridor past the front desk, she shrugged. "And you never know. It could be a slow day and the officer you talk to might get right on it."

Holly sighed as Yolanda opened a door to the squad room and led her over to a desk where a female police officer was on the phone with her back to them.

"This officer will help you," she said, pointing to a chair beside the desk.

Before Holly could sit down, the officer hung up the phone and turned to face her.

Holly's jaw dropped and her eyes widened. "Peppy?"

18 THE SQUAD ROOM

The young officer made a slicing motion across her neck as her eyes darted past Yolanda and Holly to see who might be listening.

Yolanda quickly intervened. "Officer Alvarez, this is the woman I called you about."

"Missing person report?" the officer asked, sliding the mouse across her desk, scanning the computer screen.

"Yes." Yolanda turned to Holly, winked and said, "Ms. Donnelly, Officer Alvarez will assist you from here."

"Thank you," Holly said, not fully recovered from the shock of seeing Peppy Alvarez in a police uniform.

As she took the seat alongside the desk, the young officer turned to her and leaned in close. Just above a whisper she said, "Surprised to see me, *Mami*?"

"Are you kidding?" Holly kept her voice low. "When did you become a cop?"

"Long story," Peppy replied.

"But why didn't anyone tell me?" Holly asked.

Peppy gave a slight grin as she returned her focus to the computer screen. "I think your husband didn't think it was a good idea for you to have another friend inside the Pineland Park PD.'

Holly made a sour face. "Sounds like him."

"So, who's this missing person?"

"A girl named Brittany Holzman."

Peppy typed the name onto a computer form. "Sorry, I gotta ask. How long she been missing?"

"Since Thursday."

"Good," Peppy nodded, then quickly backtracked. "I mean not good she's missing that long, but you're past the time frame for us to uh ..."

"I know what you're saying," Holly said. "You don't take these reports seriously if someone's missing for just a day or two."

"What's her address?"

Holly's phone signaled before she could reply.

"Hello. Yes, thanks for getting back to me. Listen, I need information about Brittany to file a missing person report. You know, her address, phone number–any personal information you know about her."

Peppy tapped the desk. "Photo?" she asked.

"Oh, right. By any chance, do you have a photo of her? Great. Could you text that all to me? I'm at the police station now. Perfect. I'll call you later."

"We'll have to wait for that text," Holly said after she ended the call.

Peppy leaned back in her chair and smiled. "So, what you got yourself into this time, *Mami*? Filing a missing person report for someone whose address you don't even know."

Holly sighed. "Long story."

Peppy chuckled. "Well, we got time until whoever you

talked to sends you that text. Was that your Ivy?"

"No, no." Holly shook her head. "That was a student of mine. She's in trouble and this missing girl is the reason why. Well, that's what we think anyway."

"So, how come you're not out there combing the streets looking for her yourself?" Peppy asked, her expression serious.

Holly glared back in reply.

Peppy's serious expression morphed into a grin. "Or did you try that first and your husband found out and sent you down to me?"

"I'm glad you find this so amusing." Holly crossed her arms. "I'll have you know I went to my husband first. Filing this report was his idea."

"Just teasing you, *Mami*," Peppy said as Holly's phone pinged.

"Great." Holly read the text message, then handed the phone to Peppy.

"Wait a second." Peppy looked up at Holly. "This text is from Ariana Alvarez. That wouldn't be my cousin Juan's daughter, would it?"

"Oh wow!" Holly exclaimed. "How could I forget you're Juan's cousin? Yes, this is from his daughter."

"Little Ariana? That's who's in trouble?"

Holly nodded.

Peppy quickly tapped the phone, then held it to her ear. "*Esta es tu prima. Cuéntamelo todo.*"

Holly watched Peppy's expression grow more fierce as she listened to Ariana recount what had happened. After a few minutes, Peppy began asking questions in Spanish. As she got the answers, she typed them onto the computer form. When she completed the form, she ended with words Holly was able to translate easily -- "Don't worry cousin. I got this."

After Peppy ended the call, Holly watched as she forwarded Brittany's photo and uploaded it to the form.

"What the hell was Ariana doing teaming with this Goth *perra*?" Peppy asked as she stared at the image on the screen.

"You know, I wondered the same thing," Holly said.

Peppy swiveled her chair and aimed an annoyed look at Holly. "And what were you thinking when you didn't lead with the fact that the person in trouble was an Alvarez?"

Holly grimaced. "Sorry. I don't know why I didn't make the connection sooner." But after a moment Holly returned an irritated look at Peppy. "Maybe if you kept in touch with me and let me know you were a police officer, I might not have been so surprised when I saw you, forcing everything else out of my head."

Peppy held up her arms in surrender. "Okay. You got me there. But now you know and all is well, right, *Mami*?"

Holly leaned in close. "All is well as long as you keep me informed of everything you find out."

Peppy filled her cheeks with air and blew out slowly through her lips. "You really don't want me to get in trouble with the boss, do you?"

In a low voice, Holly said, "Detective Manelli is not your boss."

Peppy shifted uncomfortably in her chair. "But ..."

"No 'buts'," Holly hissed.

"So, what you saying? Back together again?"

Holly's face wore a satisfied grin. "Back together again."

19 EXPECTATIONS

Peppy tapped on the door to Nick's office.

"What do you want?" he growled without looking up.

"Can we talk?" Peppy asked and waited by the door.

Nick finally glanced up and gave her an appraising look. "Yeah, sit down, Alvarez." He leaned back and dropped his pen on the desk.

Peppy returned his gaze, unblinking. "Detective, I don't want to get caught in the middle of a family thing. You know what I mean?"

"Then just do your job," Nick replied. "How would you handle this if it were a total stranger who reported someone missing?"

Peppy shook her head. "But your wife is not a total stranger. And you know Ariana is my cousin's daughter, right?

"Is that a problem for you?" Nick asked.

"Hell no," Peppy shook her head defiantly, then quickly caught herself. "Sorry. No, sir, it's not a problem for me. But your *esposa* wants me to keep her informed of whatever I find out and I know her. If I don't call her, she'll call me and if I don't return the call, she'll hunt me down. I can't lie to her. You know she's the reason I'm here and not just another punk hustling on the streets."

"I thought I was the reason you were here," Nick said.

"Yeah, of course. It's just that GED class she got me enrolled in is what started me on the right path." Peppy fidgeted in her chair. "You know I appreciate everything you did to get charges against me dropped and then get me accepted into the Academy. That's why I'm sitting here right now. I don't want to do anything you don't want me to."

"Then just do your job."

"C'mon, sir," she said, her tone pleading. "You never told your wife that I became a cop. Today you specifically request me to take a missing person report from her in a case that involves a relative of mine. I gotta know what you expect from me."

Nick's expression softened. "Why do you think I requested you?"

Peppy shrugged.

Nick continued. "You think I wanted to set you up? Make things difficult for you?"

"Well, no. I guess not."

"Remember what you did the last time my wife talked you into helping her?"

"Yeah, but she wasn't your wife back then."

"Never mind that," Nick said. "What did you do when you thought she was in danger?"

Peppy smiled. "I called you."

"Bingo." Nick smiled back.

"Oh, oh, oh. I get it. You want me to make sure she doesn't do anything stu–uh–dangerous." Peppy got to her feet "I got it."

She headed to the door, then turned back. "But the missing person thing. You do want me to check it out, right?"

"What do you think?" Nick asked.

Peppy stared at him for just a moment. "On it."

20 ROOMMATES

"Holly, do you really think this is a good idea?" Ivy asked as her sister pulled into a parking space in front of a two-story brick apartment building.

"Yes, I do," Holly replied.

"But from what you told me, Peppy is on the case. Why not just let her handle it?"

Holly unsnapped her seat belt. "Because this isn't the only thing she might have to work on. If an urgent call comes into the police station about a crime in progress, that will take priority. Who knows how long before she can get here?"

"But it's for her cousin. Surely, she'll get to it as soon as she can," Ivy objected.

"Well, we're here now, so let's just see if Brittany's roommate will talk to us. Besides, I think we may have a better chance of getting information than a police officer will." Holly opened her door and got out before Ivy could say anymore.

Together they climbed the front stoop. Holly pulled out her phone and checked the address.

"Apartment 2A," she said and rang the corresponding buzzer. She waited a few seconds, then buzzed again.

Ivy glanced up to the second story and saw a curtain

flutter. "Someone just came to the window," she said.

When nothing happened, Holly buzzed again. The sound of the window opening above them drew their attention upward.

"Not interested in attending your church, ladies," a young woman with messy, blonde hair shouted down to them.

"We're not church ladies," Holly replied. "We're looking for Brittany Holzman."

"Well, when you find her, let me know. She owes me this month's rent."

As the blonde started to close the window, Holly shouted. "Please. I'm a professor at the community college. I'm trying to help some students who are in trouble because of Brittany. We just need to ask you a few questions. Please."

The window closed.

"Let's go, Holly." Ivy started down the stairs but stopped when the buzzer sounded.

Holly pulled the door open. "C'mon before she changes her mind."

Reluctantly, Ivy followed her sister up the stairs. Apartment 2A was the first door on the right. The door opened only as far as the security chain allowed.

"You got an ID or something?" the woman asked.

"Yes." Holly unzipped the side compartment of her bag and pulled out her faculty photo ID. "I'm Professor Holly Donnelly. This is my sister Ivy."

Looking first at the ID, then at Holly, the woman glanced over at Ivy. "You twins?"

"No. Just sisters," Holly replied to the often-asked question.

"Come in," the woman said as she unhooked the chain and opened the door.

"What's your name?" Ivy asked as they stepped inside the sparsely furnished apartment.

"Lisa Nicastro," she replied and dropped down on a couch that showed signs of wear. "Have a seat." She pointed to two unpadded, metal folding chairs facing the couch. "Like I told those two girls who came around here the other day, I don't know where Brittany is. She hasn't been here since last Wednesday."

"What two girls?" Holly asked.

"I don't remember their names. A white girl and a Latina."

"That must have been Ariana and Debby," Ivy said.

"Yeah," Lisa nodded. "Ariana. I remember that name."

"Do you have any idea where Brittany might have gone?" Holly asked.

"No. I really don't know much about her."

"Even though you're roommates?" Ivy asked.

Lisa let out a scoffing laugh. "Roommates are just a way to pay the rent these days–not besties or anything."

"This is your place?" Holly asked.

"Yeah."

"You must have checked this girl out before you let her move in," Holly said. "Do you remember anything she might have told you at that time?"

"Look, I've been stiffed by friends, so when this college girl showed up with cash and paid three months in advance, I felt like I finally found a reliable source of rent money. I didn't ask much after that."

"You didn't check references?" Ivy asked. "You know, you really should do that."

Lisa chuckled. "Where you from, lady? Not around here I'd guess."

Ivy sighed as Holly gave her head a small shake and continued probing. "Did Brittany ever invite friends over?"

"Once," Lisa replied. "I got off work early and when I came home, a guy and a girl were here."

"Any chance you remember their names?"

"No. But I got the feeling they weren't really friends of hers. It seemed like a meeting of some kind. I know she was big into this green stuff." Lisa sat forward. "Wait. Now I remember. When she first moved in she said she belonged to some tree-hugger group. She invited me to one of those save-the-planet meetings. I told her that wasn't my thing, so she never asked again."

"Was the meeting at the college?" Holly asked.

"No, it was at somebody's house on the other side of town."

"Do you remember the name of the group?"

"Nah."

"Did Brittany leave any of her things here?" Ivy asked.

Lisa nodded. "Yeah. That kind of gave me hope she'd be back, but now that people are looking for the little weirdo, I don't think she will. She really didn't have much."

"Do you think we could have a look in her room?" Holly asked.

Lisa stared at Holly, appearing uncertain about how to reply.

"You can watch us. We just want to see if maybe there's a pamphlet or something with the name of this group she's part of."

"Three students may lose their scholarships if Brittany isn't found," Ivy added.

The young woman scratched the back of her head, sighed, then got to her feet. "Okay. But you'll need to hurry up."

She looked at her phone. "I have to get to work."

"We'll be quick," Holly said and followed Lisa as she grabbed a set of keys off a side table and walked to a closed door on the opposite side of the room.

She unlocked and opened the door of a bedroom, even more sparsely furnished than the living room. Just a single bed and a four-drawer dresser. A suitcase sat on the floor beside the bed.

Holly entered the room and walked over to the dresser. On top lay a small stack of business cards. "These might help," she said, spreading them out. She reached inside her bag, pulled out the phone and snapped pictures of all of the cards.

Ivy knelt beside the unzipped suitcase and lifted the top. "Over here, Holly." She pointed to a white sheet of paper with the number 9172022846 and a phone number.

Holly snapped a photo then turned to Lisa. "Thank you."

"Yes," Ivy said, "we've taken up enough of your time."

As they exited the room, Holly pulled out a business card. "If by any chance you hear from Brittany, would you please give me a call. That's my cell number on the card."

Lisa nodded and accepted the card. As she headed across the room, she stopped when there was a knock on the door.

"Dammit! Nobody's supposed to let anyone in that front entrance," she sputtered, walking over to the door. "Who's there?"

Holly grimaced as she heard a familiar voice say, "Pineland Park Police."

21 TOLD YOU SO

"You know, Holly," Ivy said as she stared out the back door of the police cruiser, "In my whole life I've only been in the back of a police car three times. And each of those times was with you."

"Yeah. Well, just remember," Holly said, "the last time was when they drove us home after I rescued you."

"May I remind you that I wouldn't have needed to be rescued if we'd stayed home like Nick told us to."

"Just say it already and get it over with."

"Say what?" Ivy asked.

"I told you so."

Ivy waggled her head. "Well, I did."

Holly pulled out her phone.

"What are you doing?" Ivy asked.

"I'm going to search the organizations on the business cards we found on the dresser."

Ivy leaned over and peered at the phone as Holly googled 'Ecolytes'.

"Oooh, look it this," Holly said. "Here's a group picture

at an Earth Day rally." Her fingers tapped quickly. "I'm texting this to Peppy. She can ask Lisa if she recognizes any of the people in it."

"So now you're telling Peppy what to do?" Ivy shook her head. "Bad enough she made us wait in her cruiser. You want her to take us to police headquarters too?"

Holly made a tsking sound. "She's not going to do that."

"Really? Because she seemed pretty annoyed to find us here. You do know we're going to get the obstruction-of-justice and interfering-with-a-police-investigation lecture?"

Holly sighed. "So what? It's no big deal."

"Really? The last time you got that lecture Nick arrested you."

"C'mon. He's not going to arrest me now. I'm his wife."

Ivy smirked. "But Nick's not involved here. Peppy can bring us in. Spending a night in lock-up may be okay with you, but I'm too pretty to go to jail." She tossed her hair back over her shoulder and again gazed out the window.

Holly laughed. "You can be very funny, you know."

"Here she comes." Ivy lifted her chin towards the front of the building as Peppy descended the steps.

She walked around the car and opened the door on Holly's side. Bending down she glared at Holly.

"You pull another stunt like this, *Mami*, and our deal is off. Not only will I not keep you informed of what I learn, I will tell Manelli you are interfering with a police investigation and should be charged with obstruction."

"Told you so," Ivy muttered under her breath.

"I'm sorry, Peppy, but I figured you might be too busy to get right on this," Holly said.

"Did it occur to you to text me and let me know what you were doing?" Peppy said.

"Wouldn't you have just told me not to come here?" Holly asked in her defense.

"Probably," Peppy said exasperated. "And I also could have told you I was on my way."

"Oh." Holly grimaced. "Right."

"Besides, you know how annoyed witnesses get when they have to tell their stories over and over again?"

"I didn't think of that," Holly looked down at her hands, her expression contrite. After a few moments, she again made eye contact with Peppy. "Can I tell you what Lisa Nicastro told us? I mean, just in case she left something out when she talked to you."

Peppy bit the corner of her lip. "Go ahead."

Holly recounted the conversation she and Ivy had with Brittany's roommate. "In addition to the photo I texted you, I can text you photos I took of the business cards on Brittany's dresser."

"I got them," Peppy said, clearly annoyed. "Give me some credit for knowing how to do my job."

"Sorry." Holly said, her expression again penitent.

"You're just lucky that girl identified two of the people in that Ecolyte photo you texted me, or I'd be taking you back to the station with me."

"Really?" Ivy spoke for the first time. "That's great," she said as Holly quickly brought the photo back up on her phone.

"Who did she identify?" Holly held the phone for Peppy to see.

Peppy let out a scoffing laugh. "You are a real piece of work. You think I'm going to point them out to you? And what are you gonna do? Go on a manhunt?"

Holly sighed. "No. I'd just like to know," she said in a pouty tone.

"Get out of the car," Peppy said, straightening up. She walked over to Holly's car as the two sisters climbed out of the cruiser and followed.

"Now, get in your vehicle, go home and stay there," Peppy said.

"But, Peppy," Holly began as Ivy hurried to the passenger side and got in.

"No buts." Peppy's expression softened. "I'm serious. We don't know what we're dealing with here. And besides, you're on the wrong side of town."

Holly let out a small laugh. "Yeah, Lisa thought we were church ladies."

Peppy chuckled. "Please. Let me do my job. I'll let you know if I find out anything."

"Promise?"

"Promise. Remember, it's my cousin's future on the line here. This is my first priority."

Holly tapped Peppy on the shoulder. "Okay. Maybe I'll try to call Dr. Miller and see if I can find out what the college is doing."

"Now you're talking." Peppy smiled. "I won't have to worry if you stick to your wheelhouse." She pulled something out of her pocket and reached out to Holly. "Here. Ms. Nicastro won't be needing this.

Holly sighed, took the business card she'd giving Brittany's roommate, and got in the car. As she slipped the key in the ignition, Ivy said, "Thank heaven she didn't take us to the station."

Holly smirked. "Told you so."

22 EXPLOSION

When Holly awoke the next morning, before she even reached over to Nick's side of the bed, she knew he was gone. How he managed to get out of the house without waking her, she'd never understand. Opening her eyes, she glanced over at his pillow. As she expected, a note was resting on top.

Got a call a little after midnight. Not sure when I'll be back. Will call you when I can. Ti amo.

Holly frowned. When was he going to retire? Most days she didn't worry about him. After all, Pineland Park wasn't exactly a hotbed of criminal activity. But she hated when he got these late-night calls. Nothing that required Nick to get up and out in the middle of the night was ever good.

The clock on the nightstand read 6:44. Even though she didn't have a class until one, she never slept past seven. Lucky usually made sure of that.

She got up, pulled on a pair of sweats and laced her sneakers. When she opened her bedroom door, she was surprised to see that Lucky wasn't lying in the hall. When Ivy was visiting the dog's favorite bedtime spot was exactly halfway between their rooms. Across the hall, Ivy's door was open.

"Might as well start breakfast," she said to herself and headed downstairs. She had just finished adding the coffee to the coffee maker when she heard the front door open. Lucky bounded into the kitchen, grinning from ear to ear.

Holly bent down and rubbed the dog's back. "Had a good walk, girl?" When Ivy didn't immediately follow, Holly peeked into the hallway. No Ivy. When she heard a commercial jingle on the television, she headed to the living room.

"What's up?" she asked.

"Someone in the park told me there was a bad fire on the other side of town last night," Ivy replied. "I was just wondering if there was anything on the news about it."

"Oh damn!" Holly said. "That must be why Nick left in the middle of the night."

"He did?" Ivy asked. "Why would he get called for something like that? That's not homicide."

Holly sighed. "Unless it is."

Ivy's brow wrinkled. "What do you mean?"

"Well, if the firemen determine the fire appears to be suspicious and the police first on the scene discover a body, homicide gets called in."

"Oh." Ivy sank down on the couch. "Of course."

Holly joined her as a commercial ended and the local news anchor came on the screen.

"And in breaking news, the Pineland Park Fire Department reports that the four-alarm fire at the west side Industrial Park is now under control."

"Oh wow!" Holly said as the screen shifted to a video of the site. Billowing flames soared skyward as firemen aimed their hoses at the burning building.

"I hope no one was inside," Ivy said.

The screen again shifted to a reporter holding a microphone. In the background, firemen continued their work. The fire was clearly out, but smoke clouds continued to drift upward.

The studio news anchor asked, "So, Maria. What can you tell us about this tragic fire?"

"Well, Liz, the fire appears to have started at a Green Gardyn Foods warehouse after a loud explosion occurred around 10:30 last night. A fireman I spoke to said this particular warehouse did not store flammable substances, and we're probably looking at a case of arson."

"Was anyone injured?" the anchor asked.

"No fire fighters were injured, but I understand from one of the policemen that a body was found inside. That has not been confirmed, and probably will not be until family members have been notified."

"Thank you, Maria." The anchor's somber face once again filled the screen. "Channel 4 News has just confirmed that the warehouse where the explosion occurred had been the site of a demonstration by environmental groups accusing Green Gardyn Foods of fraudulent claims about their organic growing practices. We'll continue to follow this story."

The sisters sat quietly as another commercial came on. After a moment Ivy slowly turned to Holly. "You don't think that Green Gardyn Foods is ..."

Holly nodded. "Company B."

23 ARSON

"We've confirmed that the body they found was a security guard on night duty," Nick said as Holly placed a plate of bacon and eggs in front of him.

"Oh, that's awful," she said. "Do you know how old he was?"

"Just thirty-three," Nick replied, shaking his head.

"Any chance the explosion was an accident?"

"No."

"So what do you think?" Holly asked. "Homicide?"

"We won't know until after the autopsy," he replied, biting into a crisp strip of bacon.

"I know that," Holly said. "I'm asking you what you think."

"I think we've got a case of arson."

Holly shot him a look of impatience. "You know what I'm asking."

Nick lifted a forkful of the fried egg to his mouth. "You know you've ruined me for diner breakfasts. Nobody makes bacon and eggs as good as yours."

In spite of his attempt to change the subject, an evasion

tactic that always frustrated her, Holly could not help smiling at the compliment.

"Here are the photos you took," Ivy said as she walked into the kitchen holding Holly's cell phone.

"Give me that," Holly said, grabbing the phone.

"What do you have there?" Nick asked.

"Didn't you tell him?" Ivy looked at her sister askance.

"I didn't have a chance to ..."

"Tell me what?" Nick demanded.

"We went to Brittany Holzman's apartment and talked to her roommate," Ivy replied.

"Blabbermouth!" Holly scowled at her sister.

"Didn't I assign a police officer to handle your missing person report?" Nick asked, his face stony.

"Yes," Holly bristled. "Peppy was there."

"After we already talked to the roommate," Ivy added.

"Ivy!" Holly shouted. "Can't you ever just shut up?"

Unfazed by the question, Ivy replied. "No. Not when someone has died."

Nick crossed his arms and waited. Holly's shoulders slumped as she sank down in a chair and faced him.

"Okay, here's what happened." She recounted their visit with Lisa Nicastro, then picked up her phone and tapped the screen. "I took photos of business cards on Brittany's bedroom dresser." She handed the phone to Nick. "Peppy has them too."

"Do you think one of these groups might be responsible for the fire, Nick?" Ivy asked.

"It's possible," Nick said, getting up from the table. He pulled out his cell phone and walked out of the kitchen into the hall to make a call.

"Really, Ivy," Holly said just above a whisper, "can you

never wait for me to talk to him in my own time?"

Ivy shook her head. "No. Not if you're in danger."

"What are you talking about? I'm not in danger."

"You know darn well this may be related to this GMO mess and, as always, you're right in the middle of ..."

Before she could finish, Nick walked back into the kitchen and sat down.

"Peppy confirmed that Ecolyte is the group that staged demonstrations at the warehouse two weeks ago."

"What's going to happen now?" Holly asked.

"Your missing person is now a person of interest in this arson investigation." Nick placed his arms on the table and leaned toward his wife. "If this group caused that fire and knew that the security guard was in there, they will be charged with first degree arson. Depending on what we find out, murder charges could be brought as well."

Holly locked eyes with his but said nothing.

After a moment, Nick continued. "The girl you're looking for could be in a lot of trouble if she had anything to do with this fire. More trouble than just forging a signature for a science fair project." He sighed and reached for Holly's hand. "If she and these Ecolyte people are responsible for that fire last night, they're dangerous. Please, I'm asking you. Let the police find her."

"Of course," Holly said. "I won't do anything else. I promise."

Nick gave a slight smile, kissed her, and got up. "Now, I need to get some sleep. If I'm not up in four hours, wake me."

"Hear that, Ivy?" Holly said as he left the kitchen. "I may not be back from school in four hours." She grabbed her bag and briefcase. "I've got to go."

Ivy glanced up at the wall clock. "What's your hurry?

Your class isn't for another hour."

"I have some things to do," Holly said and headed to the front door.

Ivy followed her sister and grasped her arm before she could step outside. "Don't forget your promise to Nick."

24 WHAT NOW?

"So, Professor Donnelly, do you think you'll have the papers corrected by Thursday?" a girl in the third row asked.

"Well, considering that you've just submitted them online, I don't think so." Holly's reply was greeted with a groan from the class. "But I promise to try to get them all read and returned by next Tuesday. And please come prepared to discuss the reading assignment on Thursday. Class dismissed."

As the students filed out, Holly slung her bag over her shoulder, scooped up the rest of her belongings and headed out the door. As she hurried down the hallway she wondered if she'd made a mistake contacting Ariana. Ivy was right. She did promise Nick she wouldn't do anything more–but that was about trying to locate Brittany. Surely, the promise didn't extend to warning Ariana that anyone with a relationship to Brittany might be questioned by the police.

Or would Nick call that interfering in a police investigation? Probably. But wait a minute. Anyone questioned by the police could ask to have an attorney present. How was a friend offering advice any different?

At the entrance to the cafeteria she spotted Ariana waiting for her at a table in the corner. The girl smiled and waved her over.

"Ms. Donnelly," she said as Holly sat beside her, "did you get to speak to Dr. Miller? Did Peppy find Brittany?"

Holly let out a sigh. "No, Dr. Miller's out of town this week. I know Peppy's searching for Brittany, but I haven't heard anything from her yet either."

Ariana's expression morphed from hopeful to disappointed. "When I didn't hear from you yesterday, I didn't know what to think. I wanted to call you and Peppy, but my father said not to pester the two of you. Just trust you two to get the job done."

"Your father's a good man." Holly gave her a weak smile. After a moment she said, "Something else has come up, and I just want to prepare you."

Ariana's eyes widened. "What now?"

"Did you hear about the explosion at a warehouse last night?"

"Yeah, I heard someone talking about it in my class this morning," Ariana replied. "But what does that have to do with anything?"

"The police suspect a group that staged some protests outside the warehouse two weeks ago of setting off the explosion. Brittany may have ties to that group."

"Oh no!" Ariana dropped back in her chair. As the news sank in, she shook her head. "I know she's a little strange, but you don't really think she was involved, do you?"

Holly shrugged. "I don't know, but she is what the police call a person of interest. The reason I wanted to see you was that they're probably going to talk to anyone who knew her. I think it's very likely they will want to speak to you, Debby and Luis. I just want you to be prepared."

"No!" Ariana pounded the table with her fist. "This can't be happening."

Holly placed her hand on the girl's arm. "Try to stay calm. You just have to answer the questions the police ask you truthfully and everything will be fine."

"What kinds of questions?" Ariana asked.

"Well, they'll want to know about Brittany and if you know anything about her and this group she was involved in."

Ariana slowly moved her head from side to side, her expression growing increasingly alarmed. "What's the name of the group?"

"Ecolyte."

Ariana dropped her head to her chest.

"What is it, Ariana?" Holly asked, a sinking feeling beginning in her mid-section.

"Brittany talked us into going to one of their meetings."

"You, Debby and Luis?"

"Yes." Ariana grasped the edge of the table. "We thought they were crazy, so we never went again."

"Good," Holly said without much conviction. After a moment she asked, "Exactly what do you mean when you say crazy?"

Ariana started to answer, then stopped. Swallowing hard, she finally replied. "They wanted to go after companies they felt violated the environment."

"By 'go after', do you mean through the use of violence?" Holly asked, the sinking feeling in her stomach growing stronger by the moment.

"Wait a minute," Ariana now wore a look of panic. "What was the name of the company where the explosion took place?"

Holly ran her tongue over her lips before she replied. "Green Gardyn Foods."

"Oh, *Dios Mio!*"

The expression on Ariana's face confirmed Holly's worst fears. Company B was indeed Green Gardyn Foods.

25 SKIN IN THE GAME

The next morning Holly sat between Luis and Debby outside the interview room at Pineland Park Police Headquarters. She glanced at her watch. Only five minutes had passed since Ariana stepped inside to be interviewed by Nick and Police Chief Rafael Vargas. It felt more like an hour.

Closing her eyes Holly inhaled deeply. Everything was going to be all right. Though Luis was reluctant at first, he finally agreed with her that they should talk to the police. All three students realized how much better it would be if they came in voluntarily to tell the police everything they knew.

A sniffle from Debby caused Holly to open her eyes. She reached for the girl's hand. When she did, Debby began to sob.

"It's going to be okay," Holly said, her tone soothing. "You didn't do anything wrong. You're here to offer help to the police. It's all good."

"Hmpf." Luis grunted. "Easy for you to say."

Holly turned to the boy. "I get that, Luis. As you kids say, I don't have any skin in the game, but you have to believe I wouldn't advise you to do anything that would hurt you."

"You're right." The boy smirked. "You don't have any skin in the game–brown skin that is."

"Luis!" Debby shot him a pleading look. "She's trying to help us."

The boy shook his head, got up and headed down the corridor to where a pair of vending machines lined the wall. Debby went after him.

Holly watched helplessly, too stunned to respond. She felt as if she'd just taken a blow to her solar plexus. But the boy was right. She didn't know what experiences he had in his life to make him feel the way he did. And just when these kids had completed an A+ project that assured them full scholarships, their future was in jeopardy. Worse yet, their lives were now being impacted by a crime they had nothing to do with. It just wasn't fair.

She glanced down the corridor as Luis retrieved two bottles of water from the vending machine, handing one to Debby. As he sat down in a chair along the wall, Debby turned and walked back to where Holly was sitting.

"I'm sorry, Professor Donnelly. Would you like some water?" Debby asked offering her the bottle she carried.

"No thanks." Holly shook her head, as the girl sat beside her.

"You have to understand, Luis is taking this pretty hard."

"I do understand," Holly replied. "as much as I can, anyway."

"He and I talked after our project got withdrawn from the competition. He said he worked so hard all his life, stayed out of trouble, avoided the gangs, did well in school, and for what? To have it all come to nothing because of Brittany."

"A white girl," Holly added.

Debby nodded. "I can't blame him. I'm angry too. I need that scholarship. From some of the conversations I had with Brittany, I could tell she came from money. After all this is over, she'll be taken care of and where will we be?"

Holly blinked back tears as she took Debby's hand. "I admit that I don't know how this will all turn out, but I promise you. I will do whatever I can to help all three of you."

The interview door opened and Ariana stepped out. Holly was relieved to see she seemed calmer than when she went in.

Nick appeared behind her. "Where's Luis Navarro?" he asked.

Holly frowned and tilted her head in the direction of where Luis remained seated across from the vending machines.

Holly watched as Nick slowly walked down the corridor. She smiled when she saw him extend his hand to the boy. After a brief exchange, Luis stood and together they walked back to the interview room. Nick glanced at Holly before he closed the door and gave her a quick wink. Her husband always knew the right thing to do.

As Ariana sat down, Holly's phone pinged. She reached inside her bag and clicked on the text icon. It was from Kate.

"IMPORTANT! I NEED TO TALK TO YOU ASAP CONCERNING BH."

26 REDDINGTON MANOR

Holly stared at her cell phone. BH? That had to be Brittany Holzman. What could Kate possibly have to tell her about Brittany? Although Holly was anxious to talk to Ariana about her interview, she knew Kate's request was urgent. Even Kate, the ultimate Luddite, understood that texting in all capital letters was tantamount to screaming.

"You'll have to excuse me." The two girls looked surprised as Holly got to her feet. "I have to make a call. I'll be right back."

She headed down to the lobby and through the front doors of the police station. Outside a few smokers were clustered to the right of the doorway. She tapped her cell screen as she headed in the opposite direction.

"Thank God!" Kate's voice greeted her before the end of the first ring.

"What's going on, Kate? Holly asked.

"Brittany's here," she replied in a voice just above a whisper.

"What in the ..." Holly began to exclaim.

Kate cut her off. "She's upstairs taking a shower. I don't have a lot of time to talk. She called me yesterday. Said she needed a place to stay–could I put her up for a night or two."

"Kate, listen to me. She's a person of interest in the investigation of an explosion that happened here last night."

"The one all over the news this morning?"

"Yes. You need to get her to turn herself in."

"Are you kidding me?" Kate practically spit into the phone. "You really think I can do that?"

"You have no choice!" Holly spat back, that oh-so-familiar sinking feeling returning to her stomach.

"I hear footsteps," Kate whispered. "I have to go."

"Kate ..." Holly heaved a sigh as the call ended. Only one thing to do. Talk to Nick. She quickly sent a text.

"URGENT! Brittany Holzman is at Kate's place in Reddington Manor."

Holly hurried back inside the police station. The desk sergeant waved her through. When she reached the corridor outside the interview room she stared at the closed door.

"Is something wrong, Professor?" Ariana asked as she and Debby exchanged worried looks.

Eyes on her cell phone, Holly shook her head as she resent the text and stared at the door, willing it to open.

A few seconds later, she exhaled a sigh of relief as it did, and Nick appeared. He took her by the arm and quickly led her into another room across the corridor. He closed the door and listened as she told him about Kate's call. Before she finished he pulled out his cell phone, tapped the screen a few times and held the phone to his ear.

"Jason. Nick Manelli here."

Holly sat down on a desk as Nick spoke to Jason Bascom, the Sheriff of Reddington Manor. She smiled as she remembered the last time they'd seen him at their wedding in Kate's backyard. She allowed the happy memory to distract her as Nick explained the situation to Jason.

"Call me when you have her in custody," Nick said. After he listened for a moment, he smiled. "I'll tell her."

"Tell me what?" Holly asked as he slipped the phone back in his pocket.

"He and Raquelle are finally getting married," he replied as he put his arms around her. "Said to be on the lookout for an invitation."

"Oh, that's great." Holly smiled up at him, but the smile quickly faded. "You don't think Jason will have trouble apprehending Brittany, do you?"

Nick snickered.

"What's so funny?" Holly asked.

"He has help." The corners of Nick's mouth twitched.

"Who? The last I heard from Kate, the deputy quit and the city council decided they didn't need to replace him."

"Yeah, but the Sheriff is authorized to deputize citizens on an as-needed basis." Nick again let out a small chuckle. "Did you forget who lives next door to Kate now that her former neighbor is in jail?"

Holly let out a belly laugh as she remembered Kate's new neighbors–Benny and Razor.

27 COFFEE

Kate poured herself a mug of coffee as Brittany entered the kitchen.

"Good morning," she said. "Did you sleep well?"

"Yeah," the girl replied and sat down at the counter.

"Would you like some coffee?" Kate asked.

"Sure."

"Milk? Sugar?"

"Black," Brittany replied.

Of course, she'd like it black, Kate thought. As she pulled a fresh mug out of the cupboard, she wondered what to do. She knew Holly was right and Brittany should turn herself in, but she doubted she could ever convince this girl to go to the police. And since, at this point, Brittany didn't know Kate was aware of the explosion or that the police were looking for her, she didn't even know how to start the conversation.

Placing the steaming mug in front of Brittany, Kate sat down on a stool across from her. "You seemed pretty beat last night when you arrived. I figured you didn't want to talk. So, what brings you up here to the Catskills?"

"Just passing through," the girl replied, her eyes focused

on her coffee mug.

"How'd you get here? I didn't see a car drop you off."

"I walked."

Not good, Kate thought. She'd never be able to talk about turning herself in if Brittany wouldn't even tell her how or why she got here. After a moment, Kate just decided to take a leap.

"Brittany, are you in some sort of trouble?"

The girl finally looked up and made eye contact. "No."

"Because if you are, maybe I could help if you tell me what's going ..."

A knock on the door caused Brittany's sullen expression to evaporate. Her posture stiffened, and she appeared genuinely alarmed as Kate walked over to the window and peered out to the porch.

"It's my neighbor," she said as she opened the door. "Hi, Benny. Come on in."

"Hey, Kate." Benny winked at her before he stepped inside. "We're outta milk "Could we ..." Benny stopped when he spotted Brittany. "Oh, I'm sorry. I didn't know you had company."

"Yes. This is Brittany. She just arrived here last night. Brittany, meet Benny."

"Nice to meet you." Benny smiled and extended his hand. When Brittany didn't offer hers, he smiled. "What's the matter? You a germaphone or something? 'Cause I get that. You gotta be careful this time a year, flu season and all."

Brittany stared at Benny as if he were an alien creature.

"Would you like some coffee?" Kate asked.

"Sure would," he said, giving her another wink as he walked over to the coffee pot and poured himself a cup.

Kate ignored Brittany's glare and pulled a stool over for Benny to sit down. Since he'd never before winked at her, she thought he must know something was up, though she had no idea how. At least she hoped he did. Maybe Holly called him.

"You make the best coffee, Kate," Benny said after he took a big gulp. "Don't you think so, Brittany? Nice name, by the way.

Brittany turned her glare on him, but Kate was happy that Benny continued just being Benny.

"Hey, I hope you don't mind my asking, but are you a Goth?"

Finally, Brittany responded. "Yeah, you got a problem with that?" she asked.

"Me? Ah, hell no," Benny replied, his cheerful manner unaffected by her belligerent attitude. Why, one time, me and Razor–he's my business partner and roommate. Well, we had engine trouble outside a Goth bar upstate. Those folks came out and helped us like we was old friends. Yep, I find Goths are real congenital people."

Brittany huffed. "You mean congenial. And, it's germaphobe, not germaphone," she added unable to hide her disdain.

"Oh, yeah," Benny guffawed. "If Razor was here, he'd a corrected me. He always does that. Right, Kate?"

"Yes, Benny, he certainly ..."

Another knock on the door interrupted her.

"I bet that's Razor wonderin' where the milk is," Benny said.

Kate opened the door and in stepped Sheriff Jason Bascom.

"You bitch!" Brittany shouted at Kate as she jumped to her feet and ran to the back door. When she pulled it open, she found her retreat blocked by a rock-solid figure.

"Goin' somewhere, little girl?" Razor asked.

28 CASE CLOSED

Six hours later Peppy stared in disbelief at the trio entering Pineland Park Police Headquarters. Detective Manelli smirked when he said to her earlier, "Just be prepared." She knew what the Goth girl looked like from her picture attached to the missing person report. But she certainly didn't expect the two men who accompanied her.

Benny smiled as they approached the desk, the chains on his leather belt jangling, his man-bun slightly askew. He extracted a piece of paper from the pocket of his leather vest and handed it to her.

"Hiya, Officer. I'm Benny Vinson and this is my associate, Razor Barnes," he said, pointing with his thumb to the big man beside him. "We're here to see Detective Manelli to deliver the suspect we comprehended for him."

"Apprehended," Razor said in a low voice.

"Right," Benny guffawed. "Apprehended."

Peppy looked over the paper, then back up at Benny. "You the deputies from the Reddington Manor Police Department?" she said, unable to disguise the skepticism in her voice.

"Yes, Ma'am," Benny replied, puffing out his chest. "We're not actually full-time deputies. The Sheriff, he dep ... what's

110

that word, Razor?" he asked.

"Deputizes," the big man replied.

"Oh, yeah. The Sheriff deputizes us for special assignments."

Peppy turned to the caramel-complexioned giant standing on the other side of the Goth girl. He gave his head a single nod. She narrowed her eyes as she studied the tattoo circling his left eye. He met her gaze unblinking.

"Nice ink," she said.

Razor nodded with just the trace of a smile as Peppy date-stamped the document Benny had given her and stapled it to a copy of the missing person report.

"You Brittany Holzman?" she asked the girl, who stood staring at her feet the entire time.

"Answer the officer," Benny said, his tone gentle.

Brittany, who'd been standing silently, her face downcast, looked up and glared at him.

Razor gave his head a slight shake as he handed a plastic bag to Peppy. "ID's in there."

"Thanks," Peppy said, placing the bag on her desk. "Follow me."

As she escorted them down the corridor, Benny asked, "You a full-time cop?"

"Yep," Peppy replied.

"What kinda cases you work on?"

"All kinds," Peppy replied. "Ms. Holzman here was a missing person case I been working on."

"You mean we just helped you close your case?" Benny said, unable to hide his glee.

Peppy had to smile. "Yep, I guess you did," she said as they reached Yolanda Rivera's desk.

"Officer Rivera," Peppy said, her smile widening at Yolanda's droll expression as she eyed the trio now standing in front of her. "These are the Reddington Manor deputies and Ms. Brittany Holzman. Is Detective Manelli here?"

Before Yolanda could reply, Nick appeared in the doorway of his office. "Rivera, take the suspect into the interview room."

As Yolanda took an unresisting Brittany by the arm, Peppy turned to see Nick's face break out into an uncharacteristically wide grin. She watched in amazement as he embraced first Benny, then Razor, exchanging warm greetings. How in the world did a straight-laced cop like Manelli know this truly odd couple, she wondered.

"Hey, you boys want to watch the interview?" Nick asked.

"Hell yeah," Benny answered. Razor nodded in agreement.

Nick turned to Peppy. "What about you, Alvarez?"

"Are you kidding?" Peppy said. "I'd love to see you break that little *bruja*."

"Brewha!" Benny repeated. "What's that mean?"

"Witch," Razor and Peppy replied simultaneously. Peppy glanced at Razor, surprised he knew the meaning of the Spanish word.

"More like rhymes with witch." Benny chuckled.

"Well, she's pretty mild-mannered now," Yolanda said as she returned to her desk.

"Now, maybe," Benny said, "But she was so bad when we first set out, Razor threatened to put her in the trunk of the cruiser if she didn't stop kicking the back of the seat."

"Officer Alvarez," a voice sounded over the intercom. "Please report to the front desk. Officer Alvarez. Front Desk."

"Damn!" Peppy said. "I gotta go."

Nick turned to her. "Before you go, did you thank these guys for closing the case for you?"

"No, I–uh–didn't get a chance to, sir." Peppy extended her hand to Benny first. "Thanks," she said.

"A real pleasure to meet you, Officer Alvarez," Benny said. "I hope you don't mind my sayin' this, but you look real good in that uniform."

Peppy laughed as she turned to Razor. When he took her hand, she was surprised at the gentleness of his touch.

"Uh–thank–thank you," she said, a warm feeling rising up her neck till it reached her cheeks.

"*De nada, señorita*," Razor replied softly, as he gazed into her eyes, still holding her hand.

"Okay, guys, you're with me," Nick said, heading to the interview room.

Yolanda grinned at Peppy who stood staring as the men disappeared down the corridor.

"My, my, Officer Alvarez. Are you blushing?"

29 LUNCH

"The eagle has landed." Benny grinned at Kate's face smiling back at him from the cell phone Holly had propped up in the center of her kitchen table.

"Happy to hear that. Wish I were there," Kate said as she scanned the table. "Looks like lunch was a feast."

"Well, I already had all the ingredients to make lasagna for dinner," Holly said. "When I got your call, Ivy and I immediately started cooking."

"It was–what was that word you taught me, Kate? Delishioozzo?" Benny asked as Razor just shook his head.

"Close enough." Kate laughed. "Enough of the chit chat. Now tell me everything that happened after you guys left here."

"You tell her, Razor," Benny said looking at his friend.

"Not much to tell," the big man replied. "The girl finally settled down in the back of the cruiser once we got to the highway."

"Yeah, after Razor pulled over and threatened to cuff her and put her in the trunk if she didn't stop kicking the back of his seat." Benny guffawed.

"You don't need to tell that story to everyone, Benny," Razor said.

"Oh, I'd have paid money to see that," Kate said.

Razor just closed his eyes and gave his head a slight shake. Holly had to smile. His tattoo designed to look like an eye patch was on full display.

"Naw, Kate," Benny said. "It wouldn't a been good if you were there. Actually, we wondered if your ears were burnin', cuz ..."

"Benny," Razor cut in. His mellow tone, just above a whisper, always got his friend's attention.

Holly quickly jumped in. "The bad news is Brittany's not talking. She called her father and they're waiting for her lawyer to show up."

"That figures," Kate replied.

Holly got closer to the phone. "Kate, what I want to know is how Brittany knew where you lived."

Kate grimaced. "Well, I might have given my address to her the last time we spoke at the Eco-Fair."

"Oh, Kate," Ivy chimed in. "What were you thinking?"

"Well, I certainly wasn't thinking that she was part of an eco-terrorist group, that's for sure," Kate replied in her defense.

Holly sighed loudly. "No, even I didn't suspect that."

"Sorry, I just thought the girl might need someone to talk to," Kate added, her tone less defensive.

Razor tapped the table. "Time to go."

"Yeah," Benny said. "Jason will be missing his cruiser. We'll see you in a couple of hours, Kate."

"Stop in when you get back," she said.

"We'll talk tomorrow," Holly said as the men got to their feet. Kate waved and disappeared from the screen.

Ivy got a good-bye hug from both men. "It was great seeing you guys," she said. Have a safe trip home." She started clearing the table as Holly walked the pair to the front door.

"You gotta come up and visit us–see all the work we done," Benny said. "Even Kate said she's amazed how much better the place looks, right, Razor?" His friend nodded in reply.

"As a matter of fact," Holly smiled, "we just heard that Jason and Raquelle are getting married. We'll definitely be up for the wedding."

"That's great," Benny said, giving her a hug. "Hey, you think you could get that Officer Alvarez to come up with you?"

"Peppy?" Holly's forehead crinkled.

"Peppy!" Benny hooted. "Boy does that name suit her." He leaned in close to Holly and said, "I think the *señorita* lit a fire in somebody." He winked and waved his thumb at Razor.

Holly turned to Razor, surprised to see he didn't appear the least embarrassed by his friend's remarks. Still waters run deep, she thought.

"Well, let me see what I can do," Holly said with a smile.

"See you at the wedding," Razor said. Holly marveled at the gentleness of this giant of a man as he hugged her.

"See you then." She watched them walk to the Reddington Manor police cruiser parked out front. What an unlikely twosome she thought as they drove off.

When she returned to the kitchen, Ivy was loading the dishwasher. "You've got to love those guys."

Holly nodded. "I was just thinking that next to Nick, there aren't two men I trust more than those two."

Ivy laughed. "Remember how nervous Kate was the first time we saw them when they pulled into the driveway next door."

Holly chuckled as she lifted the lasagna dish and carried

it to the counter. "And wait till you hear this."

After she relayed Benny's remarks about Peppy, Ivy said, "Really?

"Really! And you know how whenever Benny starts saying something he shouldn't, Razor just says 'Benny' in that quiet voice and stops him in his tracks? Well, he didn't seem at all bothered that Benny was revealing that Razor seemed interested in Peppy."

"Wow!" Ivy chuckled. "Razor the Romantic. Who'd have thought it?"

Before Holly could reply, Nick's ringtone signaled. "She quickly retrieved her phone from the table.

"Hello. Yeah, they left a little while ago." Ivy watched as Holly just listened. Finally, she said, "Okay. So, will you be home for dinner? All right. Love you too."

"What'd he say?" Ivy asked.

"Brittany's still not talking and they're just waiting for the father's lawyer. Nick can't leave before they talk to him."

Ivy frowned. "So, her father is sending his lawyer?"

"Yeah," Holly nodded. "This morning when I talked to Debby she told me Brittany came from money." She put air quotes around the words. "She complained about how unfair it was. After all of this is over, Brittany will be taken care of, but they'll be out of their scholarships."

Ivy patted her sister's shoulder. "Let's hope she's wrong."

30 GAME CHANGER

Holly looked down at Nick asleep on the bed as she finished buttoning her blouse. She didn't even hear him come in last night. She was dying to know if they were able to get anything out of Brittany, but she hated to wake him. Unfortunately, she had an early class. She'd just have to wait.

Out in the hall, Lucky was gone, and Ivy's door was open. Perfect, she thought. If she didn't have to walk the dog, she could leave early. She gently closed the door and tiptoed down the steps, trying not to make a sound.

When she reached the kitchen, she had to smile. Ivy had put the coffee on before she took Lucky out. She even had mugs and the milk pitcher out on the counter. What a good sister she was! Holly would miss her when she flew home later today.

As she filled a mug, she heard the front door open. Lucky rushed into the kitchen, and stood looking up at Holly, tail wagging wildly.

Holly bent down, ruffling the dog's ears. "I know. You had a great time, didn't you?"

"Good morning," Ivy said as she entered the kitchen. "I was thinking of making waffles this morning. How does that sound?"

"Fattening," Holly replied. She glanced at the wall clock. "Besides, if I leave now, I have time to swing by the police station. Maybe Yolanda can tell me if Brittany told them anything."

"Don't bother," Ivy said as she pulled the waffle iron out of the cupboard.

"Why not?"

"Because the FBI showed up at the station after Nick talked to you. They've taken over the investigation, and they took Brittany to FBI headquarters in Newark before her lawyer even got there."

Holly stared at her sister dumbfounded. "Wait a minute. How do you know that?"

"I was up when Nick got in last night." Ivy added flour to a mixing bowl.

"And you didn't wake me up!" Holly said through gritted teeth.

"I knew you had an early class. There was no point in waking you," her sister replied as she began to whisk the batter. "I'm telling you what happened now and, face it, there's nothing you can do about it."

"Hmpf," Holly grunted as she sat down and sipped her coffee. "The FBI, huh?"

"Yep," Ivy replied. "They've been monitoring Ecolyte for a while. They're on the FBI's eco-terrorist watchlist."

"No kidding?" Holly said. "Have they done this kind of thing before?"

"Well, they've mostly been responsible for organizing protests. Recently there's been an increase in cases of arson at companies where Ecolyte has staged protests, but Nick said the FBI hasn't had any proof."

"Do they have proof now?" Holly asked.

"I don't know, but this is the first time someone has died."

"Oh wow! That would definitely be a game changer." As Holly refilled her coffee mug Kate's Old Phone ringtone sounded. She put the phone on speaker. "What are you doing up so early?" she asked.

"Before I went to bed last night, I went into the guest room where Brittany slept," Kate replied. "She left her bag here."

"Did you go through it?" Holly asked.

"No. I admit I wanted to, but I thought I better not get my fingerprints on anything. What should I do?"

Holly glanced at the clock. "I have to leave for class, but Ivy can tell Nick when he gets up. He'll call you."

"Okay. Talk to you later," Kate yawned. "I'm going back to bed."

"Bye," Holly shook her head as the call ended. "Always something."

"I'll let Nick know," Ivy said, the ladle in her hand poised over the waffle iron. "One waffle or two?"

"None." Holly gulped down what was left in her coffee mug and got up. "If I leave now, I'll beat the traffic. I'll be back in time to take you to the airport this afternoon."

"About that ..." Ivy turned to face her.

"What?" Holly asked, aiming suspicious eyes at her sister.

"I've cancelled my flight. Left the return open."

Holly pursed her lips and wiggled them from side to side. "Nick's idea, right?"

"Well, we both thought it might be a good idea if I stayed a few more days."

"I'd argue with you," Holly said, a momentary glare

morphing into a smile, "but I'm glad you're staying."

"You are?" Ivy said, appearing surprised.

"Yes." Holly gave her sister a quick peck on the cheek and headed to the door. "You figure out what to cook for dinner."

31 WHAT TO DO

"Sorry. There's really nothing else I can tell you." Yolanda's face wore an apologetic frown. "The Feds took Brittany and everything else we had, which wasn't much. Just your missing person report and the recording of her interview. And all she kept repeating was 'On the advice of counsel, I am not answering any questions at this time.'"

"I was afraid of that." Holly scratched the back of her head. Suddenly her eyes widened. "You know they're going to want to talk to Ariana, Luis and Debby. Those poor kids! Like it wasn't stressful enough when they had to talk to Nick." Frowning, she asked, "Is Peppy here?"

"Hold on. I'll call the front desk," Yolanda replied, picking up her phone. "Peppy there? Okay, thanks." Hanging up the phone she said, "Peppy called in. She needed to take a personal day. A family emergency."

Holly groaned as she pulled out her cell phone and gave it a few taps. "Voice mail." She grimaced. "Peppy, call me."

Holly glanced at her watch. "I've got to run if I'm going to get to class on time. Thanks, Yolanda."

Officer Rivera just shook her head as she watched her boss's wife scurry down the corridor. She hated withholding information from Holly, but she had her orders.

****

Traffic was light so Holly arrived at school in plenty of time for her class. As she placed her briefcase on her desk, her phone signaled. She glanced around the room. Only a few students had arrived, and they were chatting with one another in the opposite corner of the room. She turned to face the windows, her back to the students. "Peppy, where are you?" she whispered into the phone.

"Chill, *Mami*. I have everything under control."

"Exactly what does that mean? Why aren't you at work?"

"I had a sleepover with three friends of mine," she replied. "You know them. My local homeys."

"Oh," Holly said, her voice tentative, unsure what to say next. "How long are they staying?"

"Not long. They need a ride to Newark this morning. I said I'd take them."

Holly let out a sigh of relief. Peppy was with Ariana, Debby and Luis. And she would accompany them to FBI headquarters. She probably spent the night prepping them for how to answer questions they'd be asked in their interviews.

"That's really nice of you." Holly turned to face the class. Several more students had arrived. "My class is about to start," she said. "Call me later?"

"You got it, *Mami*," a cheerful Peppy replied and the call disconnected.

Holly managed to maintain her focus as she taught her class, but the moment she dismissed her students her mind started racing again. Did Peppy do the right thing? But how could she fault her? The rookie police officer had taken a page right out of her own playbook. After all, hadn't she gotten the three students together and convinced them to turn themselves in to the police the day before? No, Peppy did the right thing. It will look so much better for them if they turn themselves in and volunteer to tell the FBI everything they know. Peppy also knew it would be much less traumatic to take them to FBI headquarters than to have the Feds show up at their homes, or, worse yet, at school and cart them off like criminals.

As she packed up her belongings, Holly wondered what her next move should be. She absolutely hated just waiting around. There had to be something she could do. And then she remembered she hadn't heard from Dr. Miller. Grabbing her briefcase and handbag, she headed to his office.

As she rounded a corner, reaching the corridor where Dr. Miller's office was located, she heard voices–angry voices. She couldn't make out what they were saying, but they were definitely coming from Dr. Miller's outer office. She moved to the wall, edging her way closer. She stopped when she reached the door that was slightly ajar.

Though the voices were raised, still, she could only make out an occasional word or phrase. Suddenly, one of the voices became audibly louder.

"You don't have any choice, do you?"

Holly recognized Rodney's voice. But who was he talking to?

Unexpectedly, the door flew open a moment later. The door blocked her view, but also hid her. She held her breath and prayed that whoever came out headed in the opposite direction.

"You're going to regret this, Rodney!" a second voice threatened.

As the footsteps headed off in the direction Holly hoped they would, she dared to lean forward and peek past the door as Professor McNair stormed down the corridor.

32 STALWART

Reddington Manor? What kind of a name was that for a town, Peppy wondered when Manelli asked her to drive up and retrieve Brittany's belongings. She'd never heard of the place before this case. Sounds more like the name of some rich person's estate.

As she drove, her mind returned to a question she didn't dare to ask Manelli. If the Feds took over the investigation, why was he sending her up to get Brittany's belongings? Manelli had a reputation in the police department for being a by-the-book detective, so why didn't he just call the Feds and have them retrieve whatever the Goth *bruja* left at Kate's?

But was he playing by the book when he told her to pick up Ariana, Luis and Debby, keep them at her house and take them to the FBI the next day? That was a really smart move. He even gave her advice on coaching the kids how to answer the questions the FBI would ask.

Well, whatever his reasons, she trusted Manelli. He certainly was out to protect her cousin and her friends, and that was good enough for her.

The sun had dipped almost completely below the horizon when she saw the Reddington Manor exit sign. She was glad she would reach Kate's before dark. City streets she knew how to navigate. Unlit backwoods roads–not so much.

She smirked as she drove through the center of town. A few storefronts, a non-chain supermarket and a gas station. She smiled as she passed a Victorian house with a sagging white picket fence, figuring it was about as close to a manor house as you get in a small burgh like this.

Just past the light, her GPS instructed her to make the next turn. As she did, on her right she spotted a mangy old dog chained up in front of a seedy-looking rowhouse. He eyed the police car as she passed but didn't even bother to bark.

On the left was a storefront with a small sign reading Reddington Manor Library. Not quite the building she'd expect a library to be in. How many books could they even have in there?

The GPS again indicated she needed to make the next left. As she reached the turn, she stopped and looked up a very steep hill. She wished she were driving a police cruiser and not her beat-up old car. She just hoped her Hyundai could make the climb.

The car strained as it ascended the hill. She was grateful when the GPS announced she'd reached her destination. She turned onto a steep gravel driveway. To her surprise a police car was already parked there. She pulled alongside it, grabbed her jacket, and got out.

As she started across the lawn to the house, she stopped at the sound of a voice behind her. A voice she recognized.

"Officer Alvarez," Razor said coming up alongside her. "I've been keeping watch. You have any trouble finding us?"

"No," she replied. "Just glad I got here before dark. Wait." Her brow wrinkled. "You said 'us'. You live with Kate?"

"Naw," the big man let out a gentle laugh and pointed his thumb over his shoulder. "Benny and me live next door."

"Oh," she said, looking at the small bungalow on the

other side of the driveway.

"C'mon. Let's get you inside," he said, placing a guiding hand on her back.

She felt a small shiver at his touch. They walked just a few steps when she stopped. "Why were you keeping watch? And why is there a police car in the driveway?"

Razor grimaced. "Inside," he said, again using his hand to guide her. She didn't mind.

Before they mounted the steps, the door opened. "Peppy!" Benny greeted as he held the door for her. "I can call you that, right?" he grinned. "That name suits you."

Peppy smiled as she nodded. It was hard not to like this guy. Her smile quickly faded when she entered the kitchen and saw a police officer in uniform standing beside a distraught-looking Kate holding an icepack on her knee.

"I'm Sheriff Jason Bascom." Jason extended his hand to Peppy.

"Officer Peppy Alvarez," she said, shaking his hand.

"What happened?" Peppy looked from Jason to Kate.

"A man broke into my house," Kate replied.

"Yeah, but she fought him off," Benny nodded his approval. "When she has to, our Kate can be pretty stalworth."

"Stalwart," Razor said barely above a whisper.

"Oh, yeah," Benny said undaunted by the correction. "Stalwart."

"Robbery?" Peppy asked.

"No," Kate shook her head. "He was after that." She pointed to a black tote bag lying on the counter.

"I take it that's what I'm here to pick up–Brittany's bag?"

When Kate nodded, Peppy reached inside her jacket pocket and pulled out a pair of blue nitrile gloves. "Did he get anything?"

"No," Kate replied. "I was in the garage potting up some plants. I just happened to come out when the guy was leaving by the side door that I'd left unlocked. When I saw he had the bag, I ran after him and managed to get close enough to grab onto the shoulder straps, but then I fell. He dragged me, but I wasn't letting go."

Peppy stared at Kate as she slid her hands into the gloves. After a moment, her mouth curled into a wry smile. "I get why you're friends with Ms. Donnelly."

Jason let out a small snort.

"Oh please," Kate frowned, giving her hand a dismissive wave.

"It's just lucky we came home when we did," Benny said. "The guy must a run off as soon as he heard the truck, cuz when we got out, all we saw was Kate on the ground."

Peppy shook her head and reached inside the bag, taking out items one at a time. A black pullover sweater, three black T-shirts, a hairbrush, a toiletries bag and a paperback book.

Peppy held up the copy of Stephen King's *Carrie* and said, "Role Model." She rifled the pages, but nothing fell out.

"Not much in there," Jason said. "I can't understand why anybody'd go to the trouble of breaking into a house to get it."

Peppy looked at Kate. "You sure nothing else was taken from the house?"

"My handbag over there," Kate tilted her head in the direction of the patchwork shoulder bag sitting on the counter, "was right there in plain view. Not a dime was taken."

Peppy squinted as she considered this. "Well, there's definitely something missing here."

"What do you mean?" Jason asked.

"Where's her phone?" Peppy asked. "She didn't have one

on her when you delivered her to us. The girl had to have a phone."

"You're right," Kate said. "She did have a phone with her when she arrived. I saw her checking her messages."

"You sure the guy didn't get it, Kate?" Jason asked.

"He wouldn't have fought her for this bag if he had." Peppy said before Kate could answer. "Can you show me the room where she stayed? Maybe she hid it somewhere."

Kate winced as she started to get up. Razor quickly walked over and put a hand on her shoulder. "You stay put. Did she stay in your son's old room?"

"Yes," Kate nodded.

Razor turned to Peppy. "C'mon. Benny and I will help you search."

33 RED MEAT

"I couldn't eat another thing," Nick said as he lowered his dessert fork to his plate. "That was a terrific meal, Ivy. Don't' you think so, Holly?" He glanced over at his wife, who appeared lost in thought.

"What?" Holly said, looking up from the plate she'd been staring at. "I'm sorry, I didn't hear the question."

"I said the meal was terrific," Nick replied, casting a suspicious glance at her, "Ivy, what did you call this delicious dish?"

"Swiss Steak." Ivy beamed at the praise.

"You know, we don't get much red meat around this house," Nick said.

His remark got Holly's attention. "And how's your blood pressure and cholesterol levels, *amore mio*?" she asked.

"She's got me there," Nick smiled sheepishly at Ivy. "I'm off all meds since I married your sister."

"That's great, Nick," Ivy said. "But I still say a little beef and pork once in a while is good for you."

"Oh, shut up!" Holly glared at her sister.

Ivy got up. "Just for that, you can clean up yourself. I'm

taking Lucky for a walk. C'mon, Lucky." The dog jumped to its feet and followed her out of the kitchen.

As the front door closed, Nick reached over and grabbed Holly's hand, kissing her palm. "You know I love your cooking," he said.

Holly gave him a grudging smile. "I know." She got up, gave him a quick peck on the cheek and started stacking the plates.

As she carried them over to the sink, she said, "So it looks like Peppy did the right thing."

"Yep," Nick stood and carried the meat platter over to the counter.

"I was so relieved when she called and told us the kids were questioned, released and on their way home. You know, I'm really impressed that she thought to round them up and keep them at her place last night."

Nick didn't comment as he retrieved the remaining serving bowls from the table.

"Seriously," Holly stopped and stared at the dishes in the sink. "I mean, how did she think to do that so quickly?" She turned to face her husband, a puzzled expression on her face.

"Wait a minute." She placed her hands on her hips. "Did you tell her to do that?"

"Me?" Nick frowned. "Thwart the FBI? My son works for them, remember?"

Noting that he did not say 'no', Holly scrunched up her nose at him. "You could have told me."

"Told you what?" Nick reached inside the cupboard and pulled out a container for the leftover meat. "Can I take this for lunch tomorrow?"

"No!" Holly snapped, turning back to the sink.

They continued cleaning up in silence. When Holly

pressed the start button on the dishwasher, Nick came up behind her, encircling her with his arms. As his lips glided along her neck, she nestled back against his chest. She had to hand it to him. He certainly knew how to end an argument.

After a moment, he turned her around. "So, you going to tell me what's on your mind?"

"What do you mean?"

"Holly," he said, drawing out the two syllables in that indulgent tone that made her want to scream. It was impossible to hide your feelings from a detective, especially when he was your husband.

"Let's sit down," she said, leading him back to the table. "So, after my first class I went to Dr. Miller's office."

When she finished relaying what occurred that morning, Nick asked, "And what did you do after that?"

"Well, I decided that it probably wasn't the best time to go ask Rodney if he gave Dr. Miller my message. I just went to the adjunct faculty office, corrected papers, taught my afternoon class and came home."

"You know, that argument you overheard may not have had anything to do with this case."

Holly tilted her head to the side and just stared at him. Her expression clearly communicated just how ridiculous she thought his comment was.

"Okay." Nick sighed. "Maybe it does, but ..."

The sound of the front door stopped Nick as Ivy's voice called to them from the entrance hall. "Nick, Holly, come here. I have a surprise for you."

When they stepped into the hall, they both said, "Nicky!" and rushed over to hug him.

"What a nice surprise!" Holly said.

"Why didn't you ..." Nick paused when he noticed the

man standing behind his son. Dressed in a black suit, white shirt and black tie, he clearly was an FBI agent. "You're not here to visit, are you?"

"No, Dad. This is Agent Phil Daniels. We're here on official FBI business."

"I told your agents everything I know last night when they picked up Brittany Holzman."

"We're not here to talk to you, Dad," Nicky said, his expression betraying his extreme discomfort. "We're here to question Holly."

34 QUESTIONS

"Me?" Holly stood frozen in place, unable to process what she'd just heard.

Nicky nodded. "May we sit down?"

"Of course," Nick said, pointing to the living room.

As the two men stepped through the archway, Ivy gave her sister's arm a squeeze. "I'll wait in the kitchen," she said, taking Lucky with her.

Holly could feel her heart beating. She turned to Nick. He put a reassuring arm around her.

"Just answer their questions," he said softly and led her into the living room.

The two agents had taken seats in the wingchairs on either side of the fireplace. Nick led Holly to the couch.

"Do I need a lawyer?" she asked as they sat down.

"No." Agent Daniels replied, a practiced smile on his face. "We need to see your cell phone, Mrs. Manelli."

Holly just stared at Daniels, appearing not to understand his request.

"My wife's last name is Donnelly," Nick intervened as he got up. "I'll get your phone."

Holly rubbed both her eyes, then gave her head a shake. "I'm sorry. I'm just–I don't know …"

"Relax, Holly," Nicky soothed. "We just need to clear up a few things."

"Like what?" Holly asked as Nick returned to the room.

Nicky extended his hand and took the cell phone from his father. "Your password?" he asked Holly, leaving her question unanswered.

As he tapped in the number she gave him, Agent Daniels asked, "What's your connection to Ecolyte, Ms.Donnelly?"

"There is none. I only learned about the group this past Monday when I talked to Brittany Holzman's roommate, Lisa Nicastro. Before that I'd never heard of them."

Nicky bit the corner of his lower lip as he looked up from the cell phone. He got up and handed the phone to Daniels, who studied the screen.

"Can you explain this text Agent Manelli just found on your phone?" Daniels asked, as Nicky walked over to show her the text.

Holly stared at the message. "9172022846". There was something vaguely familiar about the sequence. Where had she seen it? She looked at the phone number the text was sent to but didn't recognize it.

She gazed up at Nicky. "I don't recognize that phone number, but that sequence of numbers–I don't know."

"Are you saying you didn't send that text?" Agent Daniels asked.

"No, I definitely didn't send it," Holly replied.

"Yet the numbers in the message look familiar to you?" Daniels probed.

"Yes," Holly replied, turning to Nick. "It's weird. I just can't remember where I've seen them."

"When was the text sent?" Nick asked.

"Thursday afternoon," Nicky replied.

"Could one of your students have used your phone?" Nick asked.

"I don't think so." Holly shook her head. "Exactly what time was that text sent?" she asked.

"3:32 pm," Nicky replied.

"That was after the presentations at the Eco-Fair. In fact, we were probably on our way home about that time."

Ivy suddenly rushed into the room. "I know! I know!" She flashed a contrite grimace at Daniels. "I'm sorry, I couldn't help overhearing the conversation from the kitchen."

"This is Holly's sister, Ivy Donnelly," Nicky said to Daniels who peered over his reading glasses at her.

"So, what is it you know, Ms. Donnelly?" he asked.

Barely glancing at him, she turned to her sister. "Holly, remember when we got to the car? Kate's phone was dead. She asked to borrow yours."

"Oh, right," Holly nodded.

"Who's this Kate?" Daniels asked.

"She's my friend." Holly replied not looking at him. "Do you remember her saying who she was sending a message to?"

"No," Ivy shook her head, "because Nick's text arrived inviting us to dinner and Kate teased you about his calling you *amore mio*?"

Holly smiled. "Right. And I told her to give me the phone back or she could stay home and eat leftovers." She turned back to Nicky and reached for her phone. "Here, give me that."

"Ms. Donnelly ..." Daniels began to object as she took the phone from her stepson.

"Relax, Agent Daniels," Holly said. "We can call Kate and

get this whole thing straightened out.

"Ms. Donnelly, really …" Daniels started to get up, but Nick held out his hand palm outward, signaling the agent to hold on.

Holly walked over to Ivy, holding the phone out for her to look at. "Do you recognize these numbers?" she asked.

Ivy stared at the screen for a moment before her mouth began to curl into a smile. "Yes. Go to your photos."

Holly tapped the screen. "I knew I'd seen that sequence before." She walked over to where Daniels sat and held the screen for him to see the photo. "We took photos of business cards, and we found this piece of paper in Brittany Holzman's bedroom," she said with an air of triumph.

Daniels grimaced. "I wouldn't be smiling if I were you, Ms. Donnelly."

Holly's smile quickly evaporated. "Why?" She turned to Nicky. "What does it mean?"

Nicky sighed. "The numerical sequence is the date, time and number of the building where the Green Gardyns' explosion occurred."

35 PHONE INTERVIEW

Agent McDaniels pulled out his cell phone.

"Kate is no eco-terrorist, Agent Daniels," Holly said, not masking her annoyance. "Believe me, it will go a lot better if you let me talk to her first."

Daniels aimed a get-control-of-your-wife look at Nick.

"Holly, let's go to the kitchen and let the agents do their job." Nick took her by the arm. She resisted for just a moment, but realizing, as she had so many times before, resistance was futile, she let Nick lead her to the kitchen. Ivy followed.

Nicky gave his father an appreciative nod as he returned his attention to Holly's phone.

In the kitchen both sisters sat down at the table, their expressions grim.

"Really, Nick," Holly said, distress coloring her face. "Don't you think it would be better if I had talked to Kate first?"

"You know that's not how this works," her husband replied, sitting down in the chair beside her. "They don't want you prepping her before they question her."

Holly's eyes widened. "You mean like you had Peppy ..."

Nick quickly placed his hand over her mouth. When he

removed it, she whispered, "I knew it!"

Ivy leaned closer. "Knew what?" she asked in a hushed tone.

"I'll tell you later," her sister replied. "I just pray Kate doesn't start telling them any of her conspiracy theories."

"Yeah," Ivy frowned, looking at Nick. "That wouldn't be good, would it?"

Nick smiled. "Give these guys some credit. They know the difference between a terrorist and a ..." He hesitated.

"A what, Nick?" Holly glared at him. "A garden variety nut case? An hysterical woman?"

"I didn't say that," Nick demurred. "Besides, I know Kate."

"What does that mean?" Holly asked.

"She's Italian. She has an innate distrust of authority figures. She'll answer their questions and say as little as possible."

Ivy's left eyebrow rose. "You know, I think he's right. She lets loose when she talks to us, but I have noticed when we're in the company of strangers she never talks about anything controversial."

"Maybe." Holly crossed her arms. "I don't know."

"Really. Remember after the closing ceremonies how she wouldn't even tell us what she found out from Brittany until we were a block away from the Planetarium and no one was around us?"

"Hmpf," Holly grunted. "I never thought about it. Come to think of it, she always cautions me whenever I talk to her on the phone and say something overly critical of government."

"See." Nick wore a self-satisfied smile.

Holly stared back at him through narrowed eyes. "So, what do you think is going to happen here?"

"They'll send field agents, probably from Albany, to Kate's to get a statement. And they'll check her phone records." Nick locked eyes with Holly. "This text message and that piece of paper you found in Brittany's room is clear evidence the girl was involved in some way with the explosion at Green Gardyn Foods."

Holly's brow furrowed. "You think it's possible she didn't know what the message was about?"

"Yeah," Ivy said. "Maybe she had instructions to send that text to a phone number and that's all she knew."

"But she had the sense to get someone else to send it for her, didn't she?" Nick asked.

Holly's shoulders drooped. "Oh, yeah."

Nicky appeared in the doorway. "We're done here."

"That didn't take long," Holly said. "How'd it go?"

Both Nick and Nicky looked at her with the same amused expression.

After a moment, Nick said, "You know he can't answer that."

Holly let out a loud, impatient huff. "And you know I'll just talk to Kate and find out anyway."

"Nice to see you both," Nicky said with a smile at Holly, then Ivy.

"Can't you stay with us tonight?" Holly asked.

"Another time," Nicky replied.

"C'mon. I'll walk you out," Nick said.

As the men disappeared into the hallway, Ivy leaned toward her sister and whispered. "Let's call Kate."

Holly's face lit up, but quickly grew dim. "They've got my phone."

36 THE SEARCH

"That phone has to be here," Kate said.

"We searched every nook and granny of that room," Benny said, shaking his head.

"Cranny," Razor corrected.

"We searched the bathroom too," Peppy added. "Nada."

"Well, I'll put out a BOLO based on this description of the intruder, Kate," Jason said, closing his notebook. "Doesn't look like there's anything more we can do tonight."

Suddenly Kate's phone signaled from inside her shoulder bag. "Could you hand me that?" Kate asked.

She located her phone, glanced at the screen and quickly put it on speaker. "Hello, Ivy? What's up?"

"It's me, Holly," came the reply.

"What happened to your–oh, never mind. Just so you know, I've got you on speaker. I'm here with Benny, Razor, Jason and Peppy."

"Peppy?" Holly's voice conveyed her surprise. "What's she doing there?"

Peppy's eyes widened and she shook her head at Kate, who shrugged, uncertain what she was supposed to do.

"She came up to visit me." Razor quickly came to the rescue.

"Oh, that's nice," Holly said, sounding confused. "But I'm calling to find out how it went?"

"Well, I've got a bruised knee, but I managed to save the bag."

"What are you talking about?" Holly asked.

"What are you talking about?" Kate replied.

"Are you kidding me?" Holly said with an air of impatience. "I want to know how the call went with Agent Daniels."

"Who's Agent Daniels?" Kate asked, her tone equally impatient.

"Wait. Are you telling me you didn't just talk to the FBI?"

"I think I'd remember that," Kate replied. "What's this all about?"

"Well, Nicky was just here."

"Surprise visit?" Kate asked as lights from outside and the crunch of gravel in the driveway sent Jason, Razor, Benny and Peppy to the windows. "Wait, Holly. Someone just pulled in the driveway."

"Looks like an FBI vehicle," Jason replied.

"Uh-oh," Peppy said as the black SUV came to a stop behind her Hyundai. She turned to Razor. "I can't be here," she said.

"Holly, I gotta go," Kate said, ending the call as Razor quickly took Peppy by the hand and led her across the kitchen through the mudroom to the back door.

"When we let these guys in, you go over to our place. The back door is open." He released her hand and returned to the doorway. "I'll tell you when."

After just a few seconds, a knock sounded at the kitchen

door. Jason glanced back at Razor who nodded. As Jason opened the door, Razor said, "Now."

Peppy slipped out silently.

"Can I help you?" Jason asked.

"I'm Agent Fred Higbee." A man appearing to be in his fifties held up an FBI badge. Pointing to the younger man behind him, he said, "This is Agent Ross Conrad. We need to speak to Kate Farmer. May we come in?"

Jason nodded and opened the door. "I'm Sheriff Jason Bascom," he said. "What brings the FBI here?"

As the two men stepped inside, Higbee surveyed the room. "I might ask you the same question, Sheriff."

"Attempted robbery," Jason replied.

Higbee looked from Benny to Razor.

"These guys?"

"These men are my neighbors," Kate said indignantly. "They're the reason I've only got a bruised knee and nothing was taken."

"Sorry, Ma'am," Higbee replied chagrined.

"I'm Kate Farmer. Now what is it you want to see me about?"

"Can we talk privately?" the agent asked.

"Absolutely not," Kate replied. "I don't know you. And if these men weren't here, I wouldn't have even let you into the house."

Higbee locked eyes with her for a moment, but finally said, "We're here about Brittany Holzman."

So, this is what Holly was calling about. Kate just nodded. She wasn't volunteering any information. He was going to have to work for it.

"Show her," Higbee said to his younger partner.

Conrad took out his phone, tapped the screen, then walked over and let Kate take a look.

"You recognize that message?" Higbee asked.

Kate felt her stomach flip. It was the text Brittany had asked her to send the day of the Eco-Fair. She thought it was an odd message at the time. But why would the FBI be interested in it?

"Yes, I recognize it," she replied, again not offering any more than she was asked.

Higbee appeared to be growing annoyed. "Ms. Farmer, could you please tell us about your relationship to Ms. Holzman and the organization known as Ecolyte?"

Suddenly Kate realized this had to have something to do with the warehouse explosion. She had no choice.

"I met Brittany Holzman the day before the Eco-Fair at Pineland Park Community College," she began.

Conrad took notes as she told them everything she knew. When she finished, Higbee gave her an appraising look.

"So, you're telling us Ms. Holzman just showed up at your door, a hundred miles from Pineland Park," he said, "and, even though you'd only just met her, you invited her to stay overnight in your house?"

"Yes," Kate replied. Her stomach was beginning to churn. Even she realized how lame her story sounded.

"Did you know she was wanted for questioning in the Green Gardyn warehouse explosion?"

"No. Not until I talked to my friend Holly Donnelly the morning after Brittany arrived."

"And when you found out, did you call the the Sheriff here?" Higbee asked, tilting his head in Jason's direction.

Kate could feel her heart rate speed up. "Well, Jason did come and ..."

144

"Did you call him?" Higbee asked.

"No, but ..."

"Okay, Ms. Farmer," Higbee said as he got to his feet. "You'll need to come with us."

37 QUICK THINKING

Once inside Benny and Razor's place, Peppy pulled out her phone and tapped the screen. Manelli's number was at the top of her recent calls list. She tapped it.

"Damn!" she said under her breath when the "Can't talk now" message appeared.

She knew he'd call her back as soon as he could. Slipping the phone in her back pocket, she finally lifted her eyes from the screen and took in her surroundings. The kitchen was old-fashioned, but neat and spotless. White metal cabinets covered the back wall. The countertop was faded and worn, a brownish hue she'd never seen in a kitchen. Whatever it was made of, it pre-dated Formica.

The side wall was bare sheetrock. On the floor, paint cans, a paint tray and a roller were neatly lined up on top of a plastic tarp. Peppy smiled. Who was the do-it-yourselfer, she wondered. Benny or Razor?

She crossed the room and peeked through the door into the living room. The furniture was also vintage. It reminded her of pictures she'd seen of her grandmother's house. The only new item in the room was a 55-inch television screen sitting atop an antique credenza. That, too, made Peppy smile.

These guys weren't gay. Not that that mattered. But what was their story, she wondered, when her phone signaled.

"Boss, the Feds are at Kate's."

"Where are you?" Nick asked.

"I'm next door at Benny and Razor's place. Kate was on the phone with Holly when they pulled up. Razor snuck me out the back door."

"Good. Quick thinking."

Peppy was glad he couldn't see the goofy grin on her face at his praise. "So, what's going on?"

"Well, two FBI agents, one of them my son, just left here."

"What!"

"Remember that piece of paper with the numbers on it, the one you brought back from Brittany's room?"

"Yeah," Peppy replied.

Nick explained the significance of the numbers and the connection to Holly and Kate.

"That's not good, but I got something to tell you, too," Peppy said after he finished. "When I got here, a police car was in the driveway." She relayed Kate's encounter with the intruder.

"I searched the contents of the bag, but there was no phone. Now, she didn't have one on her when we booked her. Kate said she saw her checking messages the night she arrived. Benny and Razor helped me search the bedroom she slept in and the bathroom, but we didn't find it."

Peppy waited as Nick remained quiet. After a few moments, he said, "You're onto something, Alvarez. She had to have hidden that phone there some …"

"Hold on, Boss. I hear a car starting." Peppy walked to the side window. "Uh-oh."

"What is it?" Nick asked.

"The FBI SUV is lit up and it looks like an agent is leading Kate out to the vehicle."

"Great," Nick said, disgust in his voice. "I knew there was going to be a problem when Nicky told me they were sending the Albany field agents to talk to Kate."

"You knew they were coming?" Peppy asked, trying to keep an accusing tone out of her voice.

"Not until a few minutes ago. I walked my son and the agent he came with out to their car. That's why I couldn't take your call. When the other agent got in the car, Nicky tipped me off about the Albany agents."

Peppy grimaced. She should have known better than to think he would have sat on that information. "What do you want me to do?" she asked.

"Have they left?"

"Pulling out now," she said as she watched the SUV back down the driveway.

"Is Jason still there?" Nick asked.

"Yep."

"Get back over there. I have a plan."

38 BACKSTORY

Peppy had just closed a dresser drawer in Kate's bedroom when she heard the shout.

"Hot damn!" Benny exclaimed. "I found it."

She hurried to the game room that Kate called 'the attic'. Razor, who'd been searching the mudroom downstairs, mounted the back steps two at a time.

"Can I get a hallelujah?" Peppy walked over to where Benny sat on the floor holding up the cell phone. She pulled a plastic evidence bag out of her pocket and he dropped the phone inside.

"Nice work," Razor said to his friend extending his hand to help him up.

Peppy pulled out her phone. "Hello, Boss. We got it. Benny found it. Yeah. Okay. See you tomorrow."

"What'd he say?" Benny asked.

"You know him," Peppy replied. "Great work. Get some sleep. See you in the morning." She glanced at her phone again. "Oh boy. I didn't realize the time. It's after midnight. No wonder he wasn't very chatty." She headed to the stairs. "Not that he ever is."

Down in the kitchen she placed the evidence bag near her jacket. Turning to face the men, she said, "I owe you guys big time. I'd have been at it all night if I had to search by myself. As we say back home, '*muchas gracias*'."

Benny beamed. "We're always happy to help."

"Well, your work is done here. Go home and get some sleep," Peppy said.

Benny stretched and yawned. "Yeah, I'm ready to turn in."

In a quiet, yet commanding voice Razor said, "I'm not leaving you here alone."

Peppy felt a warm sensation rising up her neck as her eyes met his. "Hey, that's really not necessary," she shrugged, quickly averting her gaze. She patted her holster sitting on the counter. "See. I'm fully armed."

"And dangerous," Benny guffawed. He cast a momentary glance at Razor. Peppy sensed that some telepathic communication had occurred because Benny immediately headed to the door. "Don't let the bedbugs bite," were his parting words.

Razor walked over and locked the door.

"Really," Peppy said, "you don't need to stay here."

"*Me quedaré*," Razor said as he stood by the door watching. When Benny was safely inside the bungalow next door, he turned to face her. "I'm staying because that intruder who was here earlier is still out there."

"Oh, yeah," Peppy nodded.

"He came for that phone, and my guess is he'll be back before this night is over. Why don't you go upstairs? Get some sleep. I'll stay down here and keep watch. If he does come back, he won't get past me."

Peppy let out a soft laugh.

"Go on," he urged softly.

Peppy lingered, staring at the big man. After a moment she asked, "So, what's your story? You and Benny."

Razor went to the refrigerator and peered inside. "You drink beer?"

"What d'you think?" Peppy replied.

He pulled out two cans of Blue Moon and popped open the tops. Handing her one, he headed to the living room. Peppy followed.

Dropping onto the couch, he took a long swallow of the beer. After Peppy sat down in the armchair, he said, "Me and Benny been friends since first grade. We always had each other's backs."

Peppy took a sip of the beer and aimed a droll smile in Razor's direction. "That's it? You opened two beers just to tell me that?"

"What else you want to know?" he asked.

"Where'd you learn to speak Spanish?"

"My mother."

Peppy leaned back in the chair and sighed. "More please."

"My mother was Puerto Rican. My father was Irish. They met in Brooklyn. A guy my father was in the Navy with offered him a job up here as a mechanic. Moved here when I was six." He raised the bottle to his lips again.

"Okay, that explains the Spanish and the–uh–perpetual suntan. But if I walked into a room full of people, the last two I'd think were friends are you and Benny."

"Well, people with my skin tone weren't exactly welcomed into the neighborhood when we moved here. The local bullies liked to–well, you know. One day a group of older guys ganged up on me. Benny happened to be walking home with his pit bull and he threatened to let him loose on them if they didn't stop. We been lookin' out for each other ever since."

"Male bonding. I get that." Peppy took another swallow.

"So, what's your story, Officer Alvarez?" Razor asked. "How'd you become a cop?"

"That I owe to Detective Manelli and his wife. But that's a long story for another time." Peppy yawned.

"Another time?" Razor smiled. "I like the sound of that."

Before she could control her expression, she returned the smile. Quickly, she got to her feet. *"Buenos noches, amigo,"* she said and headed to the stairs.

With her back to him, Peppy was glad he couldn't see her face when he said, *"Buenos noches, cariño.'* Only her father had ever called her *cariño*–darling. She liked the sound of it.

39 NEXT MOVE

"You're going to call Nicky, right?" Holly gave her husband a pleading look as he adjusted the Windsor knot of his tie.

Nick turned to her. "Holly, you know I can't do that. I need to wait for him to call me." Placing both hands on her shoulders, he said, "Relax, will you? I guarantee Kate will be released this morning–this afternoon the latest. When they review her phone records, they'll see she had no other contact with Ecolyte. They'll confer with Agent Daniels and they'll let her go."

"I hope you're right." Holly frowned as she followed him out of their bedroom and down the stairs. When they reached the kitchen, she asked, "Why won't you tell me what that midnight call was about?"

Nick poured himself a mug of coffee. After he took a sip, he said, "Some things you don't need to know."

"Oh, c'mon, Nick!" Holly stamped her foot. "How many times are we going to have this same argument?"

Nick gave her his indulgent smile, the one that infuriated her because she knew he wasn't going to budge. "Were you questioned by the FBI yesterday?"

She glared at him. "You know I was."

"And you know it's a crime to lie to federal agents, right?"

Holly let out a resigned sigh. "Right."

"Well, you can't lie about something you know nothing about, can you?" he said giving her cheek a light tweak.

Holly didn't reply as he gulped down what was left of his coffee and placed his mug in the dishwasher. She followed him to the front door. Grabbing his keys from the key rack, he kissed her on the cheek. "Trust me. Everything will be okay. Go teach."

Holly gave him a feeble smile. "Call me if you hear anything."

He kissed her again and walked out the door. Holly watched as he headed to his Malibu parked out front. Of course, he was right.

She returned to the kitchen and filled her mug. As she added milk, the front door opened. Lucky rushed in, Ivy behind her.

"Any news about Kate?" Ivy asked.

"Not that he'll tell me." Holly sighed.

"I heard the phone ring last night," Ivy said, pouring the last of the coffee in a mug. "Was that Nicky calling?"

"I don't know. One of several questions Nick wouldn't answer." Holly sank down into a chair at the table. "Another one is what was Peppy doing up at Kate's."

Ivy sat down across from her sister. "Well, that's easy. He sent her up there to get Brittany's bag."

Holly appeared confused as she considered what her sister just said. "That's right! I forgot all about Kate's call telling us she found it. After a moment she gave her forehead a slight tap. "Gosh, what's wrong with me? I can't seem to think straight these days."

"Well, getting questioned by the FBI could sort of push other things out of your mind," her sister said.

"Thanks for giving me an excuse." Holly flashed her a lame smile.

"You know, Nick never mentioned Brittany's bag to Agent Daniels and Nicky, did he?"

Holly's pursed lips slowly turned into a smile. "No, he did not." She tapped the table. "That sly devil withheld evidence. That's why he didn't want me to know. If the FBI questioned me about it, I couldn't tell them what I didn't know!"

"But withholding evidence. That's not like him," Ivy's forehead puckered. "Why do you think he did that?"

"Well, I do know the cops never like it when the Feds come in and take over their case."

"Ooooh," Ivy's brow became smooth again. "I get it. That warehouse explosion took place on his turf."

"Exactly. And he had to hand over his suspect and all the evidence he had to them." Holly glanced up at the clock. "Oh boy. I've got to go, or I'll be late for my class."

"You only have one class today," Ivy said. "Will you be home right after you finish?"

"I don't know. I'll call you," Holly said heading to the hall.

"You don't have a phone, remember?" Ivy said.

"Oh right. Let me borrow yours."

Ivy handed her phone over and followed her sister to the front door. Putting a hand on her forearm, she said, "Please come home right after class. Don't do anything stupid."

"Me? Stupid? Please." Holly smiled as she hurried out the door, wondering exactly what her next move should be.

40 THE PARKING DECK

Holly stopped for a red light at the intersection in front of the Planetarium. Looking over at the gleaming, glass façade, she let out a sigh. How different the drive here felt just a week ago. The Eco-Fair held such promise. How could things have spun so far out of control?

Was Brittany really involved in the Green Gardyn explosion? Or was she an unwitting dupe? Same with the forgery on the release papers allowing Ariana's team to use Green Gardyn seeds in their experiment. Did she forge the signature on the forms allowing the students to use Green Gardyn seeds in their experiment? But she had to know that sooner or later the forgery would be discovered.

Holly's thoughts were interrupted by the sound of Kate's ringtone. She quickly tapped the screen.

"Kate, hi. How'd you know to call me on this phone?"

"When I got no answer on your cell, I called your house phone. You and I have to be two of only a handful of people who still have them. Anyway, Ivy told me you had her phone. So, the FBI still has yours, huh?" Kate said, a smug edge to her voice.

"Never mind that. Are you home? Are you okay?" Holly

asked as the light turned green.

"I'm home, but I'm not okay," her friend replied, the edge in her voice decidedly sharper.

"I'm so sorry," Holly said as she continued the drive to the parking garage. "I hardly got any sleep last night thinking about you."

"Really? Well, how'd you like to be me? They kept me up all night asking the same questions over and over and over. I actually thought I was guilty of something."

Holly unsuccessfully tried to stifle a laugh as she approached the parking garage.

"It's not funny, Holly!" Kate growled.

"I know. Hey, is Peppy still there?"

"No. She must have gone back last night or left really early this morning."

"She was there to get Brittany's bag, right?" Holly asked.

"You didn't know that?"

"No, I ..." Holly stopped the car halfway up the first level ramp when she spotted Ariana running towards her. "Hold on," she said as she lowered her window. "Ariana!" she shouted, but the girl ran past without stopping.

"What's going on?" Kate asked. "Where are you?"

"In my car. I'm in the parking deck at school," Holly looked in the rearview mirror. "Darn. There's a car behind me. Hold on until I park."

As she rounded the turn, she spotted an empty space and quickly pulled in. "Okay. I can talk now."

"So why were you shouting to Ariana?"

"She was running down the ramp. She ran past like she didn't even hear me. I wonder what's wrong."

"She's probably just late for class."

"No. First period doesn't start for another twenty minutes. And she was running like …"

"Like someone was chasing her?" Kate asked. "Are your doors locked?"

Holly sighed. "Seriously, Kate, it's 8:00 am and broad daylight."

"School shooters don't wait until dark! They act when school is in session."

In spite of her skepticism, Holly checked the door locks, peered out her window, then the passenger side window. "Really. There's no one around."

"You stay in that car until you see someone you know," Kated ordered. "Can you call for a security guard to walk you to the building?"

"I'm not going to do that," Holly replied. "Let's get back to last night. Did you find out what was in Brittany's bag?"

"Not much. But guess what wasn't in the bag?

"What?"

"Her phone. Peppy said she didn't have it on her when they brought her in. It wasn't in the bag, and I saw her checking her phone messages the night she arrived here."

"So, it's somewhere in your house?"

"Yes, and if I weren't so tired, I'd start searching for it." Kate yawned.

Holly looked at the clock on the dashboard. "Look, I gotta go. My class starts soon."

"You better be careful. Stay on the line with me until you reach the building."

"Oh Kate, you are so dramatic," Holly said as she grabbed her bag and briefcase and got out of the car.

"Humor me," Kate said.

"This coming from the woman who invited an eco-terrorist to stay in her home," Holly teased, glancing at the cars parked on the opposite side of the aisle from where she parked.

"How many times do I have to say, I didn't know ..."

"Hold on," Holly said as something caught her eye in a car parked across the aisle.

"What is it?" Kate asked, alarmed at Holly's tone.

"I don't know." Holly crouched down as she approached a silver Toyota. "Oh no!" she gasped when she reached the driver's side of the car. She dropped the phone and her bags and tried to open the door, but it was locked. She began pounding on the window. Her shoulders sagged when she got no response.

"What's going on?" Kate's voice shouted from where the phone lay on the concrete.

Holly retrieved the cell phone. "I think I just found a dead body."

41 HOMICIDE

Holly thanked the security guard who handed her a cup of coffee. She glanced at the wall clock. Nearly two hours had passed since they escorted her to the Campus Security Office across the street from the parking deck.

Although she felt shaken, she had the presence of mind to call the English Department admin as soon as they brought her there. They needed to get someone to cover her class. She doubted that would be possible on such short notice, so she gave the admin instructions for a writing assignment the class could work on in her absence.

She really would prefer to be across the street teaching her class instead of watching the police cordon off the parking deck entrance with crime scene tape. She sipped her coffee wondering why they were keeping her here so long. She'd answered all the questions the local police asked and agreed to write up a statement for them.

Suddenly the door opened, and Nick walked in. Holly felt a wave of relief wash over her when she saw him. She started to stand, but her legs felt wobbly, and she sank back down into the chair. Nick rushed over and sat down in the chair beside her.

"You all right?" he asked, putting a comforting arm around her.

Resting her head on his chest, she could feel the tears she hadn't realized she'd been holding back as they began to run down her cheeks. After a few moments, she lifted her head and brushed at the tears with the crumpled napkin she'd been given with the coffee.

"The policemen brought me over here before they opened the car," she said, feeling the blood drain from her cheeks. "If you're here that means it was a homicide."

Nick nodded.

Holly moaned and lowered her head again.

"Tell me what you know," Nick said softly.

"There's not much to tell." She sat up, inhaled deeply and recounted her discovery of the figure slumped over the steering wheel. When she finished, she grasped Nick's hand.

"How?" she asked.

"Stabbed in the chest. Bled out."

"Do you know who it was?"

"Rodney Blakely."

Holly gasped. "That's Dr. Miller's assistant. He's an annoying little guy, but still–I can't imagine why anyone would want to kill him." After a moment, her eyes widened. "Do you think it had anything to do with that argument I overheard the other day?"

Nick gave a non-committal shrug. "Did you see anything else? Anything suspicious? Anyone who didn't look like they belonged here?"

Holly felt a stitch in the pit of her stomach at the memory of Ariana running past her, not stopping when she called out to her. Holly's eyes met Nick's.

"I can see you did," he said when she didn't reply. "You

have to tell me."

"Ariana," she said. "I saw her running down the ramp toward the pedestrian bridge when I was driving in."

Nick grimaced as he stood and reached into his chest pocket for his phone. He walked across the room out of earshot to place a call.

She suddenly felt cold and hopeless without his arm around her. She closed her eyes and leaned back in the chair.

This could not be happening. Ariana was incapable of killing someone. But why had she been running? Running so hard that she didn't even stop when Holly called out to her.

Maybe she discovered the body and was running to report it. Holly nodded to herself. That had to be it, she thought, feeling a bit comforted by the idea.

Nick finished his call and returned to where she was sitting. Offering his hand, he said, "Let's get you home."

She reached for him and stood. His hands were always warm–always reassuring. But as they walked out the door, the momentary respite from her worst fears waned. If Ariana was running to report the body, why hadn't she also been sitting in the Campus Security Office with her?

42 CONFLICT

Despite Holly's objections, Nick arranged for an officer to drive her car, and insisted she ride with him. He knew she needed to talk, so he had her tell him everything she knew about Rodney Blakely. Although she'd said she couldn't imagine anyone wanting to kill him, Nick thought he sounded like just the kind of guy lots of people would want to murder.

After he dropped her off at home, he drove back to the Pineland Park Police Station. On the drive he considered his next move. Though he wouldn't admit it to Holly, he felt pretty certain Rodney Blakely's murder was somehow related to the Green Gardyn explosion. But how? There was no real evidence linking the two.

And how was he going to handle his investigation when the FBI was involved? He didn't want to do anything that would reflect badly on Nicky. Besides, if he shared with them his suspicions that Rodney's murder might be related, that could further tie his hands. They already had custody of a prime witness in the Green Gardyn case who might have information that could help find Rodney's killer.

And why, oh why, did his wife have to be caught up in the middle of this mess? There was no way to sideline her, not when Ariana Alvarez's future was at stake.

"Damn!" he muttered under his breath, as he realized he was going to have to pull Peppy off the case. Though he was ninety-nine percent certain Ariana did not murder Rodney, having her cousin work on this case could later call into question the integrity of their investigation.

No, he did not want to sideline Peppy. The rookie had street smarts. He'd become increasingly impressed with her ability to think on her feet. He'd given her no special instructions when he sent her up to Reddington Manor to pick up Brittany's bag. Still, she knew she would have a hard time explaining to the FBI what she was doing there since they had taken over the case. She had good instincts. Besides, he knew he could count on her to keep Holly safe.

When Nick arrived at his office, Yolanda looked up from her computer screen and smiled. "Good news. Dr. Wisnieski will conduct the autopsy. He said he'll get right on it."

"Good," Nick replied, walked into his office and dropped into his chair. Yolanda followed.

"Bad news. No word on Ariana yet." She frowned.

"Does Peppy know we're looking for her cousin?" he asked.

Yolanda shook her head. "I don't think so."

Nick let out a loud sigh. "You better tell her to come see me."

Yolanda nodded, but before she reached the door, Peppy appeared, a huge smile on her face.

"Boss, we been going through Brittany's phone. After they checked for prints, I started reading the emails and texts. There's a whole lot of back-and-forth between her and a burner phone number," she said, her voice brimming with excitement. "They seemed pretty careful not to say anything real specific, but there was a flurry of messages the day of the explosion and they were clearly planning to get out of town."

When Nick didn't react, Peppy appeared confused. "Well, this is good, isn't it? And I got more."

"Sit down," Nick said.

Peppy's expression shifted from puzzled to wary. She glanced at Yolanda, whose face remained impassive.

"Did I do something wrong?" Peppy asked as she sat down.

"No," Nick replied, then told her about Rodney's murder and Ariana's fleeing the scene of a crime.

"Who said she fled the scene?" Peppy asked, her voice calm, but her tone combative.

"Holly."

Peppy jerked her head back as if she'd been slapped. After a moment, she sat forward and pounded her fist on the desk. "No!"

Nick glanced at Yolanda, who quickly closed the door to prevent anyone from overhearing the conversation.

Peppy began to shake her head. "No! Ariana is incapable of killing anyone. How was this guy murdered?"

"Stabbed to death."

Peppy hooted. "Boss, that's impossible. Ariana doesn't know one end of a knife from the other. Me! I was the one with the blade. She ran away whenever I practiced." Her expression grew somber. "Boss, you know she couldn't have done this, don't you?"

"She didn't report the crime, and we can't find her," Nick said without emotion.

"That doesn't mean she killed the guy!" Peppy appeared increasingly frustrated.

"We need to talk to her," Nick said, his voice calm and even as he studied the young policewoman in front of him. He decided to take a chance. "Can you find her and bring her in?"

The conflict Peppy felt was clearly reflected on her face.

Yolanda placed a hand on Peppy's shoulder. "You know this is the only way."

After a moment, Peppy stood. "I'll find her."

After she was gone, Yolanda turned back to Nick who was already reading a report she'd put on his desk. "For what it's worth, I think that was the right thing to do."

Without looking up, he said, "Let me know when the autopsy results are in."

"Yes, sir," Yolanda smiled and headed to the door. Once again, Peppy appeared, out of breath, not smiling this time.

"I almost forgot," the rookie said. "We found something else on the phone. Photos. I sent some to Kate Farmer to look at. She identified one of the men as the guy who tried to get away with Brittany's bag." She held out her phone with a copy of the photo of Brittany with the unknown intruder.

Nick glanced at the screen, then turned to his assistant. "Yolanda, go with her and get that phone."

As the two policewomen turned to leave, Nick called out. "Alvarez."

When Peppy turned to face him, he said, "Good work. Now go find Ariana."

43 FBI HEADQUARTERS, NEWARK

Nicky was hard at work doing background checks on a list of Ecolyte members when his phone signaled. The agent who reviewed Holly's cell phone and social media activity told him she was in the clear. They failed to turn up anything linking her to Ecolyte or Brittany Holzman.

He thanked the agent for letting him know, feeling the tension in his neck recede. Though he was certain his stepmother was no eco-terrorist, he felt on edge until he got the official word that she was cleared of any connection to the group.

He still remembered the horror he felt when he discovered that the text message signaling the time, date and address of the Green Gardyn explosion had been sent from Holly's cell phone. Why, of all the agents working on the case, did he have to be the one assigned to examine the burner phone they found at the explosion site?

Last night he wanted to call his father when he got back to the hotel, but Agent Daniels made it clear that he was not to discuss the details of the case with anyone, especially his father. The only way that was possible was if he had no contact with him. He was grateful his dad hadn't tried to call him either. Nicky knew that, after a career in law enforcement, he understood the position his son was in.

As a rookie agent Nicky had certainly proven himself his first few months on the job. He succeeded in foiling a few cyber attacks on government agency computer networks. Still, he was too new to take a risk and violate protocol by discussing the case with anyone outside the FBI.

Nicky rubbed the back of his neck. At least now that Holly was cleared he would be able to give his undivided attention to the background checks he was working on. As he began to review an Ecolyte member's Facebook page, his phone again signaled.

"I need you in the conference room, Agent Manelli," Agent Daniels said.

"Yes, sir. I'll be right there," Nicky replied.

As he approached the glass-walled conference room where Agent Daniels had set up his war room, Nicky was more than a little surprised to see his father sitting at the table. This could not be good he thought, as he opened the door. Nodding in his father's direction, Nicky quickly turned to Agent Daniels for direction.

"Here." Daniels held up a cell phone with a photo of Brittany Holzman and a man who appeared to be slightly older than her. "This is Brittany Holzman's phone. Stop whatever you're doing and find out who this guy is. We need to know his connection to Brittany Holzman."

"I'll get right on it, sir." Nicky took the phone, again aimed a slight nod in his father's direction, and quickly left the room.

Mixed emotions clamored for his attention as he hurried back to his desk. He looked at the photo on the cell phone screen and felt a vague spark of recognition, but couldn't quite place where he'd seen the face. As he began to run the facial recognition program, he wondered how his father got his hands on the phone.

It had to have been left at Kate's place up in the Catskills. If Kate found it, she would have called Holly and Holly would have told his father. His father should have contacted the FBI immediately. But he didn't. His father would know that the FBI didn't need a warrant to access Brittany's phone records and internet activity. Then why bring in the phone at all? Nicky smiled. He needs our help finding out who this guy is.

Nicky's smile widened. He couldn't wait to hear the story his father concocted for Agent Daniels as to why he had the phone and why he knew the man who's face they were searching for was a person of interest.

44 A KNACK FOR MURDER

"Here. Drink this." Ivy handed her sister a cup of tea.

"Thanks," Holly replied. "Stop looking at me that way."

"What way?" Ivy asked.

"The way you do when you are concerned about me. I'm fine. Really."

"I know." Ivy sat down across the kitchen table from her sister. "Still, finding a dead body isn't something that happens every day–though with you ..."

"Stop." Holly frowned at her sister and took a sip of the tea.

"Who do you think killed Rodney?" Ivy asked.

"Well, I told you about that argument I overheard between him and Professor McNair," Holly replied. "But honestly, I can't imagine the professor killing anyone–and stabbing him to death?"

"Yeah, that is a rather barbaric way to commit murder. I'd expect a professor to be a little more imaginative."

"Ivy! What a thing to say."

Ivy shrugged. "Sorry, it's just that stabbing someone seems like a passionate thing to do. I think of scientists as more analytical–that they'd be more methodical if they were planning to murder someone."

"If they were planning to murder someone," Holly repeated. "But what if he wasn't planning ..."

The ring of the house phone interrupted her. She grabbed the cordless phone and tapped the speaker button. "Hi, Kate. I'm home, here with Ivy."

"Oh that's a relief. I haven't been able to stop thinking about you since you had to hang up on me. So, whose body was it? Anyone you know?"

"Yes," Holly answered. "Rodney Blakely, Dr. Miller's assistant."

"The nerdy guy with the horn-rimmed glasses?"

"That's the one."

"Suicide?" Kate asked.

Holly glanced across at her sister.

"No, Kate," Ivy replied. "He was stabbed to death and bled out."

Kate gasped. "Another murder? I can't believe you, Holly."

"Oh c'mon," Holly objected. "You make it sound like I had something to do with it."

"No, but you have to admit, you have developed this knack for–oh, I don't know–being in the vicinity when a murder occurs. Don't you agree, Ivy?"

"It certainly seems so," Ivy replied.

Holly glared at her sister, then at the phone. "Is there anything else you wanted before I hang up?"

"Yeah, there is," Kate replied. "Have you talked to Peppy?"

"No. Why?"

"Well, she sent me some photos they found on Brittany's phone and ..."

"Brittany's phone? So it was in the bag she left at your house."

"No, it wasn't. After the FBI arrested me ..."

"They didn't arrest you, Kate."

"Okay, okay. After they took me–against my will–for questioning, Peppy, Benny and Razor searched the house. Benny found the cell phone between some books on a bookshelf in the attic. I didn't know that until Peppy called me not long after you and I were on the phone. And get this–I identified the guy who tried to get away with Brittany's bag in one of the pictures."

"Oh, wow," Holly said. "That's great. Any idea who he is?"

"No. Maybe a boyfriend."

"Hey, Kate," Ivy broke in. "Has it occurred to you that that guy might still be around–waiting for another chance to get the bag?"

"No, but now that you've put that in my head, I probably won't be able to sleep tonight. In fact ..."

Holly and Ivy smiled as they could hear the sound of a door slamming shut.

"... I just closed and locked the door."

"Maybe you should drive down and stay with us until this guy is found," Holly suggested.

"Yeah, we could start a game of Clue," Ivy said, a gleeful lilt to her voice.

Holly groaned. "No, we're never doing that again. But seriously. Ivy's right. That guy might still be around, and if he tries to get in again, you could get hurt."

"Well," Kate hesitated. "Let me think about it. Tonight is my book club at the library and I don't want to miss that.

172

Maybe tomorrow."

"Could you ask Benny and Razor to sleep over?" Ivy asked.

"That's not a bad idea," Kate replied. "Hey, I see Benny out in his driveway. Let me go talk to him. Call you later."

"Bye," Holly said as the call disconnected. "I'll bet that's what that call was about last night." She huffed. "As usual, Nick isn't telling me everything."

Ivy chuckled. "You think by now he'd know you're going to find out anyway."

Suddenly, Holly locked eyes with her sister. "You know you're right. That guy who tried to get Brittany's bag could still be lurking around up there, and who knows what's on that phone? Or to what lengths he'll go ..."

Both sisters jumped when Lucky let out a sharp bark. The sound of the doorbell quickly followed.

"Who could that be?" Holly said as she and Ivy followed the dog to the entrance hall.

Holly opened the door and said just one word. "Ariana."

45 ARIANA

Ivy put the tea kettle on as Ariana and Holly sat down at the kitchen table.

"I'm sorry," Ariana said. "I didn't know where else to go." She was pale and her hands shook.

"I saw you run past my car when I pulled into the parking deck. I yelled to you. Why didn't you stop?" Holly asked.

"You did? I'm sorry. I didn't hear you. I was so ..."

Ivy brought over the tissue box as the girl began to cry. Holly exchanged a quick glance with her sister. They'd been in this situation before. In a gentle voice, she said, "Tell us what happened."

"That's just it." Ariana's eyes had a wild look as she sliced the air with her hands. "I don't know."

"Did you talk to Rodney?"

Ariana lowered her eyes and just shook her head.

Holly once again looked at Ivy, giving her shoulders a slight shrug. The tea kettle began to whistle, and Ivy turned her attention to the stove. Holly waited as her sister prepared a cup of tea and brought it over to the table.

"Drink this, Ariana," Ivy said, her tone soothing.

After the girl had taken a few sips, Holly tried to match her sister's calming tone. "You're going to have to tell me what happened if you want me to help you."

Ariana nodded and began, her eyes on the teacup. "Rodney asked me to meet him in the parking garage before my class. When I got to his car, I tapped on the window. I thought he'd fallen asleep." She looked up at Holly. "I tried to open the door, but it was locked. I ran to the passenger side of the car, but that door was locked, too. I banged harder, but he didn't move." The girl's eyes teared up and she began to tremble. "Then I saw the blood."

Holly reached across and took both of Ariana's hands in hers. "Then what did you do?"

"I ran."

"Where did you go?"

"I went to the bus stop and got on a bus that was waiting there. I didn't even know which bus it was. I just wanted to get away."

"Why didn't you go to the Security Office?" Holly asked.

"I–I was afraid." Ariana pulled her hands loose from Holly, then lowered her head. "With everything that's happened–you know–with our experiment being withdrawn from the competition–I just didn't want any more trouble."

Holly's left eyebrow arched as she again exchanged a knowing look with her sister.

"Why did Rodney want to talk to you?" Holly asked.

"I–uh–I don't know." Ariana glanced up, but quickly averted her gaze, focusing on the teacup.

"The truth, Ariana," Holly said gently.

Ariana took a deep breath, and this time her eyes met Holly's. "Rodney asked me out last month. He seemed nice enough, so I said yes. He took me to a posh restaurant. After dinner I should have known what was up when he asked the valet for his keys and didn't have him bring the car to us. When we got back in the car, he ..." Ariana paused, visibly distraught.

"Did he molest you?" Holly asked, just barely keeping her voice controlled.

"He tried," Ariana shook her head. "Lucky for me, my neighbor Manny works as a valet at the restaurant. He saw us get into the car. When we didn't pull right out, Manny came over." Ariana gave a weak smile. "He was like a big brother to me growing up. Well, when he got near the car, he heard me yelling at Rodney to stop. He pulled open the door. Rodney let go and I got out. I waited with Manny until his shift was over and he drove me home."

The tension building in Holly's neck eased. "So that's why you tensed up when Rodney appeared that day your display got vandalized."

Ariana nodded.

"Hey, do you think Rodney vandalized the display?" Ivy asked.

"I don't know," Ariana replied. "Maybe."

"I remember he was less than helpful at the time," Holly said. "Dr. Miller had to order him to get help for you guys."

"And he certainly would have had access to the display area when no one else was around," Ivy added.

"Good point." Holly smiled at her sister. After a moment, she turned back to Ariana. "What about the morning of the closing ceremonies? I saw you talking to him. You told me nothing was wrong, but clearly it was."

Ariana sighed. "He stopped me in the hall when I was

on my way to see you. He told me our project was being withdrawn, but that he could help me if I ..."

"If you slept with him," Holly said.

Ariana nodded.

"Did he explain how he could help?" Ivy asked.

"No. Just that if I wanted his help, I knew where to find him."

Holly looked up at the ceiling. "I wonder what ..."

Lucky barked, and a moment later the doorbell rang.

"I don't even know why you have a doorbell," Ivy said as she got up and followed the dog to the front door. When she opened it, Peppy was standing on the front stoop.

"Let me guess," she said. "Looking for Ariana?"

46 DANGER

After Nicky left with Brittany's phone, Agent Daniels gave Nick an appraising look.

"I suppose we owe you one, Detective Manelli," the agent said.

Nick shrugged. "You could say that."

Daniels let out a small laugh. "What do you want?"

"Well, I'd like to know the identity of the man in the photo."

"Why? The FBI is now in charge of the case," Daniels said.

"Well, here's the thing," Nick began. He gave the agent a quick recap of Holly's involvement in trying to help Ariana and her teammates and their belief that Brittany and this unidentified man were the key to saving their reputations and their scholarships. He left out the fact that he believed they might also help solve Rodney Blakely's murder.

Before the agent could reply, Nicky appeared at the glass door of the conference room. Daniels signaled for him to enter.

"Facial recognition got a hit that fast?" Daniels asked.

"No. It's still running," Nicky replied, tapping the screen

of a tablet he held in his hand. "When I looked at the photo, I thought I recognized the face, so while I was running the facial recognition program, I searched through some of the photos I'd been looking at doing background checks."

"This is one of Ecolyte's members?" Daniels asked.

"No," Nicky replied showing Daniels the tablet screen. "He's a former Green Gardyn employee. George Holzman."

"Ah," was all Nick said as he nodded.

Daniels smiled. "Well, Detective Manelli, since you've dropped this significant lead in our laps, would you care to observe our interview with Ms. Holzman?"

This time Nick smiled back as he nodded his affirmation.

****

From inside the observation booth, Nick watched Brittany. She sat back with her arms crossed, her expression as sullen as the day he interviewed her before the FBI took her off his hands. He felt pretty certain she would talk this time.

Agent Daniels and Nicky entered the interview room and took their seats opposite the girl.

"What am I doing here without my lawyer?" Brittany asked. "You know I'm not going to answer any questions you have without him here."

"Oh, we know that," Daniels replied. "We called him. We thought we'd just wait here with you until he gets here." Daniels glanced over at Nicky. "Agent Manelli, just to give Ms. Holzman some time to prep, maybe you want to show her what we're going to be asking her about." Looking back at Brittany, he said, "And just to be clear, you don't have to talk to us until your lawyer arrives."

Nicky tapped the tablet screen and turned it toward Brittany, who stared silently at it, the blood draining from her cheeks.

Ignoring Brittany, Daniels turned his chair toward Nicky, "So, what's your best guess, Agent Manelli?"

"Well, sir, I'd guess Mr. Holzman here is a disgruntled employee. I've requested his employee file and we should have that by the time Ms. Holzman's lawyer gets here."

From the observation booth, Nick could see Brittany's knuckles turning white as she gripped the table.

"Yes, that should confirm it," Daniels said. "And that would go to motive for why he blew up the Green Gardyn warehouse."

"It really is unfortunate that the security guard was murdered in the explosion." Nicky frowned. "Exactly how many years will that add to the sentencing, sir?"

"Stop it!" Brittany banged the table with both fists. "George had nothing to do with the explosion!"

Bingo, Nick thought. Brilliantly played.

Agent Daniels leaned towards Brittany. "Ms. Holzman, you really should wait until your..."

The girl's expression turned to one of pleading. "George is my brother, and I'm telling you he had nothing to do with the explosion."

"Did you?" Daniels asked.

"No. Of course not."

"Your brother knows you're in custody," Agent Daniels said. "Why hasn't he turned himself in?"

"Because he's in danger."

"Care to explain?" Daniels asked.

Brittany placed her elbows on the table and covered her face with her hands. After a few moments, she again looked at the photo of her brother on the screen, then back at Daniels.

"George discovered that Green Gardyn Foods was using GMOs even though they claimed they were non-GMO. He got me the seeds and the signed release paper allowing us to use them in our Eco-Fair experiment."

"He forged the signature?"

"No. He was an administrative assistant to the man who signed the forms. George said he rarely looked at anything he gave him to sign on a Friday afternoon. He just included the paper in a bunch of forms and his boss signed them all."

"That's still fraudulent, Ms. Holzman."

"Oh, and saying your product doesn't contain GMOs when it does–that's not fraudulent?" Brittany again banged the table with both fists.

"You still haven't explained how your brother is in danger."

Brittany huffed. "Somehow Green Gardyns found out about our project. His boss fired him. He didn't mind. Figured he'd quit after the experiment was presented to the public anyway. But the day after the explosion someone sent George a video–a time-stamped security video showing him and me at the warehouse the day of the explosion."

"And were you there?"

Brittany's expression reflected the torment she clearly felt. Before she could answer, the interview room door opened, and her attorney walked in.

47 PILLOW TALK

Holly was reading in bed when she heard the front door open. She glanced at the clock. Midnight. When was this man going to retire? Unfortunately, she had so much else she wanted to talk to him about she didn't dare bring it up tonight. She turned off her Kindle just as Nick entered their bedroom.

"Long day, huh?" she said.

"Yep," he nodded wearily. "For you too. What are you still doing up?" he asked as he hung his jacket in the closet.

"Please. With everything that happened, my mind just won't shut down." Holly sat up. "Will you tell me what happened with Ariana?"

Nick walked over and caressed her cheek. "Do I have a choice?"

Holly got up on her knees and hugged him. "Look, if you're really tired ..."

"Give me a minute," he replied as he entered the bathroom. When he returned and got in bed, he began, "Nicky says hello, by the way. You'll be happy to know they're finished with your cell phone. I brought it home for you."

"That's great, but when did you see Nicky?" Before he could answer, she said, "Oh, it must have had something to do with that photo Kate identified on Brittany's cell phone."

"Well, it looks like you already know everything," Nick said, rolling on his side with his back to her.

"Oh, c'mon. Kate told me about it." When he didn't reply, she slid her hand up and down his back. "Did you find out who the guy in the picture is?"

"You know I'm not going to tell you that, so let's just get some sleep."

Holly tugged at his shoulder in a futile attempt to roll him over to face her. "Okay, okay. Just please tell me one thing, Nick. What happened with Ariana? I've been trying to reach Peppy, but she hasn't returned my calls."

Nick let out a fake snore. Not to be put off, Holly nestled closer and ran her lips along his neck. That always worked.

In just a few seconds he rolled over to face her. "I questioned Ariana and sent her home."

"She told you about her date with Rodney?"

"Just like you told her to," Nick replied.

"Well, she kept it a secret from me until this morning. I didn't want her to think keeping it from the police was a good idea." Holly laid her head on Nick's chest. "You don't think she had anything to do with it, do you?"

"We'll see what the physical evidence shows."

"What do you mean? Like fingerprints? Nick, if she was in his car on that date, her fingerprints are bound to be in the car."

"Holly ..." Nick said in the tone she knew meant this was not up for discussion. So she decided to change topics. "Where's Peppy? I haven't heard from her since she left here with Ariana."

"I sent her up to Kate's."

Holly lifted her head in alarm. "Why? Did something

happen?"

"Relax. Nothing happened. We just think Kate's intruder might still be in the area."

"That's what Ivy and I said. We told her to come down here and stay with us until the guy is found, but all we could get her to say was she'd think about it." Holly lay her head back down. "We told her to invite Benny and Razor for a sleepover. They'd keep her safe. Peppy didn't have to drive all the way up there."

After a moment, Holly lifted her head again. "Wait a minute. You had to take Peppy off the case because her cousin is a suspect. That's why you sent her up there, isn't it?"

"Yeah, and I'm thinking maybe I should send you up there too," Nick said.

Holly sat full up. "What's that supposed to mean?" she asked with an air of indignation.

"I'm just sayin' you find more dead bodies than a cadaver dog, *amore mio*."

"That's not my fault!"

Nick propped himself up on his elbows. "Yeah? Well, tell me this. Why whenever you're involved in a murder investigation, do most of the suspects or their family members end up in our living room?"

"That's not true," Holly objected fiercely.

"Really? Let's see." With his right hand he began the count using his fingers. "There's Juan Alvarez. Elena Gomez. Becky Powell ..."

Holly knew this was an argument she couldn't win, so she resorted to Nick's favorite argument-ending ploy. She pushed him back down on the pillows and placed her mouth firmly on his.

48 OUTSIDE AGITATORS

"So, what's it like to live up here?" Peppy asked as she and Kate stepped out of the coffee shop onto Reddington Manor's Main Street.

Kate chuckled. "I get that it's not everyone's cup of tea, but I like it. You know everybody in town. Nice and peaceful."

"Really?" Peppy said, sarcasm in her voice. "And that's why Manelli had to send me up here—not once, but twice."

"Okay, but you know this isn't typical," Kate said. "Besides, problems are usually caused by out-of-towners, like Brittany and her brother."

"Ah, the old 'outside agitators' argument," Peppy scoffed. "Well, for what it's worth, I think George Holzman is long gone."

"You really do? Then why did Nick have you drive all the way up here last night?"

"Because Ariana is a suspect in Rodney Blakely's murder and he knew the only way to keep me from working the investigation was to get me out of town."

"Oh, that would definitely be something Nick would do," Kate said. "But then who's watching Holly?"

Both Peppy and Kate laughed loudly as they reached

Kate's driveway. Making their way up the gravel-covered stretch, Peppy glanced up at the house, then grabbed Kate's arm.

"Go wait on the porch over there," she said giving Kate a nudge in the direction of Benny and Razor's bungalow.

"Why?" Kate asked.

"Just do it!" Peppy said, giving her a harder push this time before she broke into a trot across the lawn to Kate's side porch.

As she suspected, the side door was ajar. Whomever she'd seen in the window upstairs had gotten in that way. It had to be George Holzman, and she didn't intend to let him get away.

If he'd seen them coming up the drive, he knew he couldn't leave the way he'd come in. He risked running smack into them if he tried to get out the kitchen door. He'd most likely try to exit by the front door. Why did these old homes have so many damn doors?

Slowly, she edged her way along the back of the house and peeked around the side. Nothing. Staying close to the house, she continued to make her way towards the steps to where the wrap-around porch began. She mounted the steps, then got on her hands and knees, crawling below the windows. Suddenly she remembered that she left her gun buried under some clothes in the dresser in the guest bedroom. What if old Georgie boy searched the drawers looking for the phone and found it?

As she reached the front corner of the house, she could hear the sound of the doorknob jiggling. Well, there was only one thing to do, she thought, as she got her feet under her.

When the door opened, Peppy stood up straight. As Holzman stepped outside, she ran straight at him, knocking both him and her off their feet, her gun skidding across the

186

porch.

Holzman was considerably larger than she was, but Peppy was relieved that her gun was out of play. She was already standing as he still struggled to get on his feet.

"Stay down," she said, delivering a kick to his backside, causing him to sprawl spread-eagle.

Quickly, she retrieved her gun. "George Holzman, you're under arrest," she said, placing her foot on his back.

Kate came running across the lawn brandishing a broom over her head. Peppy laughed. "What are you gonna do with that thing?" she asked with a droll smile. "Sweep him into submission?"

"Go ahead, laugh," Kate sneered. "But you'd be surprised what a broom can do."

"Yeah, I'll have to take your word on that. Now, can you please go upstairs and get my handcuffs. They're on the dresser."

The sound of an engine drew their eyes to the road. Razor's Silverado spit gravel as the truck drove up the driveway and came to an abrupt stop. Razor's door flew open.

As the big man ran toward them, Benny in his wake, Peppy aimed a questioning look at Kate.

Kate shrugged. "I called them," she said as she turned and unlocked the kitchen door.

As Razor took the steps two at a time, Peppy's captive tried again to get up. This time she stepped on his shoulder. "I said, stay down."

Razor glanced at the man lying on the porch floor, then cast a smoldering look of admiration at his captor.

When Benny reached Razor's side, he chuckled as he poked the big man in the ribs. "I told you Peppy didn't need our help."

49 THE NOTEBOOK

Razor reached down and pulled the vanquished intruder up by his collar. As he did, a small black notebook fell to the floor. Holzman tried to make a lunge for it but was unable to break free from Razor's grasp.

Benny scooped up the notebook and quickly leafed through the pages. "You know, I came across this book on the bookshelf when we was searching for the phone," he said. "I didn't think nothing of it. Just a bunch of dates and numbers."

"So, that's what you were looking for, not the phone," Peppy said.

Holzman swallowed hard. "My life depends on it," he said, barely above a whisper.

The kitchen door opened, and Kate appeared with the handcuffs. Razor turned Holzman with his back to Peppy.

"Put your hands behind your back," she said.

Holzman's shoulders sagged. "You don't need to bother. I'm not going to try to get away. As a matter of fact, why don't you just shoot me now? My life's over anyway."

Peppy's eyes met Razor's communicating an unspoken message.

"Let's go inside," Peppy said, stuffing the cuffs in her

jacket pocket.

Kate pulled open the door. "I called Jason when I was inside. He's on his way."

Keeping his hold on Holzman's collar, Razor guided him inside and over to a chair at the counter.

Once everyone was inside, Benny was the first to speak. "So, who is this guy?"

"George Holzman."

"Naw." Benny shook his head in disbelief. "Can't be. He looks too straight to be the little Goth's husband."

"He's her brother," Kate said.

Benny let loose a belly laugh. "Wow. I bet there was a lot of sibling riflery in your family."

"Rivalry," Razor quietly corrected his friend.

George Holzman glared at Benny as Peppy looked at the notebook he'd tried so hard to get his hands on. "We know you worked for Green Gardyn Foods, George," she said. "Care to tell us what these dates and numbers refer to?"

"No," he replied.

"Suit yourself," she said.

Benny walked over and looked out the door. "Jason's here."

Peppy turned to Razor. "I'll need to talk to him–outside. You'll keep an eye on my prisoner?"

He tipped his head. "My pleasure, *señorita*."

Peppy nodded and turned quickly, once again feeling a warm flush starting at the base of her neck. What was it about this guy that made her feel all mushy inside? She didn't like it. Or did she?

Outside she met the Sheriff as he got out of his car.

"We need to talk before we go inside," she said.

Jason smiled. "What's Manelli got you mixed up in now?"

He listened attentively as she explained why she'd been sent to Reddington Manor, who George Holzman was and how, once again, the FBI might not look kindly on their involvement.

When she finished, Jason looked upward as a hawk glided above the line of trees that marked the edge of Kate's property. After a few moments, he said, "Well, we can handle this the same way we did when you came up for Brittany's bag. Kate spotted the intruder on her way home. She called Benny and Razor. They apprehended him and called me. Being the dim-witted country sheriff that I am, and not knowing federal protocols, I called Manelli instead of them."

"Only one problem with that. Manelli should immediately call the FBI after he hears from you. And you know what would happen if he did that."

"Yeah, they'll send the guys from Albany to get him." Jason frowned.

"Unless you don't call Manelli first," Peppy grinned, "and being the dim-witted country sheriff that you are, you just pack him in a car with your deputies and send him to Pineland Park."

"Yep, that ought to work. I can say I meant to call, but just got so darn busy." Jason smiled. "Just one thing. You notice how in this version of the account I look stupid, and you, who captured the guy, don't get any credit?"

Peppy nodded. "My *abuela*–that's grandmother -- always says, do the right thing and God will reward you in the end."

Jason laughed. "If that's the case, all I know is there better be a heaven."

50 WHAT IF

Holly watched through the glass panes of her front door as Peppy's car pulled up in front of the house.

"They're here!" she called to Ivy who was preparing a plate of sandwiches in the kitchen. She opened the door and walked to the front gate as Kate got out of the passenger side.

"Benny!" Holly said as his head appeared above the roof of the car on the driver's side. "I didn't expect to see you."

"Yeah," Benny grinned. "Somebody had to drive Peppy's car back. She insisted she ride in the police cruiser with her prisoner, but if you ask me, I think she and Razor just wanted–what did you call it Kate?"

Kate grinned. "Alone time."

Benny chuckled. "That's it. I ain't seen Razor like this in a long time. He's smit–what's that other word you said, Kate?"

"Smitten."

"Yep. Smitten."

Holly laughed. "You know, at first blush, they seem an unlikely pair, but I think they might just be right for each other." She reached for Kate's overnight bag. "Benny, you coming in for some lunch?"

"No thanks. I got to get over to the police station. We got Jason's cruiser and he'll be wanting it back before the date night crowd gets out on the roads. Fridays and Saturdays are his busiest nights."

"Wait a minute, Benny!" Ivy called from the front stoop where she'd been listening. She ran inside as Holly and Ivy made their way up the walk.

"Thanks for driving me, Benny," Kate said.

"Sure thing," he replied as Ivy came back out the door with a brown paper bag in one hand and two bottles of water in the other.

"Some sandwiches and cookies for the drive back," she said handing the bag and bottles over the fence.

"You're a doll," Benny said taking the items. "Be seein' ya." He waved as he returned to the car and drove off.

Once they were settled in the kitchen, Holly said, "Okay, now tell us everything that happened."

When Kate finished describing the events of the morning, Holly gave her a wry smile. "You and that broom."

Kate just made a sour face in return.

"So, if Brittany's brother is to be believed, the seeds Ariana's team used in the experiment were genuine and Green Gardyn Foods is guilty of fraud," Ivy said.

Holly nodded as Kate sat back and crossed her arms. Her expression conveyed her smug satisfaction. "And so, Holly, admit it. I was right."

"Okay," Holly conceded. "You were right about Brittany."

Kate sneered. "Of course, I was right about the girl. I'm talking about a company sabotaging the students' Eco-Fair project!"

Holly simply stared at Kate, appearing lost in thought.

Kate glanced at Ivy, "See. She knows I'm right."

After a few moments, Holly said, "If you are right, how did Green Gardyn Foods find out about the project?"

"And is that what got Rodney killed?" Ivy asked.

"And did it have something to do with that argument between Rodney and Professor McNair?" Holly said.

Kate's expression changed from smug to thoughtful as she uncrossed her arms and sat forward. "What if Rodney somehow found out the signature wasn't legitimate and–I don't know–blackmailed McNair?"

Holly shook her head, clearly perplexed. "That's a lot of 'what-ifs'. The question remains, how did he find out about the signature in the first place? Only Brittany and her brother knew the truth."

"Still, it sure seems like Rodney's murder is somehow linked to the student experiment," Ivy added.

"And who knows?" Kate crossed her arms, her smug expression back in place. "Maybe the warehouse explosion too."

Suddenly, Holly slapped the table with both hands. "I need to talk to Nicky."

Ivy shook her head. "No, Holly. You know Nick said he's not allowed to talk to him about the case."

Holly grinned. "Maybe Nick can't. But I can."

51 GEORGE HOLZMAN

Peppy was elated that Manelli asked her to observe his interview of George Holzman, but she felt her heart start to beat faster as she entered the viewing cubicle, Razor right behind her. On the drive back from the Catskills, with Holzman in the back seat, they stuck to safe topics like the weather, movies they'd seen, the music they liked. Nothing too personal. Nothing flirty.

She hated to admit that she felt a little disappointed. By the time they reached Pineland Park police headquarters, she actually began to wonder if maybe his calling her 'cariño' the last time she'd seen him really didn't mean anything. It was probably a term he used with all women. Like waitresses when they served his meal–"*Gracias, cariño*" –"Thank you, darling." Just something you say. Yeah, that had to be it.

Still, she felt a tad nervous as he closed the observation booth door. Glancing at George Holzman through the one-way glass window, she said, "I kinda feel sorry for this guy."

"Why is that, *cariño*?" Razor asked, his eyes on her, not on Holzman.

That word! Had he read her mind? Peppy felt a warm flush edging its way up her neck. Not trusting herself to make eye contact, she kept her eyes on Holzman. "I–uh–I think he's just a whistle-blower wannabe who got in over his head."

"You don't think he was involved in the explosion?" Razor asked.

"No," Peppy replied, then got the courage to turn and face the big man. "No, I don't. Do you?"

Razor shook his head. Before he could say more, Detective Manelli entered the interview room and sat down across from Holzman. He placed a manila folder, a yellow legal pad and the suspect's black notebook on the table.

"Mr. Holzman, did you murder Rodney Blakely?" Manelli asked.

Holzman blanched and his eyes widened. "What are you talking about? Who's Rodney Blakely?"

Nick pulled a photo out of the manila folder. "That's Rodney Blakely. His body was found yesterday morning in the parking deck at Pineland Park Community College. Stabbed to death."

Holzman rocked his head from side to side. "I have no idea who that is. I've never even seen him. Why would I kill him?"

"Where were you yesterday?" Manelli asked.

"I was up in Reddington Manor."

Razor lowered his head close to Peppy's ear. She got a tingly feeling along her neck. "Why is he asking him about Blakely's murder? He knows the guy had nothing to do with it," he asked, his voice low.

"Because that's our case," Peppy whispered. "Just watch how Manelli gets him to start talking about the explosion, the FBI's case." She placed her hand on the wall to keep from swaying as she glanced over and saw Razor's smile.

"Brilliant," he said.

Manelli lifted the notebook and fanned through the

pages. "I understand you broke into Kate Farmer's home to retrieve this book. Why? What do all these dates and figures signify," he asked.

Holzman just sat staring at his hands resting on the table.

"I understand that you feel, for some reason, you're in danger and this book somehow contains information that can keep you safe. Is that right?"

The young man gave Manelli a mournful glance. "Yes."

"I sat in on an FBI interview with your sister yesterday. She said there's a photo of you and her at the scene of the Green Gardyn explosion. Were you there?"

Holzman gripped the edge of the table with both hands, "Oh, what the hell?" he said, an air of desperation in his voice. "Yes, I was there, but I went there to stop them."

"Stop who?"

"Ecolyte." Holzman fidgeted in his chair. "Look, Brittany got involved with that group. She didn't know how radical they were. When she realized what they were planning, she came to me. We went there to stop them. I swear it."

"And this notebook?" Nick asked.

"It contains dates and numbers of GMO seed batches that Green Gardyn Foods shipped to their growers. This information could ruin them. They know I have it and they're looking for me."

Manelli slid a yellow pad and pen across the table. "Write it all down."

"Just brilliant," Razor said.

As he opened the observation booth door and stepped out in the corridor, Peppy felt all the warmth in the room exit with him.

52 A PLEASANT AUTUMN AFTERNOON

Ivy and Kate entered Military Park in Newark and found an empty bench to sit on.

"I still say this is a big mistake," Ivy said with a frown.

Kate shrugged. "I don't know. I think it's pretty clever to be honest with you."

"Yeah, well when Nick finds out, he's going to hit the roof." Ivy got out her phone and began to tap the screen.

"What are you doing?"

As she scrolled down, Ivy said, "You know, from here I can get a taxi to Newark Airport and be back in South Carolina in a few hours."

"Oh, no!" Kate put her hand across the front of Ivy's phone. "You're not going to leave me here alone to deal with the Manelli fallout."

"See! You know this is a bad idea."

"Think about it, Ivy," Kate said. "You got to hand it to your sister. The way she planned it, Nick will never even know she was here." Kate smirked. "She really thought of everything. No phone, no email, no text. Just a handwritten note in a sandwich bag. Unless Nicky tells his father, how's he going to find out?"

"Seriously?" Ivy said, exasperation in her voice. "*Unless* Nicky tells his father? Of course, he's going to tell him. Or Nick will find out somehow. He always does."

"Shh," Kate said. "Here comes Holly."

"Well?" Ivy asked as her sister joined them on the bench.

"We'll see," Holly smiled. "The security guard working the front desk was very nice. He said he'd send the bag of food right up to Nicky. He was so cute. Said he wished he had a stepmother to bring him a homemade lunch. I told him next time I'd bring a bag for him."

"So now what?" Kate asked.

"So now we wait," Holly replied.

Ivy huffed. "What if he doesn't open the bag right away, Holly? Or what if he doesn't find the note inside? Are we going to just wait here for hours?"

"I am," Holly said. "You can go sit in the car if you like."

Ivy pulled out her phone again. "Or I can cab it to the airport and fly home."

Holly glared at her sister. "Why don't you ..."

"Stop it!" Kate cut in. "Both of you. The weather's nice, it's a pleasant autumn afternoon. Let's just try to enjoy ourselves."

Holly took a deep breath and looked back in the direction from which she'd just come. Her sister turned in the opposite direction. Sitting between them, Kate sighed and looked straight ahead at the buildings across the street.

"Hey, Ivy," Kate pointed across the street, "doesn't that look like a gift shop over there?"

"Where?" Ivy peered in the direction Kate pointed.

"C'mon." Kate got to her feet. "Let's go check it out."

Ivy turned to her sister. "You'll be okay waiting here alone?"

Holly nodded. "Yeah. Go shop."

Holly watched the pair as they crossed the street and entered the store, grateful to be alone. She pulled out her phone and scrolled through her email as she waited, grateful Nicky had seen to it that the phone was returned to her. She'd been lost without it. After replying to just a few questions her students sent her, she sensed someone approaching.

"Nicky." She smiled and stood to greet him.

Her stepson gave her a hug and they both sat down. "So, Mata Hari, what's this all about?" he said with a grin.

"First of all, your father doesn't know I'm here and I'd like to keep it that way."

Nicky's grin widened. "I figured that."

"And I'm not sure if you and your father have been able to talk about what happened at the community college Eco-Fair, or the murder that happened on campus on Friday."

The grin disappeared from Nicky's face. "No, I haven't been able to talk to him about anything. There was a murder on campus?"

"Yes," Holly frowned, "and I discovered the body."

"Of course you did," Nicky sighed.

"Stop. You sound just like your father." Holly sat forward. "I think there's a link between that murder and the warehouse explosion. Here's what I know."

Nicky listened attentively as she told him about Ariana's project and the argument she'd overheard between Rodney Blakely and Professor McNair. "I don't know how it's all connected, but I just know it is, and I think your father does too, but he won't talk to me about it."

Nicky sat back and looked skyward at the top of the office building across the street. Holly sat quietly, having seen his father in the same contemplative mode as he digested the information he'd just heard.

After a few moments, he looked over at her. "I don't know exactly what I can do with this information. Let's say I tell Agent Daniels that I got this from an anonymous tip. You know, he'll have the FBI take over the murder investigation, and Dad will not be happy."

"Oh," Holly said, feeling like a deflated balloon. "I didn't think about that." She turned and put her hand on his arm. "I've put you in a terrible position, haven't I? If Daniels finds out you knew this and didn't tell him, you'll be in trouble."

"Yeah, and if this were any other case, I'd call Dad to get his advice."

"Well, you may get to see …" Holly caught herself before she mentioned George Holzman's capture. She'd already told him too much. "Can't you say you read about the murder? It was in the papers."

Nicky appeared thoughtful again. After a few moments, he said, "I have to think about this."

"Oh!" Holly grasped his arm. "I just thought of something else. The college said they would turn over the documentation of the student experiment to the federal agencies in charge of GMO oversight. Could that maybe help you?"

"I don't know." Nicky shrugged and got to his feet.

Holly got up and gave him a hug. "I'm sorry, Nicky."

"Don't be." He smiled. "I'm looking forward to the lunch you packed me."

She smiled back as he kissed her on the cheek and headed back in the direction of the FBI office.

Under her breath, she said, "What have I done?"

53 THE ASSIST

Outside the interview room, Manelli gave instructions to the officer standing guard to return George Holzman to a holding cell after he completed writing his statement. Turning to Razor and Peppy, he said, "Good work, you two."

He extended his hand to Razor. "Thanks again for the assist."

"I just drove the car." Razor shook his hand, tilting his head in Peppy's direction. "Officer Alvarez here apprehended the suspect without any help from me."

Manelli nodded as he glanced at Peppy. "Good work. Now go home, Alvarez. Get some rest." Turning back to Razor, he said, "Have to go. I've got some calls to make."

As Manelli headed down the corridor, the big man turned to Peppy. "Walk me to the car?"

"Sure," Peppy said as they moved in the opposite direction Manelli had gone.

"So, Officer Alvarez, you have any plans to come up to the Catskills when you're not on official business?" Razor asked.

"Not really." Peppy let out a small laugh. "I mean what's there to do up there?" As soon as the words were out of her mouth, she regretted it.

"Oh, I can think of a few things we could do," he said softly.

Peppy felt the skin on her neck starting to warm. Why had she given him that opening? And "we". He said the word "we". Was he asking her out on a date? What was she supposed to say now?

"Here comes Benny with my car," she said, looking past Razor to the parking lot entrance, grateful for the opportunity to avoid replying to his leading remark.

They watched as Benny drove up to where they were standing and rolled down the window.

"Your car, Officer!" he said offering a mock salute. "And not a scratch on it."

"Thanks, Benny." She smiled and pointed to a space across the lot. "You can park it over there."

As he did, a police cruiser pulled into the lot, lights flashing. It came to a stop directly in front of the entrance to the station. A patrolman got out of the passenger side and opened the back door. Peppy gasped as she saw the officer assist a young man in handcuffs out of the back seat.

"Something wrong?" Razor asked, concern in his voice when he saw the expression on Peppy's face. "You know that boy?"

"Yes," Peppy said taking off at a jog toward the cruiser as the officer walked his prisoner inside the station. Razor followed her.

She tapped on the driver's side window and the officer inside lowered the window.

"Ortiz, what's going on?" Peppy asked. "Why is that kid in handcuffs?"

"He's a suspect in the Blakely murder," Officer Ortiz replied.

"No way," Peppy snarled.

"Sorry. All I know is his fingerprints were found in the victim's car."

"Damn," Peppy said as Ortiz shrugged and slowly drove off.

"So what's up?" Benny asked as he joined them.

Peppy just lowered her head and stared at the ground. Benny looked to Razor for an answer.

Instead, Razor placed a hand on Peppy's shoulder and asked, "Who's the boy?"

After a moment, Peppy looked up. "Luis Navarro. He's my cousin Ariana's friend. I know that kid my whole life. There's no way he committed murder."

"This Manelli's case?" Benny asked.

"Yes," Peppy replied.

Benny's mouth expanded into a wide grin. "Then you got nothing to worry about. Manelli always gets it right."

Not feeling the consolation Benny intended, Peppy's expression remained grim.

Undaunted, Benny said, "Hey, come on. With you and Manelli on the case, the kid'll be cleared in no time."

"That's just it." Peppy clenched her fists. "I'm not on the case. Manelli took me off because my cousin's involved." Unclenching her fists, she extended her hand, palm outward. "Gimme my keys," she said, a determined tone to her voice.

Benny held the keys out, but Razor snatched them before she could get her hands on them.

"Hey," she shouted. "What do you think you're doing?"

"Hold on a minute," Razor said calmly. "What are you planning to do?"

Peppy jutted her chin out. "I don't know yet, but I'll think of something," she said again reaching for the keys.

As she and Razor locked eyes, Benny's phone signaled. "Oh man," he said as he looked at the screen. "It's Jason. That's the third time he called. He's getting anxious about us getting back with the cruiser."

Razor pulled the cruiser keys out of his pocket and handed them to Benny. "You go. I'm staying."

54 QUÉ PASÓ

Peppy and Razor sat in her car, Peppy's eyes glued to the door of the police station.

"You should have gone back with Benny," she said. "You didn't need to stay."

"Mm-huh," was Razor's reply, his eyes also fixed on the door.

Peppy pursed her lips and turned an annoyed look on the big man. "What's that? Mm-huh? Don't patronize me!"

His 6'3" frame packed rather tightly in the passenger seat of the Honda, Razro turned just his head to face her. "Nope. I'm not one for arguing is all."

Peppy's expression softened. After a moment she started to laugh. "You know, even with the seat moved all the way back you look a little–uh–cramped in this car."

He smiled, reached over and gave her hand a gentle squeeze. "So, you want to tell me why we're sitting here?"

"I'm waiting for Manelli to leave. He's got to take Holzman to the FBI office in Newark."

"Then what?"

"Then I go in and talk to Luis. Find out why the hell his

fingerprints were in the victim's car." She tapped the steering wheel with open palms.

Razor just nodded and they both continued their watch of the police station door. They didn't have to wait long. Manelli appeared at the back door followed by two patrolmen with George Holzman between them. Manelli spoke briefly to the officers, then headed to his car. The two policemen walked Holzman to a cruiser.

As soon as Manelli and the police car left the parking lot, Peppy jumped out of her car. By the time Razor got out, she was halfway across the parking lot. He broke into a trot and caught up with her at the bottom of the steps to the station entrance.

Peppy turned to face him. "You should wait in the car."

Razor shook his head. "I stayed here to be with you."

"What?" Peppy waggled her head. "You going to babysit me?"

Razor took hold of her left forearm. In a calm voice, he said, "You don't have a plan. Sometimes it helps to have someone to bounce ideas off of, especially when you're ..."

Peppy jerked her arm away. "When I'm what? Emotional? *Una chica loca*?"

This time he gently grasped both her forearms. She tried to pull away but couldn't get loose.

"*Cariño*," Razor said, his tone pleading. "Manelli took you off this case for a reason. Let me help you."

Peppy stopped resisting and remained absolutely still. As her eyes met Razor's, she found herself wanting to give in, wanting to accept his help. Her past experience with men taught her to rely only on herself. She felt this guy was different. Someone she could count on. Was she kidding herself? Only one way to find out.

"Okay," she said. "Let's go."

Together they entered the police station and Peppy headed directly to the holding cells.

Officer Tim Sullivan was on duty. The young officer always put Peppy in mind of a Boy Scout. Clean shaven, short hair and a genuine smile.

"Hey, Peppy," he greeted her. "What are you doing here on a Saturday?" he asked as he eyed Razor.

"Listen, Tim. I need to talk to Luis Navarro."

The young policeman tilted his head as he grimaced. "He hasn't even been questioned yet. You know Manelli doesn't allow visitors until he's gotten a statement."

"C'mon," Peppy's tone was pleading. "I know this kid my whole life. Just ten minutes."

Sullivan glanced at Razor, then back at Peppy. "Who's he?"

"He's a friend."

If Sullivan had reservations about this hulk of a man with an eye patch tattoo, he didn't show it.

"Please, Tim." Peppy begged. "Let us talk to him."

"Both of you?" Tim's eyebrows squished together.

"Yes, both of us."

The young officer appeared conflicted. After a moment, he said, "Okay. But five minutes only."

"You're a pal, Tim," Peppy said as he opened the door behind him and allowed them inside. When they reached the cell where the boy was sitting, his head in his hands, Peppy said, "*Luis, qué pasó?*"

"Peppy!" Luis stood and hurried to the door of the cell. Grasping the iron bars, he said, "You have to help me. I didn't do it."

55 TANGENTIAL

Nick sat across from Agent Daniels as the agent read George Holzman's statement. When he finished, Daniels sat back, removed his reading glasses and threw them on the desk. Leaning back in his chair, he skewered Nick with a penetrating stare.

Having been the person delivering that stare to countless others over the years, Nick just sat calmly and met the man's gaze. He'd already explained to the agent how George Holzman came to be in his custody and how, in questioning the suspect, he learned there was a connection to the FBI's case.

Daniels hadn't questioned Nick's account. After all, it was perfectly plausible that a small-town sheriff would not realize he should have contacted the FBI when he apprehended Holzman. But Nick knew the agent didn't believe it for one minute.

After a few moments, Daniels said, "I suppose we owe you one–again, Detective."

"Just doing my job," Nick replied with a disarming grin.

Daniels shot one more sharp glance at Nick, then let out a resigned huff as he sat forward. Placing his elbows on the table, he perused the statement again. When he looked up, he asked, "So you believe this guy?"

"I do," Nick replied.

"And what about this murder you're investigating? You think it's connected to our investigation?"

Nick paused. He'd expected this question. He did not want the FBI to take over the Blakely murder case. But he didn't want to antagonize his son's boss either. After a moment, he inhaled deeply and said, "I'm not sure how, but my feeling is yes, there's some tangential connection."

Daniels squinted as he considered Nick's response. "Tangential, huh?"

Nick just nodded.

The agent scratched the back of his neck, glanced down at the statement again, then back up at Nick.

"Okay, Detective. In spite of the fact that you've managed rather successfully to skate your way around the edges of our case, you have proven yourself to be a first-rate investigator and a team player."

He paused for effect. Nick didn't react.

"Tell you what," Daniels continued. "I'm not going to take over your case–that is–if you agree to continue sharing any information you uncover pertinent to the Green Gardyn explosion."

"Of course," Nick replied, concealing the relief he felt.

Daniels tapped the cell phone lying on the conference table. "Agent Manelli, could you come into the conference room?"

Nick's feeling of relief evaporated. Was Daniels' conciliatory offering just a teaser? Were Nick's actions going to negatively affect Nicky's position? Was Daniels going to somehow take things out on his son?

After just a few moments, Nicky appeared outside the

conference room glass door. Daniels waved him in.

Nicky entered the room and faced his boss, ignoring his father.

Daniels pointed across the table at Nick. "Detective Manelli here says he thinks a murder investigation he's working on in his jurisdiction may be related—how'd you put it, Detective?"

"Tangentially," Nick replied with the sinking feeling he was being baited.

"Yes, tangentially related to our case. And he has just agreed to share with us any information he acquires in the course of his investigation that might help us with ours."

Nicky nodded to his boss, allowing himself only a quick glance in his father's direction. Daniels smiled and Nick got the distinct impression he was enjoying their discomfiture.

After a moment, the agent turned to Nick. "Detective, do you have the time to brief Agent Manelli on your investigation to date?"

Nick sniffed, the corners of his mouth twitching. "Yes, I can do that."

"Now, get out of here, both of you," Daniels grumbled, as he opened a manila folder on his desk and began reading the contents.

On the walk down the corridor, Nicky said, "You care to tell me how you pulled that off?"

"Yeah," Nick replied. "How about I take you out to lunch?"

"Sorry, Dad, I have a lot to do, and I was eating my lunch when Daniels called," Nicky said as they reached his desk.

Nick looked down at the half-eaten sandwich on his son's desk.

"That's your stepmother's honey oat bread, isn't it?" he

said.

56 A GAME OF CLUE

On the way back from Newark, Holly stopped at the supermarket. Kate and Ivy walked around the store as she picked up the few items she needed. When they met up at the checkout counter, Ivy perused Holly's shopping cart.

"Oh, you are so transparent, Holly," Ivy said.

"I don't know what you're talking about," Holly said as the items she placed on the conveyer belt reached the cashier.

Kate's nose wrinkled. "What *are* you talking about?"

"Look what she's buying." Ivy pointed at the food items. "Mozzarella, ricotta, eggplant, tomatoes."

"Guess she's cooking Italian tonight." Kate smiled.

"She's not just cooking Italian. She's making Nick's favorite–Eggplant rollatini."

"Oh, shut up," Holly said as she retrieved her credit card and the cashier handed her a receipt.

Ivy and Kate laughed as they followed Holly through the automated doors out to the parking lot.

Kate scurried beside Holly. "I'm on your side. A good offense is the best defense."

"Oh please," Holly said. "You just like rollatini as much as Nick."

****

After they returned home, Kate and Ivy took Lucky for a walk, and Holly started dinner. As she lowered the heat under the tomato sauce, her mind returned to Rodney Blakely. What had he done to get himself killed, she wondered.

She had witnessed the altercation with Professor McNair, but Rodney was a distinctly unlikable guy. He may have crossed others as well. Look how he treated Ariana. If he'd molested other young women, their fathers, brothers or boyfriends might well have had it in for him. Maybe his murder really had nothing to do with Green Gardyn Foods. She shook her head and started slicing the eggplant, forcing herself to focus on the meal she was preparing.

Yes, Ivy was right. She let out a small laugh. Her sister knew her too well. Preparing Nick's favorite dish was meant to assuage his annoyance with her if he found out she went to see Nicky. And if he didn't find out, well, the rollatini and a bottle of wine that cousin Mateo sent from his Tuscan vineyard might at least get him talking to her about the case.

She heard the front door open and, as always, Lucky raced into the kitchen, Kate in her wake.

"Oh, it smells divine in here," Kate said. "What can I do to help?"

"Would you like to set the table? I thought we'd eat in the dining room tonight. You can use the dishes and silverware in the breakfront."

"I can do that," Kate said with a smile.

"Where's Ivy?"

"Uh–she went upstairs," Kate replied. "She'll be right down."

As Kate set the table, Holly breaded and fried the eggplant. Half-way through, Ivy appeared in the doorway laden with legal pads and pens.

"Let me guess," Holly said, a trace of sarcasm in her voice. "A game of Clue?"

Ivy grinned. "Good guess," she said and sat down at the kitchen table.

Kate popped her head in through the dining room door. "Safe to come in?"

"Yeah," Ivy said. "She didn't even arch an eyebrow."

Holly made a face. "You two are very funny," she said. "I know I've objected to this so-called 'game' in the past, but my head is spinning. I keep bouncing between what happened at the Eco-Fair, the Green Gardyn explosion and Rodney's murder. I can't seem to keep anything straight. Maybe this will help me see the connections that I just know are there."

Kate rubbed her palms together, grabbed a pad and pen, and sat down beside Ivy. "Okay, she said. "Let's start at the very beginning."

"That would be the vandalism of Ariana's display the day before the Eco-Fair," Ivy said.

"Okay," Holly nodded as she opened the refrigerator and reached for the cheeses. "Now, who did that?"

"I think it was the kids wearing those GMOs Rock T-shirts," Ivy said.

"And I think it was someone from Green Gardyn Foods," Kate said jotting it down on her pad.

"I get the motive in both cases, but I find it more likely the students did it," Holly said. "I mean, did Green Gardyn Foods even know about the experiment at this point?"

"That's a really good question," Ivy said. "And one that's been puzzling me. The first call about a potential lawsuit was made the day of the presentations. Supposedly, the caller was anonymous. The call about the signature, the call that got the project disqualified, came in the day after the presentations."

"That second call had to be from Green Gardyn Foods," Kate said.

"Yeah, that makes sense," Holly said. "But who made the first call? If Green Gardyns had known about the experiment the day before, why wouldn't they have identified themselves and lodged an official complaint right then and there?"

The trio silently considered the questions they just posed when Lucky suddenly barked and headed out into the hall. A moment later the doorbell rang.

"Who could that be?" Holly asked, drying her hands with a dish towel, as she exited the kitchen and went to the front door.

"Peppy," she said, then snapped her head back when she spotted Razor standing behind her, both wearing bleak expressions.

Holly opened the door wide. "Well, I guess you better come in."

57 LUIS' STORY

"Kate, set two more places for dinner, please," Holly said as she entered the kitchen.

"Hi, Peppy," Ivy greeted her when she appeared in the doorway.

"Razor!" Kate said as he followed her in. "What are you doing here?"

"He thinks I need his help." Peppy frowned and plopped into a chair beside Ivy.

Holly glanced at the big guy who simply winked by way of explanation. "Sit down, Razor," she said. "Beer?"

Peppy shook her head. Razor nodded and took the seat next to her.

"I'll get it," Ivy said. As she got up, Holly turned to her guests. "Well, you two look like your dog just got run over. What's up?"

"They've arrested Luis Navarro for the murder of Rodney Blakely," Peppy replied.

Holly closed her eyes, threw her head back and let out a mournful sigh. The smell of burnt eggplant caused her to open her eyes and quickly move to the stove. "Damn!" she said as she lowered the flame under the cast-iron frying pan.

"Okay. Ivy, Kate, as Peppy tells us what's going on, I'm going to need you two to spoon the cheese and roll the eggplant, while I finish frying."

Ivy grabbed the baking dish, and ladled some sauce in the bottom as Kate stirred the cheese mixture.

Satisfied they had everything under control, Holly returned to the stove. "Okay, Peppy, talk to us," she said as she dredged a slice of eggplant through a shallow bowl of flour.

"Luis admits he talked to Rodney early the morning of the murder and that's why his fingerprints were in the car."

"How did they identify the prints as his?" Kate asked. "Does he have a record?"

"No," Peppy replied. "He applied for TSA pre-check."

"Oh, yeah." Ivy nodded. "I forgot they fingerprint you for that."

"So, what did Luis have to talk to Rodney about?" Holly asked.

"The day before he overheard Ariana agreeing to meet Rodney in the parking lot the next morning. Luis knew Rodney tried to–uh–take advantage of

Ariana in a restaurant parking lot a couple of weeks ago."

"How did he find that out?" Holly asked.

"He's friends with Manny, the valet at the restaurant where it happened. Anyway, he showed up early and found Rodney already sitting in his car. The doofus was so fixated on his phone Luis was able to get in the passenger side before he even looked up. Luis told him if he tried anything like that again, he'd ..." Peppy hesitated, "he'd pay."

Holly held back a sigh as she turned over a slice of eggplant. "And how did that work out?" she asked.

"Rodney laughed at him. Luis warned him when he least expected it, that's when he'd get him—the same way he got in the car before Rodney even looked up. Luis could see that scared him. After that he said he just got out of the car and left."

"Why didn't Luis offer to go with Ariana in the first place?" Holly asked.

"I don't know." Peppy shrugged.

"He's got a thing for Ariana," Razor said in his low voice. "My guess is she treats him like a brother."

"What are you talking about?" Peppy looked at Razor as if he had sprouted a second head.

"No," Holly said. "I get that. Plus, he probably figures he can't compete with a guy like Rodney."

"And he obviously found out about their arranged meeting by eavesdropping," Ivy added.

"Yeah, yeah," Kate agreed. "Poor guy."

"Men!" Peppy shook her head. "All I know is Luis says he didn't do it and I believe him."

Holly turned off the stove and brought the last pieces of eggplant over to the table where Ivy and Kate were working. "I don't believe that boy is capable of murder either," she said turning on the oven.

Kate got up and handed her the first pan of rollatini. "I'll bet Rodney knew something about Green Gardyn Foods and that's what got him killed."

As Ivy rolled the last slice of eggplant and placed it in the second pan, she said, "Kate, get the legal pads and let's get back to work sorting out the facts we know."

Lucky suddenly got to her feet and headed to the hallway, tail wagging.

At the sound of the front door opening, Holly whispered, "No, hide those. Lucky didn't bark. That's Nick."

58 SUSPENSION

"Looks like the gang's all here." Nick smiled as he paused in the doorway to the kitchen. "What smells so good?" he asked glancing at the stove.

"Eggplant rollatini." Holly smiled back as she walked over and gave him a kiss on the cheek.

"My favorite," Nick's smile widened.

"Hey, why don't you all go sit down in the living room while I get the pasta started," Holly said as she turned on the fire under the stockpot. "Kate, Ivy, would you get everybody something to drink please."

"Sure," Ivy said as the guests got up and moved into the other room.

"I'll decant the wine." Kate said, opening a drawer, searching for the corkscrew. When everyone had left the kitchen, Kate whispered, "Looks like you pulled it off."

Holly took a deep breath. "We'll see."

****

Throughout dinner, no one mentioned Green Gardyn Foods or Rodney Blakely. Most of the conversation consisted of Peppy and Holly teasing Kate and Razor about life in Reddington Manor.

"Come on," Peppy said. "What do you have, like a dozen books in your library?"

"Oh stop it," Kate huffed. "I'll have you know we can request books from anywhere in the county, and I've been able to get whatever I want to read, even the latest best sellers."

"I'll give you that," Holly said. "But other than the library, you have to admit there's not much to do up there. How many miles are you from the nearest movie theater?"

"Only twelve," Razor replied, wearing a deadpan expression. After a moment, even he couldn't hold in the laughter.

"Hey, Razor," Nick said. "What do you say you come with me to walk the dog?"

Razor looked to Holly. "Can I help you clean up?"

"No," Holly replied. "You guys go. We got this."

As soon as the door closed behind the men, Holly shook her head. "This cannot be good."

****

Outside Nick said, "So, I assume you stayed to keep Peppy out of trouble."

Razor just shrugged as they headed down the street to the park.

"I know she talked to Luis right after I left for Newark. He told me. When we go back in there, I'm going to tell her she's suspended for the duration of this investigation for failure to follow protocol."

Razor let out a small groan. "She's not gonna like that."

"Don't worry. I'm not really going to suspend her. I just can't have her working on this case because of her relationship to Ariana. It's the kind of detail that a defense lawyer will pounce on to claim we doctored the evidence, Nick explained.

"I get that."

"And this is just between you and me. Holly can't know the truth either," Nick cautioned.

"I get that too."

"I'd ask you to take Peppy upstate with you, but I know she won't leave town. Can you stick around? Make sure she doesn't do anything that will force me to have to issue an official suspension that could affect her future in the department."

"Sure."

"She's a good cop with great instincts."

"Yep."

"You got a thing for her, right?" Nick asked.

"Right."

"Okay, then we're clear here?"

"Crystal."

"Okay, let's go back so I can break the bad news."

****

At the sound of Peppy's raised voice coming from the living room, Ivy and Kate excused themselves and went upstairs to bed. Holly waited in the kitchen with Razor who told her about the suspension.

Holly blanched. She'd suspected that Nick's jovial mood was not entirely genuine. During dinner, he'd casually mentioned that he'd been to Newark that afternoon. She'd been on high alert since that moment. Was she next in line after he finished with Peppy?

"Yes, sir." Peppy's angry voice came from the hallway.

Razor quickly exited the kitchen, Holly on his heels. As Peppy opened the front door, he nodded at Nick and followed her out.

"I had to suspend her," Nick said as he locked the front door and headed upstairs.

"Razor told me," Holly said. "I'll be right up as soon as I shut off the lights."

Nick was in the bathroom when she stepped inside their bedroom. She changed into her nightgown and waited on the bed. Should she just tell him she'd been to see Nicky and get it over with? This uncertainty was making her skin crawl.

No. Nicky wouldn't have ratted her out. Let sleeping dogs lie.

The bathroom door opened. As Nick stepped out, Holly got up and crossed the room. As she was about to pass him, he reached out and wrapped his arms around her. Her heart skipped a beat.

"That was a great meal." He smiled. "Why'd you make my favorite today?"

Holly smiled back. "Do I need a reason?"

"Not usually," Nick replied. "You want to tell me about your trip to Newark today?"

Holly lowered her head and let out a huge sigh. After a moment she frowned and looked her husband in the eye. "I can't believe Nicky told on me."

"He didn't. I saw the sandwich on his desk. I'd know that honey oat bread anywhere."

Holly's frown turned into a grin. "Oh, honey, that's so sweet."

59 BARBARA GILLIS

After breakfast Sunday morning, Holly, Kate and Ivy drove to the garden center to pick up some more bulbs.

"I still can't believe Nick wasn't mad at you for talking to Nicky," Kate said from the back seat. "We expected to hear an explosion after Peppy and Razor left."

"Well, the fact that Agent Daniels has given Nicky the green light to talk to Nick about the case made it less of an issue."

"Yeah," Ivy smirked at her sister. "That and the rollatini."

"And don't forget the Manelli vineyard wine," Holly chuckled as they pulled into the garden center parking lot.

"I just love this place," Ivy said, her attention immediately focused out the window where colorful hanging baskets lined the porch of the building that housed the gift shop and greenhouse.

"Flowering plants and a gift shop," Holly laughed. "Your idea of heaven."

"Mine too," Kate added as they got out of the car. "Oh, look at the Halloween display," she said pointing across the parking lot to where hay bales were stacked, surrounded by pumpkins, scarecrows, witches and goblins.

"I'm going to start with the bulb bins. I want to add to my ..." Holly just shook her head as Kate and Ivy headed to the display, paying no attention to her.

Holly slowly walked down the porch perusing the contents of the large cardboard bins filled with spring-flowering bulbs. She always liked to see the entire selection before she made her choices. When she arrived at the end of the porch, she turned and headed back to the boxes of hyacinth bulbs. As she reached for a bag, a woman came up behind her.

"You love hyacinths too?"

Holly looked up, surprised to see Barbara Gillis, the Physical Sciences Department admin standing beside her.

"Barb! Hi. Yes, I do love hyacinths. I think their scent is what heaven must smell like."

Barb laughed. "Well, I hope I get to find out whether or not you're right about that," she said as she lifted a bag of assorted colors. "Do you force them indoors?"

Holly grinned and nodded. "I do. Isn't it

amazing how powerful the smell is inside?"

"Oh yes," Barb nodded. "Do you have a lilac bush in your yard?"

"Yes," Holly replied, "and I always bring the flowers inside when they're in bloom, too. I see we both like the scented blooms."

Barb picked up a second bag from the bin. "I have another one for you. Honeysuckle."

"Yes," Holly giggled. "I have it growing on a trellis near my patio. Hey, Barb, you'll have to come over and see my garden one day. Who knew we had so much in common?"

"I'd love that," Barb agreed. "And you must come see mine as well."

"It's a deal." Holly grabbed a second bag of hyacinths.

"Well, see you around school," Barb said as she moved to the tulip bins.

"Yes, good talking to you." Holly moved in the opposite direction toward the daffodils.

As she rooted through the box, Barb came back alongside her. "Holly," she said, placing her hand on Holly's forearm. Making direct eye contact, she said, "I–uh," then dropped her eyes to the bag of bulbs in her hand. "About the students who got disqualified ..."

Holly held her breath as she waited for Barb to continue. She didn't dare say anything that might make this woman reconsider what she was about to say.

After a moment, Barb again made eye contact. "You asked me if I knew who called Professor McNair about the signature on the release forms the morning of the awards ceremony."

"Oh, Barb, I know I shouldn't have asked. Besides, we found out that it was Green Gardyn Foods."

The admin blinked rapidly. "The morning of the awards ceremony, the only calls the Professor got were from Dr. Miller and–and Rodney Blakely."

"Oh," Holly said. "I suppose he could have gotten a call on his cell phone."

Barb shook her head. "No. He complained to me when he arrived that he left his cell phone home. He was always doing that and having me place calls for him when he did."

"Could he have gotten a call the night before?" Holly asked.

"No. When he came in, he asked me to print up his concluding remarks for the closing ceremony. Ariana Alvarez's team was the winner of the competition."

"So, are you telling me that when he arrived the students were still in the running? They had actually won, and he got no outside calls that morning?"

Barb just nodded.

60 COFFEE

Peppy woke to the delicious aroma of freshly brewed coffee. She smiled as she stretched out on her futon. Suddenly, she shot up to a sitting position. Who made coffee?

She reached for the pistol she kept under her pillow and panicked when she couldn't find it. Turning ever so slowly, she looked across at the mini-kitchenette on the opposite wall of her studio apartment. She relaxed when she saw Razor standing near the two-burner stove.

"*Buenos dias, Cariño,*" he said. "Looking for this?" He held up the missing pistol.

"How did you get that?" she asked, glaring at him.

"I saw you put it under the pillow. Just waited until you fell asleep and rolled over. I didn't want to risk you waking up groggy and shooting me because you forgot I was here." He poured a cup of coffee from an old-fashioned tin coffee pot into a mug he'd found in the cupboard and brought it over to her.

Peppy took the offered cup and sipped. Glancing over at the stove, she said, "That's a coffee pot?"

Razor laughed. "How do you not know something you have in your own cupboard?"

"It was there when I moved in."

"So you didn't know that was a coffee pot, but you had coffee in the cupboard."

"I had a Mr. Coffee, but it broke. I just haven't had a chance to get a new one." Peppy took another sip. "How'd you know how to use that tin can anyway?"

"We have one for camping trips," Razor replied.

"Camping," she guffawed. "What a hick you are."

Peppy felt a tinge of regret when Razor just gave her that good-natured smile of his in reply. Didn't he ever get mad? She didn't want to ask, but wondered whether or not he got any sleep sitting in the beat-up armchair in the corner, another item left in the apartment by the previous occupant. As she gulped down the last of her coffee, Razor got up and brought the pot over to refill her mug.

"Look, don't try to be nice to me," she snapped. "I'm not a happy camper this morning." She put air quotes around the word "camper".

Razor ignored the pun. "You know Manelli

had no choice," he said, his tone soothing.

"That may be, but what am I supposed to do for the next two weeks? Just sit here while my cousin loses her scholarship and Luis sits in jail because he can't afford bail."

Razor looked at his phone. "Well, we're invited to watch the Giants game this afternoon at the Manelli's."

"You can't be serious," Peppy said, getting up and setting her mug down on a side table that wobbled. "I'm not going there." She gave the futon a rough pull, quickly converting it from bed to couch.

Razor watched as she folded her blanket. "You want to go up to the Catskills and stay with Benny and me until your suspension is over?"

"Hell no! What would I do up there? Watch the leaves fall?" Jabbing an index finger in his direction, she added, "But I think that's exactly where you should go. I can take you to the bus station."

Razor ignored the suggestion. "Shall we go visit your cousin?"

Peppy stopped and considered this option. After a moment, she nodded. "Yeah, that's what I'll do." She cast a fierce expression at Razor. "And let's get something straight. There's no 'we' here."

The big man got to his feet. Peppy froze as he crossed the room and stopped just inches from her. He grasped her upper arms gently, but firmly. She could feel his warmth, smell his distinctly masculine scent. She felt her heart start to race as he gazed into her eyes with an expression of–she wasn't sure what–affection?

"I'm not playing," he said. "I want there to be a 'we'. Now, I'm going to go out and get us some breakfast, while you get dressed and figure out what you want to do today."

Before she could reply, he pulled her even closer and kissed her. She felt powerless to resist, as if she were melting. When he released her, she wasn't ready. Surprising herself, she grabbed his shirt and pulled him to her, initiating the kiss this time.

When they paused, he smiled. "Glad that's out of the way." Suddenly, his expression turned serious. "And just to be clear, I'm not leaving you alone until this is over."

61 ANONYMITY

"Did you get everything you wanted?" Nick asked when Holly entered the living room. The Sunday paper lay on the floor and a sports announcer was on the television making predictions about tonight's game. Nick looked so comfortable nestled on the couch that she hated to interrupt his one day off.

"Yeah," she replied. "I got the hyacinths and daffodils I wanted."

"Where are Ivy and Kate?" he asked, his eyes on the television.

"It's so nice out, they decided to put the bulbs in the shed for me and said they wanted to sit outside for a while. And um, I uh ..."

Nick glanced over at his wife, muted the television and sat up. "What happened?"

Holly sighed and walked over to the couch, sitting down beside him. "I ran into Barbara Gillis at the garden center."

"Who's she?"

"The admin for the Physical Sciences Department."

"And ..." Nick prompted.

"Okay, here's what she told me."

When she finished, Nick said, "So, you're saying there was no outside phone call, anonymous or otherwise, that morning? Nothing to alert McNair to the fact that the signature allowing the students to use Green Gardyn's seeds in their experiment was illegally obtained?"

"Exactly." Holly's forehead wrinkled. "Why would McNair lie about that?"

"Well, my guess is Miller got the call and didn't want to be the one to make the announcement. He called McNair and told him he had to do it."

Holly's expression morphed into a disappointed scowl. "Oh, I can't believe that about Dr. Miller. I mean, even if he instructed McNair to be the bad news bear, why would he have the professor say he got the call? That doesn't make sense."

"You're right, it doesn't. But my experience has been that smart people do lots of things that don't make sense. Miller was leaving town for that conference. Maybe he just wanted to avoid anything that might cause him to delay his trip. Or he just didn't want to have to answer questions and, since not verifying the signature was McNair's screw-up, he made him the point of contact."

Holly scratched her head. "I don't know. That just doesn't sound like Dr. Miller."

"Has he returned any of your emails?"

"No." Holly sank back against the couch. "Well, tomorrow he's back and I'll try to talk to him after my class." After a moment, she sat up straight. "Wait a minute. McNair also got a call from Rodney the morning of the closing ceremonies."

"What are you saying?" Nick asked.

"Well, we know he was rejected by Ariana. I feel pretty sure he was the type to hold a grudge. Maybe this was his way of getting even with her."

"But even so, the signature, while not technically forged, was not legitimate. Let's say Rodney was the one who got that phone call. He'd have to tell his boss. When Miller finds out, he calls McNair. Tells him he'll have to deal with the mess. He leaves for the airport and lets Rodney handle it from there. That would account for their two phone calls."

"Hold on," Holly said. "I'm having a déjà vu feeling." She looked up at the ceiling. "I'm forgetting something."

Nick waited as she appeared to be searching her memory bank. After a few moments she smiled. "Yesterday, Kate, Ivy and I were talking about this right before Peppy and Razor showed up. One of the last questions I asked before they arrived was who made the anonymous call that forced the students to keep the company names confidential when they made their presentation. Two days later Green Gardyn Foods calls the school claiming the signature on the release papers was obtained dishonestly. It just doesn't make sense."

"No, it doesn't." Nick reached for his phone and tapped the screen. "Nicky, how did Green Gardyn Foods find out their seeds were being used in the student experiment and how did they find out their employee was tricked into signing the release document?"

Holly sat and watched as Nick listened to his son's answer. After a moment, he said, "Well, Holly just found out that the Professor who said he got the phone call the morning of the closing ceremonies didn't receive any outside calls that morning." Again, Nick paused to listen. Finally, he said, "Yep. Okay. Hey, you sure you can't come up to watch the game with us. No, I understand. Talk to you tomorrow."

"What did he say?" Holly asked.

"You're gonna love this. Green Gardyn Foods said they got an anonymous tip the day before alerting them that their seeds were being used in a college experiment. That would be the day after the school got their anonymous call. After they did some checking they discovered the release document and determined an employee–whom we know to be George Holzman–obtained the signature under false pretenses. Then they called Dr. Miller."

"So, you were right. I'm really disappointed to know Dr. Miller left Professor McNair to deal with the mess." Holly frowned for a moment. Suddenly her eyes got wide. "But that leaves us with the question, who placed the anonymous call to Green Gardyn Foods?"

"I was hoping you wouldn't ask that?" Nick sighed.

"What did Nicky say?"

"The call came from a burner phone."

62 HOME-MADE TORTILLAS

The aroma of Pork Posole cooking in the kitchen filled the Alvarez apartment when Peppy and Razor arrived. Peppy said they just stopped by to talk to Ariana, but Juan and his wife, Maria, insisted they stay and join them for their midday meal.

Ariana entered the small living room carrying a tray of glasses and cans of Coca-Cola. Juan followed with a bowl of tortilla chips and salsa. As he placed the bowl on the coffee table, he said, "Help yourself, *por favor.*"

Peppy moved to the edge of the couch where she sat next to Razor. "You don't have to ask me twice, cousin," she said as she reached for a paper plate and handed it to Razor. "When's the last time you had home-made tortillas?"

Razor ran the tip of his tongue across his upper lip. "Too long," he replied and scooped a handful of the golden chips onto his plate. He dipped one into the chunky salsa. After a taste, he closed his eyes and muttered a sigh of contentment.

Juan laughed. "*Bueno, no?*"

Razor smiled and nodded. "*Muy bueno.*"

"My wife, she make the best." Juan beamed with pride. At the sound of his wife calling for him, he excused himself and returned to the kitchen.

"He's not kidding," Peppy said, smiling at Ariana as she dipped her chip into the salsa. "Your mom really does make the best tortillas."

Her cousin gave her a weak smile and was about to say something when there was a knock at the door. "That must be Debby," she said and walked over to let her science project partner in.

"Debby, this is my cousin, Peppy, and her friend, Razor."

"Nice to meet you," Debby said. She sat down, an air of anxiety surrounding her. "Listen, I heard something from one of my old friends. I don't know if it can help us."

"Just tell us," Peppy said.

"Well, this girl told me that it was the GMOs Rock crew that vandalized our booth."

"And how does she know this?" Peppy asked.

"Because she was part of their group. She dropped out when she found out what they were planning."

"Is your friend willing to report this to someone at the school?"

"I doubt it." Debby frowned.

Ariana lowered herself into the chair next to Debby. "Ms. Donnelly advised us to go to the Student Government Association, but I don't see how that can help us if no one is willing to testify on our behalf." Her eyes began to tear up. "What does it matter anyway? It certainly doesn't help Luis." She clenched her fists. "I just don't understand why he went to talk to Rodney anyway."

Debby, Peppy and Razor all looked at her with varying expressions of disbelief.

"You're kidding, right?" Debby said.

"What do you mean?" Ariana appeared dumbfounded.

"He's in love with you, *Chica*," Peppy said.

"What?" Ariana shook her head as she turned to Debby. "No."

"C'mon. How could you not know that?"

When even Razor cast an indulgent smile at her, Ariana began to cry. "Peppy, can't you do something?"

Peppy sighed. "Look. Manelli took me off the case because I'm related to you. But I trust him. I think he knows Luis didn't kill Rodney."

"Oh, oh!" Debby sat forward, excitement in her voice. "There's something else I forgot to tell you."

"What?" Peppy and Ariana said simultaneously.

"My friend said she thinks Rodney had something to do with the vandalism."

"What do you mean?" Peppy asked, tension in her voice. "What makes her think that?"

Debby shrugged. "I don't know. I asked her, but she said that was all she could tell me."

"Come." Juan called from the kitchen doorway. "The meal is ready."

"We need to talk to that girl," Peppy said, her voice steely this time.

Razor nodded. "After we eat."

63 THE PARK

"Basta!" Peppy chided as Razor accepted a second slice of Tres Leches cake. "Enough already. You're going to explode if you eat anymore."

"Leave him, Peppy," Juan said smiling. "A big man need *mucho* food."

Maria gave Peppy a stern look. "Time you learned to cook. I teach you."

Razor smiled as he savored the creamy dessert. Peppy shook her head and looked to Ariana. "We need to get going."

Ariana jumped to her feet and started stacking empty plates.

"Let me help," Debby said, collecting the glasses and silverware from her side of the table.

Maria lifted a platter and followed the girls into the kitchen. Juan leaned across the table. "*Gracias*, Peppy."

"Thank me? What for?" she asked.

"For helping Ariana."

Peppy frowned. "But I haven't been much help."

"I know you do all you can." Juan grasped her hand, his eyes glistening. "*Gracias.*"

Peppy locked eyes with her cousin and nodded. As Razor finished the last bite of cake, she said, "Gimme that." She grabbed his fork and plate and carried it to the kitchen.

When the dishes were all washed and put away, Peppy, Ariana and Debby returned to the living room.

"*Muchas gracias,*" Peppy said to Maria, kissing both her and Juan. Turning to Razor and the girls, she said, "*Vamos.*"

Out in the car, Peppy asked, "Where to, Debby?"

"My friend said she was going to the park this afternoon. There's supposed to be live music there today."

"What if she won't talk to us?" Ariana asked.

"Let me worry about that," Peppy said, giving Razor a sideways glance.

Everyone lapsed into silence as they drove across town to the community park. The sun was setting and the traffic slowed to a crawl as they reached the park entrance. Lowering their windows they could hear the music playing. Once inside the park they were directed to the grassy expanse next to the completely full, paved parking lot.

All around, people swayed to the enticing rhythm of the salsa music on their way to the bandstand.

"Sounds good," Peppy said as they followed the crowd.

When they reached the band stand, they stopped and surveyed the people gathered on the great lawn. Many sat on blankets and folding lawn chairs they brought from home. In front of the stage, couples showed off their dance moves. The smell of peppers and onions wafted invitingly from the row of food trucks that lined the back perimeter of the great lawn.

"Why don't you two go look for your friend?" Peppy said. "We'll wait here. If you find her, Debby, you stay with her. Ariana, you come and get us."

Ariana nodded and the two girls skirted the edge of the crowd, heading in the direction of the food trucks.

As Peppy and Razor stood watching, the couples in front of the stage stopped dancing, yielding the dance area to an older couple who moved with commanding style and grace.

"I guess this isn't their first dance together," Peppy said smiling.

"Good guess." Razor nodded.

When the music finished, the crowd roared with applause. The couple responded with an elegant bow, then returned to their lawn chairs.

"You dance?" Razor asked as the band started up the next number.

"Yeah," Peppy replied. "You?"

Razor grabbed her hand. "C'mon. *Bailamos*."

Peppy pulled back. "No way. Look, we're here with a purpose."

"No reason we can't enjoy ourselves," Razor said. Looking over her head, he grabbed her hand again, this time pulling toward the food trucks. Peppy resisted until he said, "Ariana's waving to us."

Peppy quickly fell into step beside him. When they reached the girls, Debby faced them, her friend's back turned toward them. Razor stopped a few feet behind the girl. Peppy came up alongside Debby.

"Hi, Debby." She smiled in greeting.

"Oh, hi," Debby replied. "Teresa, this is Ariana's cousin, Peppy."

"Hi," the girl replied, appearing taken aback by Peppy's arrival. She cast a nervous glance at Ariana, then said, "Look, I gotta go."

As she turned, she bumped straight into Razor. "Hey!" she said. Clearly annoyed, she turned a fierce look at Debby.

Debby grimaced. "They just want to talk to you."

64 CHICKEN WINGS

A few minutes before half-time, with the Giants leading by six points, Holly got up and went to the kitchen to check on the chicken wings she had roasting in the oven. As she opened the oven door, her phone signaled. When she saw Peppy's name, she quickly closed the oven and answered.

"Peppy, how are you?" she asked, keeping her voice low.

"I'm fine, but listen, *Mami.* We found out something. The guy who got killed."

"Rodney?"

"Yeah. He's the one who got those preppy students to wreck Ariana's exhibit."

"What!" Holly exclaimed. "How'd you find that out?"

"Never mind that. We just did."

"But why did he do it?" Holly asked. "Just to get even with Ariana?"

"No. That's the thing. He was dating one of those girls, the leader of the pack. They had a fight, and she accused him of using her and her friends just to get back at Ariana. He told her no. He had orders to destroy the exhibit."

"Orders from whom?"

"The girl didn't know. He just said it was somebody important and assured her none of them would get in trouble."

"Did you get the leader of the pack's name?" Holly asked.

"*Mami*, c'mon. You're not talking to an amateur here," Peppy chided. "Her name is–get this–Ashley Whitmore."

Holly smiled, imagining the expression of amusement Peppy wore as she delivered this information. "Good work, Officer Alvarez."

Suddenly, a loud cheer came from the living room. "Look, I've got to go," Holly said. "This is important information ..." She hesitated when she heard footsteps heading in her direction. "Thanks. Bye, Ariana," she said as Nick, Kate and Ivy entered the kitchen.

"That was Ariana?" Ivy asked as she opened the refrigerator and got out the potato salad.

"Yeah." Holly grabbed the hot pads, opened the oven door and slid out the golden chicken wings.

"How's she doing?" Kate asked as she replaced Ivy in front of the refrigerator and pulled out a tray of dipping sauces.

"She's doing okay," Holly said, sliding the still-sizzling wings off the baking sheet onto a platter.

Already seated, Nick had his eyes on her as she placed the platter in the center of the table. "And?" he said when she took her seat.

Holly sighed. Was he the best detective in the world, or had she completely lost her ability to conceal things from him? She wondered if he even knew that it was Peppy, not Ariana, she'd spoken to.

"Why don't we eat first and then we can talk about what she told me."

"Holly." He had a way of saying her name that made it clear there was no point resisting or delaying the inevitable. She had to tell him.

She took a deep breath. "Okay. Ariana and Debby talked to a girl from school. She said the GMOs Rock group was behind the vandalism and that Rodney Blakely was the one who got them to do it."

"Oh my," Ivy said.

"Not Green Gardyn Foods?" Kate said, her face reflecting her disappointment.

Nick said nothing as he speared chicken wings and piled them on his plate.

"Oh, and he also said he had orders to vandalize the booth," Holly added.

"Well, there you go," Kate said, her disappointed expression morphing into a smile of vindication. "I'll bet his orders came from Green Gardyn Foods."

Nick dipped a wing in Holly's homemade honey mustard sauce and took a bite. "Delicious," he said.

"Thanks, Honey." Holly recognized that this conversation was over–until later. "Would you pass me the potato salad?" she said to Ivy. "So, what was the reason for that final cheer I heard before you all came in here?"

The conversation during the rest of the meal focused on the game and the Giants' chances of making it to the Super Bowl.

****

"So, what do you think about what Ariana told me?" Holly asked as Nick got into bed.

"I think I want to talk to the girl who talked to Ariana. Did you get her name?"

"Ashley Whitmore." As he lay down, Holly snuggled close. "Nick, you don't believe Luis killed Rodney, do you?"

Nick let out a long sigh. "No, I don't."

"And there's got to be a connection between Rodney's murder and the Green Gardyn's explosion, right?"

"Holly." His intonation this time let her know she'd asked one question too many and this discussion was over.

65 SALSA

Peppy grinned as she ended the call with Holly and slid the phone into her back pocket. She hated being sidelined like this, so it felt good to actually get some information that might help the case.

She headed to the spot where she'd left Razor, Ariana and Debby. They said they'd watch the dancers while she found a quiet spot to make her call. Scanning the crowd, she finally spotted Debby standing alone.

"So, what happened to Ariana and Razor?" she asked.

Debby grinned and lifted her chin in the direction of the dance area in front of the stage.

Peppy caught her breath as her eyes reached the center of the crowd and saw Razor spinning Ariana in time to the music. How could a man that big move so smoothly, she wondered. She watched the pair wind their arms in sinuous motion, their feet moving back and forth in sync.

She bit her lip. This was worse than she thought. She could resist anything, but not a man who could dance. When the song ended, Razor hugged Ariana, lifting her off the ground. The dancing couple laughed as they returned to where Peppy and Debby waited.

"Oh, that was fantastic!" Debby gushed. "You have to teach me how to dance, Ariana."

As the band started to play the next song, Razor extended his hand to Peppy. Shaking her head, she said, "No. I–uh–I think we should leave."

"Oh, c'mon, Peppy," Ariana coaxed. "This is the most fun I've had in weeks. I'm not leaving," she said and pulled Debby by the arm. "Come. Let's have your first lesson."

"*Vamos, Cariño,*" Razor said as he reached for her hand.

Not wanting to make a scene, Peppy followed as he led her to a spot on the edge of the crowded dance area. Starting slowly, he took both her hands in his, moving her to the right, then to the left. When he spun her towards him, her back against his chest, she felt her heartbeat quicken.

She hadn't been out dancing in a while, but the moves she'd learned when just a young girl came back to her with ease. And it felt so good. Still, she didn't dare make eye contact with Razor. Suddenly she felt herself stiffen as she worried this whole thing was moving too fast.

After their kiss this morning, he seemed to think everything was settled between them. But throughout the day, she'd been thinking this thing–whatever it was–was a mistake. And she worried about what would happen when they got back to her place later.

When the music stopped, Peppy braced herself for a hug that didn't come, as Razor released her and Debby and Ariana walked over. Had he read her mind? Or maybe he was having second thoughts too.

"Listen," Ariana said, "Debby has an early morning class tomorrow. Maybe we better go."

"Yeah, sure," Peppy said. "Let's go."

****

On the drive home, Ariana and Debby chattered on about the dancers and how good the band was. Razor agreed with their comments about the music and who the best salsa groups were. Peppy drove in silence.

When they finally exhausted the topic, Ariana asked, "Peppy, you got to talk to Ms. Donnelly?"

"Yeah," Peppy said. "She said she'll tell Manelli what your friend told us."

"Oh, okay," Ariana said. "Do you think any of this will help Luis?"

"It can't hurt," Razor replied.

Debby sighed. "Well, I'll be happy if it helps find Rodney's real killer, but I don't think anything can help us."

"What do you mean?" Peppy asked. "Look, the Holzman confessions cleared you of any role in faking the signature of your experiment documents. That's all good."

"Yeah, but the experiment results are now tainted and winning the Eco-Fair competition ensured our scholarships." Ariana groaned. "Seems like no one can help us there."

"Wait a minute," Debby said. "What about the federal agencies? I mean, Professor McNair said they would be turning over all of our work to them. Won't they have to launch an investigation of Green Gardyn Foods. Won't that clear us?"

"Good question," Peppy said. "Let me see what I can find out about that."

****

When they got to her apartment, Peppy pulled out her phone. "I have to call Holly. Maybe she can find out from her stepson what the Feds are doing?"

Razor reached for the phone. "Tomorrow."

"But ..."

"Talk to me," he said as he put the phone down on the end table. "I could feel you pull away from me in the middle of the dance. What are you afraid of?"

Peppy turned her back to him. "I'm not afraid of anything," she said walking over to the kitchenette.

"Okay," he said, his voice soft, like a caress. "Then tell me what you're feeling."

Peppy turned a fierce look at him. "That's just it. I don't know what I'm feeling. And–and this is all too ..."

"Okay," he said and sat down in the chair he'd slept in the night before.

Peppy's eyes misted over and she felt an ache of longing as she realized he was right. She was afraid. Her track record with men was not good. She promised herself after her first broken heart that she'd never give a man that power over her again. But this man–this man who had that power wouldn't use it without her consent. This was a good man.

She walked over to where he sat and put her hands on his shoulders. As he lifted his gaze to meet hers, she traced the side of his face with her fingertips. Sinking down on his lap, she surrendered to his embrace.

66 MONDAY MORNING

Nick walked into the kitchen just in time to hear Holly say, "Okay. I'll ask him." When she saw him, she said, "Thanks, Ariana. Bye." By the look on his wife's face, he knew she was talking to Peppy, not Ariana, just as he knew the call she'd gotten the night before was also from the "suspended" Officer Alvarez.

Of course, he had no intention of challenging her on the topic. It worked to his and Peppy's advantage. If he were to be questioned about her involvement in the investigation, he could truthfully answer that she was not involved in any official capacity. She was on leave and he had no direct contact with her throughout the investigation. He would have plausible deniability.

"So, what's up?" he asked as he walked over to the coffee pot and poured himself a cup.

"Well, that was Ariana again," Holly replied.

Nick fought back a smile at her apparent

discomfort. She really was a terrible liar.

"And?"

"She wondered if you could find out if the federal agencies that their experiment results were turned over to had launched an investigation of Green Gardyn Foods. She and her friend Debby were thinking that a government probe might show that their experiment was valid in spite of the fraudulent signature and improve their chances of getting their scholarships."

"I'll call Nicky and see if he can find out anything." Nick pulled out his notepad from his jacket pocket and sat down at the table. "What agencies were the results supposed to be turned over to?"

"APHIS ..."

"What's that? I never heard of it," Nick said as he started to jot down the acronym.

"That's the Animal and Plant Health Inspection Service," Holly replied. "The other two agencies are the EPA, and the Food and Drug Administration."

"So, what's on your agenda today?" Nick asked as he closed the notepad.

"Well, after my morning class, I'm hoping I finally get to talk to Dr. Miller."

"Still no reply to your emails?"

"No." Holly grimaced. "But he is a busy man."

"You ever consider that he doesn't want to

talk to you?"

Holly sat down across from her husband. "Yes, that thought did occur to me. But it's hard for me to think ill of Dr. Miller. I can't help it. I've always thought so highly of him, and after working with him on the Eco-Fair my respect for him only grew. He's brilliant and always the quintessential professional. I can't forget how kind and helpful he was to Ariana's group after the vandalism. Even if he did leave Professor McNair to deal with the fallout from the ill-gotten signature, I have to give him the benefit of the doubt and accept that maybe he really has been just too busy to reply to me."

"I get that," Nick said.

"Besides, he's the only one I trust to give me straight answers, and I think he's the only one who could help these kids out."

"And exactly how do you think he can do that?"

"Actually, I've given that quite a lot of thought. I mean, now that the kids are in the clear about the illicit signature, I was thinking that maybe he could write a personal letter of recommendation for them. He could say that in spite of the controversy caused by one team member, their work was still exemplary."

Nick nodded as he considered her answer. "Sounds like a good idea."

"Right?" Holly's face appeared to brighten at his endorsement of her suggestion.

Nick downed the last of his coffee and stood up. "What if he won't see you?" he asked.

"I don't know." The brightness left Holly's face, but only momentarily. "I know! I'll write him an impassioned plea asking him to write an endorsement letter. I'll even offer to write a draft for him."

"Atta girl." Nick bent and kissed her cheek. "Who's cooking tonight?" he asked as he headed to the front door.

"Kate," Holly replied, following him.

"Great. Italian." He turned and kissed her again, this time more than a peck on the cheek.

"I love you," she said.

"Love you more."

****

On the drive to the station, Nick hoped Holly stuck to the plan. He felt pretty sure this Dr. Miller had no intention of seeing her. Over the years Nick had been involved in his share of cases involving institutions. When they faced controversies and bad press, they generally pulled inward and limited access to anyone asking questions. The Eco-Fair controversy was one thing, but on top of that Rodney Blakely's murder clearly just added to the bad press. They couldn't have the public thinking their campus was unsafe for students.

That's what worried him most. If Blakely's murder was connected to the Green Gardyn Foods explosion and also to the students' experiment, his wife was smack in the middle of the whole mess. When he assigned Peppy to work with her, he felt fairly assured she would be safe, but now what?

And what about Peppy? Suspended, she was a wild card. He knew she wouldn't stop working the case, but at least she was sticking to her neighborhood. That was a good thing. She would be most effective there anyway. He just had to count on Razor to make sure she didn't do anything crazy. He needed to give Razor a call.

As he neared the station, his phone signaled, Yolanda's ringtone.

"What's up?" he asked.

"They located Ashley Whitmore."

67 BRIBERY

"Good morning," Ivy said as she padded into the kitchen, still in her pajamas and slippers.

"Good morning," Holly replied, glancing at the clock. "A little late for you, isn't it? Even Lucky stood staring at your door when I got up to walk her this morning."

"Sorry, Lucky." Ivy bent down to pet the dog. "Kate and I stayed up late streaming episodes of *Dark Shadows*," she said as she walked over to the coffee pot.

"You two and those vampire shows." Holly shook her head.

"Not all vampire shows." Ivy sat down across from Holly who had her laptop open. "What are you doing?"

"Trying to grade some essays. I'm really behind."

"Shouldn't you get going? Your class starts in

thirty minutes, doesn't it?"

"Yeah," Holly nodded, tapped a few more keys and closed her laptop. "You and Kate have any plans for today?"

"Not really. Will you be home right after class?"

"Well, I'm going to try to see Dr. Miller," Holly replied as she got up, "but I still should be back sometime after lunch."

"Maybe we could all go to a movie," Ivy suggested.

"Maybe. Remind Kate she volunteered to cook dinner today. I told Nick and he's expecting Italian."

Ivy smiled. "I'll tell her. And, Holly ..."

"What?" Holly said as she put on her blazer.

"Don't do anything stupid."

Holly did not reply.

****

"Okay, class. See you all on Thursday," Holly said as she packed up her briefcase. She was grateful that the students all headed to the door, and no one approached her with last-minute questions.

She'd rehearsed her speech for Dr. Miller on the drive to school. She was ready. When she reached the corridor where Miller's office was located, she spotted him coming from the opposite direction, reading what looked like a memo. Perfect.

Picking up her pace, she arrived at the door a

moment before him. "Dr. Miller, welcome back."

The scientist looked up from the paper in his hand. Holly tried her best to keep smiling, but his expression lacked any of his usual warmth. Her worst fear realized. He was not happy to see her.

"Professor Donnelly. Thank you. It's good to be back." With an air of dismissal, he walked through the door and over to what had been Rodney's desk. Another young man was now seated there, Rodney's nameplate gone.

Ignoring the tacit dismissal, Holly followed.

"Here are the messages you asked about, sir." Rodney's replacement handed the stack to Miller.

"Dr. Miller ..." Holly began.

"As you can well imagine," he cut her off without turning to face her, "after a week away, I have much to contend with this morning, Professor. You'll have to excuse me."

Holly stood crestfallen as she watched him enter his office, closing the door behind him. She glanced over at the young man who quickly dropped his eyes to his desk surface, appearing uncomfortable at what he just witnessed. Not at all the smug reaction she imagined his predecessor would have worn if he were sitting there–if he were still alive.

After a moment, Holly recovered from the snub and walked over to the young man. "I'm Professor Donnelly," she said, extending her hand, giving him her warmest smile. "What's your name?"

"Uh, I'm–I'm Ted Dombrowski," he replied, shaking her hand.

"Nice to meet you. You know, Ted, I feel so silly. I should have realized Dr. Miller would be too busy to speak to me this morning."

Ted gave her a weak smile, appearing relieved at her concession.

"But I really do need to talk to him," she said reaching into her handbag and pulling out her card. "I know your job isn't easy, but do you think you could let me know whenever a free 10-minute opening occurs in Dr. Miller's schedule."

Ted just stared at the card she offered, appearing torn about accepting it.

Holly leaned in closer. "It really is important. Just ten minutes."

The boy finally nodded and took the card.

"Thanks, Ted. I really appreciate it." Holly again reached into her bag and pulled out a Starbuck's gift card someone had given her for her birthday. "And here. Have a latte on me," she smiled.

Out in the hall, she wondered if bribing a student was a violation of the faculty code of ethics.

68 IMMUNITY

Nick and Yolanda entered the interview room and sat down facing Ashley Whitmore.

The blue-eyed blonde sat with her arms crossed, her expression communicating just how annoyed she was. Her hair, highlighted to perfection, was swept up into a messy bun that looked as if it had been styled by a professional. Her make-up too. Underneath a denim jacket, she wore a T-shirt so white, it had to be brand new. When she tossed her head, her diamond stud earrings sparkled under the fluorescent lights.

"I'm Detective Manelli and this is Officer Rivera," Nick said as Yolanda opened a notepad, her pen poised to start writing. "Thank you for coming in, Ms. Whitmore,"

"Hmpf. Like I had a choice," Ashley grumbled.

"Officer Rivera," Nick said, turning slightly in Yolanda's direction. "Didn't you tell me that Ms. Whitmore said she preferred to come to the station?"

"Yes, sir," Yolanda answered without looking up.

"Well, of course I agreed to come here." Ashley unfolded her arms and clasped the edges of the table with perfectly manicured hands. "Do you think I wanted my neighbors to see the police knocking on my door? Really!"

"Ms. Whitmore, what was the nature of your relationship with Rodney Blakely?"

"I went on one date with him."

"Is it true you vandalized an Eco-Fair exhibit at his request?"

The girl's eyes grew wide as she stared at Nick. "Do I need a lawyer?" she asked.

"Not unless you killed Mr. Blakely," Nick replied.

"Kill Rodney!" she exclaimed. "Why would I kill him?"

"You still didn't answer my question, Ms. Whitmore," Nick said, his tone a calm antidote to the girl's growing agitation.

"And I'm not going to." Ashley's hand slapped the table. "Not without a lawyer. I thought I was here just to answer some questions about Rodney. Not that I was a suspect in his murder."

"Where were you last Friday morning?" Nick asked.

Ashley rummaged through her Luis Vuitton handbag and pulled out her phone. After a few taps on the screen, she broke out into a smile. "I wasn't even in town. Thursday night I drove up to Vermont. We own a cabin up near the ski resorts."

"Were you alone?"

"No, I went with my friends." Ashley gave the phone screen a few more taps and slid it across the table towards Nick. "See. There's a picture I posted on Instagram when we arrived."

"Okay, Officer Rivera will need the names and contact numbers of your friends before you leave." Nick slid the phone back to her. "If your alibi checks out, and it looks pretty certain it will, you're not a suspect. So, now are you willing to answer our questions?"

"No." Ashley replied, again crossing her arms.

Nick got up and tapped the table next to Yolanda. "Get the names and then show Ms. Whitmore to a cell."

"A cell!" Ashley sputtered. "You can't do that. I have an alibi."

"Well, that's true," Nick said in his most amiable tone, "but you see we consider you a material witness in a murder case and we can hold you up to 24 hours." He headed to the door.

"I want my lawyer," Ashley demanded.

Nick paused and turned back to Yolanda. "Let her make her call. Then put her in a holding cell until he arrives."

"Wait! Why can't I just sit here?" Ashley whined.

Nick gave her an indulgent smile. "Ms. Whitmore, this room is reserved for questioning. Now if you'd like to re-consider and cooperate with us, well ..."

Nick could almost see the wheels turning in her manipulative little head as she considered what to do.

After a moment, she said, "If I cooperate, I want immunity."

Yolanda coughed and covered her mouth as she glanced up at Nick. He lowered his head as if he were in deep thought. After a few moments, he returned to his seat.

"Deal. You have immunity. Now tell us about your relationship with Rodney."

"I went on a date with Rodney—okay, two dates. I didn't really like him, but I figured being Dr. Miller's admin he could maybe have some pull in helping my GMOs Rock group win the top prize at the Eco-Fair. He knew how much winning meant to me."

"He suggested you vandalize Ms. Alvarez's booth?" Nick asked.

"Yeah. He was the one who told me her project had negative things to say about GMOs and her team was our stiffest competition. If we got her out of the way, we were sure to win."

"And so you agreed to vandalize the booth?"

"Well, not exactly. I talked to my teammates and one of the girls said she didn't want to get in trouble just so Rodney could get even with Ariana. That's when she told me he dated her before me."

"So what did you do?"

"I confronted him about it. We had a big fight. I said how dare he suggest I do something that would get me and my friends in big trouble, just so he could get back at another girl. That's when he swore to me that wasn't the case. He said someone in an important position wanted Ariana's group to lose."

"Who?

"He wouldn't tell me. But he did say that he had something on this important person and promised me we wouldn't get in trouble. He'd make sure of it."

"Thank you, Ms. Whitmore," Nick said. "After you give Ms. Rivera your friends' names and contact information, you're free to go."

"Great," she said, scooping up her phone.

The girl was rattling off names and numbers in quick succession as Nick stepped out of the interview room. Now all he had to do was find out who Rodney Blakely was blackmailing.

69 SUBWAY

What to do, what to do, Holly wondered as she headed away from Dr. Miller's office. Should she try talking to Professor McNair? No. That didn't work out so well last time. No reason he'd be open to talking to her now.

And doggone Nick! He tried to prepare her for this. He knew Miller didn't want to talk to her. She smiled, suddenly remembering the rest of their conversation that morning. Heading to the adjunct faculty lounge, she began formulating the "impassioned plea" she would write asking Dr. Miller to provide letters of endorsement for Ariana, Debby and Luis.

Luis? He was still in jail. That poor boy. Would including him in her letter be a mistake she asked herself as she reached the lounge. Two of the computer stations were occupied. She was happy to see the station in the farthest corner was free. Sitting down, she logged in and began, "Dear Dr.

Miller."

She'd written several paragraphs when her phone signaled. Peppy's name appeared on the screen. She scrambled to her feet and hurried out into the hall.

"Hi, Peppy. What's up?"

"Just wondering if you got to talk to Dr. Miller?"

Holly sighed. "No. I saw him, but he said he was very busy and wouldn't talk to me."

"That's not good, is it?" Peppy asked.

"No, but I'm composing a letter asking him to write letters of recommendation for Ariana and Debby now that they're cleared of having anything to do with the signature on the release form."

"So, are you just giving up on Luis then?" Peppy said, her tone a tad judgmental.

Holly felt the sting. "No, of course not. It's just ..." She glanced at her watch. "Where are you? Do you want to meet for lunch? I'd rather talk about this face to face."

"Where?"

"How about the Subway shop next to the parking deck?"

"We'll be there in fifteen," Peppy replied.

****

"So, you can see, I just think for the time being, leaving Luis out of the letter until he's cleared is the best thing," Holly said apologetically.

"You know she's right," Razor said softly, putting his hand on the nape of Peppy's neck.

Holly could see Peppy's posture ease, as if his touch released the tension in her body. She lowered her eyes, fighting back a smile. Clearly, their relationship had entered a new phase.

After a few moments, Peppy said, "Okay. I get it. But you'll do the same for him when he's cleared?"

"Absolutely."

"And what about Ashley Whitmore?" Peppy asked.

"Nick's talking to her today," Holly replied, then took a sip of soda.

"Do me one favor? When you talk to your husband, find out what Ms. Whitmore looks like. You wanna bet she's a blue-eyed blonde who looks like she just stepped off of Adolf Hitler's vision board?"

Holly covered her mouth struggling not to spray her soda across the table in reply.

Razor laughed as he quickly handed Holly some napkins.

"*Cálmate, Mami,*" Peppy chuckled.

When she stopped giggling and dried her mouth and hands, Holly said, "That's the best laugh I've had in days."

After the laughter subsided, Peppy asked,

"Hey, did you find out anything about what the Feds are doing with the experiment results?"

"I asked Nick to ask Nicky. Not much we can do until we hear back from him."

"So what should we do?" Peppy asked. "I hate just sitting around."

Holly frowned as she considered the question. "I know Luis said he didn't see anyone else in the parking deck when he talked to Rodney the morning of the murder, but do you think there's any chance someone saw them talking?"

"You mean, someone who saw that Rodney was still alive when Luis got out of his car?" Razor asked.

"Exactly." Holly nodded.

'I guess we could ask around," Peppy said, sounding less than enthused at the prospect. "But I'm sure the cops did that."

"Frustrating, I know," Holly said. "I guess I better get back to writing my letter to Miller." She crumbled the sandwich wrapping paper, grabbed her soda cup and got to her feet. "I'll let you know if I hear anything from Nick."

As she crossed the street and re-entered the school building, Holly pulled out her cell phone and tapped the screen. "Darn!" she said under her breath as the call went straight to voicemail. "Nick, did you get to talk to Nicky?"

70 RECOMMENDATIONS

Holly corrected the last typo in her email to Dr. Miller, attached the draft recommendation letters for Ariana and Debby and hit "send". She sat back and stretched her neck from side to side. Glancing at her phone she saw it was almost three o'clock. No wonder her neck and shoulders ached. She'd been hunched over the keyboard for two solid hours.

Suddenly it occurred to her that Dr. Miller might not even read his emails. What if he had his assistant screen them first? Was that Starbuck's gift card enough incentive for Ted Dombrowski to ensure Miller read her message?

Holly remembered a saying from her days as a marketer–when in doubt, use a belt and suspenders. Sitting forward, she opened the email and sent it to the printer. Next, she printed the recommendation letters, then saved everything to the thumb drive she'd inserted into the USB port.

As the printer purred, she wondered if she might not be further alienating Dr. Miller by providing him with hard copies in addition to the emails. She sighed as she retrieved the pages from the printer, neatened the stack, and slid it into a manila envelope. Nope. All that mattered was that she help the students obtain their scholarships. If she damaged her relationship with Dr. Miller, then so be it.

When she arrived at Miller's office suite, Holly was surprised to find Professor McNair seated in a chair across from Ted's desk. Ted was on the phone and blanched as she approached. The professor appeared to clench his jaw when he saw her, then quickly lowered his eyes to the floor.

Awkward, thought Holly as she waited for Ted to finish his call. As he placed the phone receiver back in its cradle, the young man shifted uncomfortably in his chair.

"Me again," Holly said, struggling to maintain a cheerful smile. "Could you please give this to Dr. Miller?"

Ted stared at the envelope, clearly reluctant to accept it. Had he already seen her email? Had Dr. Miller reacted badly to it? Had he instructed his admin not to accept anything else from her?

Without making eye contact, Ted took the envelope, saying nothing.

"Thank you." Holly frowned. No need to smile at someone who wouldn't even look at her. She headed back the way she came but stopped at the door. Turning back she said, "Professor McNair, I was wondering if you'd heard anything from APHIS or any of the other government agencies about the GMO experiment?"

The professor, too, declined to speak and simply shook his head. Holly actually felt sorry for him. His discomfort was pitiful to witness. Why couldn't he even look her in the eye?

"Professor, I'm sorry about our last conversation. Just so you know, the envelope I handed Ted here contains two drafts of letters of recommendation for Ariana Alvarez and Debby Lewandowski. Now that the students have been cleared of any wrongdoing related to the signature on the release form, I'm simply requesting Dr. Miller write letters on their behalf so they don't lose their scholarships. I'd appreciate it if you would ..."

Holly stopped as McNair looked past her, the blood draining from his face. She turned and saw Dr. Miller standing in the doorway to his office, his expression stony-faced, just a hair shy of a glare.

"Professor McNair, step into my office please," he said.

Appearing slightly relieved, the older man got to his feet and quickly shuffled past Holly.

"Dr. Miller, I ..." Holly began.

"Professor Donnelly." Miller said, his voice controlled, but stern. "Rest assured that the college has turned over all of the information on the

GMO experiment to the proper authorities. And," he paused for effect, "I am in receipt of your email and will take it under advisement. Now, I strongly recommend," he placed significant emphasis on the last word, "that you allow me to do my job."

"Yes, sir," Holly nodded as he turned and re-entered his office, closing the door more softly than she expected.

She glanced over at Ted who appeared frozen in place, her recent delivery still in his hands. She let out a loud sigh and reached for the envelope.

71 PESTO

"I just hope I haven't made matters worse for those kids," Holly said as she poked at the pasta on her plate.

Nick knew it was going to be a long night. He exchanged a knowing glance with his sister-in-law.

"Let's talk about something else," Ivy said casting a sympathetic glance at her sister.

"Yeah," Kate agreed and turned to Nick. "So, you like the pesto?"

"*Delizioso*," Nick replied, reaching for the pasta fork and piling another helping on his dish.

"Nick, did Nicky find out if the federal agencies are going to launch an investigation of Green Gardyn Foods?" Holly asked.

Ivy groaned. "Really, Holly. Give it a rest–at least until we're finished with dinner."

Holly ignored her sister and continued to look to her husband, awaiting his reply.

"Not yet," he said as he lifted another forkful of pesto to his mouth.

Kate sat forward. "As long as we're on the topic, I'm dying to know what you found out from Ashley Whitmore."

"Hey, not you, too." Nick shot her a piercing glance.

"Sorry." Kate held her hands up in surrender as she got to her feet. "Ivy made tiramisu for dessert," she said with an apologetic smile.

"You should have told me that before I took another helping of pesto!" Nick said in a mock gruff tone. He looked over at Ivy. "Did I tell you you're my favorite sister-in-law?"

Ivy laughed as she started to collect and stack the dinner plates. Her expression turned serious as she saw that her sister was lost in thought, staring absently at her plate.

"Holly, hand me your dish please," she said. "Do you want dessert?"

Holly looked up at her sister as if she'd just returned from someplace far away. "What?" she asked.

"Dessert. You want some tiramisu?"

Holly shook her head, stood and said, "Excuse me."

As she left the kitchen, Nick sighed. "Save me a big piece of that," he said as he got up and followed her.

When he reached the bedroom, Holly was sitting on the bed opening her laptop. He sat down facing her and took her hands in his.

"You did the right thing."

"Did I?" she asked.

The pain on her face hurt him. The optimism she'd felt this morning had totally evaporated.

"You know you did. Dr. Miller is probably under a lot of pressure right now. Just give it some time. If he's the guy you described to me this morning, he'll do the right thing."

Holly's brow wrinkled as she considered his words. "You're right," she said, giving him a weak smile. "He will do the right thing."

"Yep." Nick smiled back, then leaned close and kissed her. "Now, c'mon back downstairs. I've never known you to say no to tiramisu."

Holly giggled and tossed her laptop to the side. "Okay."

As they headed to the hall, Nick's phone signaled. He pulled it out of his pocket and checked the screen. Nicky.

"I got to take this," he said. "You go down. I'll be right there."

Holly nodded and reluctantly headed down the stairs. Nick waited until she reached the bottom and was out of sight before he lifted the phone to his ear. "What's up?"

"Hey, Dad. Listen, my contact at APHIS says

nothing was sent to them from Pineland Park Community College?"

"What about FDA and the EPA?"

"My contact checked with both of them."

"Holly talked to Dr. Miller today and he told her everything had been turned over to what he called 'the proper authorities'. You think what they sent might just be tied up in some bureaucratic red tape?"

"I guess that's possible, but I don't think so. My friend says anytime they get a complaint concerning GMOs, they log it into a central database even if they don't get to work on it right away."

"Hmm." Nick paused. "That means somebody is lying. You up for a visit to the college tomorrow morning?"

"Uh ..." Nicky hedged. "Not sure this has anything to do with the explosion investigation, Dad."

"No, but you have to admit I've been a great help to the FBI with their investigation, and ..."

Nicky laughed. "And you'd like a little FBI heat to help with your murder investigation. Is that it?"

"You could say that," Nick replied.

"Okay. When and where?"

72 DR. MILLER

"So, who we going to see?" Nicky asked as he got into Nick's car the next morning.

"Dr. Miller. He's head of the Physical Sciences Department."

"He's the one who told Holly everything was turned over to the Feds."

"Yep."

"You think he's lying?" Nicky asked.

"We'll see."

****

Ted Dombrowski appeared frozen in his chair as Nick introduced himself and held out his ID. When Nicky flashed his FBI badge, the young man swallowed hard.

"I–uh–I'm sorry, but Dr. Miller is on a conference call right now. He can't be disturbed."

"We can wait," Nick said. "Maybe you'd like to

answer some questions in the meantime."

"Me?" The young man gripped the edge of his desk and started to breathe rapidly.

Fearing he might hyperventilate, Nick said. "Son, why don't you just go inside and put a note in front of Dr. Miller letting him know we're here."

Ted's breath began to slow as he considered Nick's suggestion. Grabbing a pen, he quickly jotted something on a yellow sticky note, got up and walked over to Dr. Miller's office door. He paused for a moment, took a deep breath, slowly opened the door and stepped inside.

"You enjoyed that didn't you?" Nicky asked.

"Yes, I did," his father replied.

Before he could say more, Ted reappeared. "Dr. Miller will be with you in a moment. Please have a seat."

"We'll stand," Nick said.

Ted just nodded and returned to his desk, his breathing restored to normal. After just a few moments, the intercom buzzer sounded causing him to jump and let out a small squeak. He picked up the phone. "Yes, sir." Looking at Nick and Nicky, he said, "You can go right in."

Dr. Miller got to his feet and smiled warmly at the two law officers as they entered his office. "Good morning," he said, with an affable smile.

"Good morning. I'm Detective Manelli with the Pineland Park PD and this is Agent Manelli with the FBI," Nick said as they held up their badges.

"Have a seat," Miller said, then squinted as he looked first at Nick, then at Nicky. "You're related?"

Nick gave a quick nod but didn't waste time with small talk. "Dr. Miller, we're here about a student science fair project."

The scientist's brow crumpled reflecting genuine puzzlement. "Really. I wouldn't think a student project would merit the attention of the local police, let alone the FBI."

"I'm investigating the murder of Rodney Blakely and Agent Manelli is investigating the Green Gardyn Foods' warehouse explosion," Nick said. "We have reason to believe there may be a connection to that student project."

"Oh, I see," Miller said, sitting back in his chair. "How can I help you?"

Nicky sat forward. "I checked with APHIS, FDA and the EPA and all three agencies say they haven't received any information from Pineland Park Community College regarding the GMO experiment that was withdrawn from the Eco-Fair competition."

"And," Nick added, "we understand you've stated that the documentation of that experiment was turned over to the proper authorities."

Dr. Miller didn't react immediately. He turned to his computer and after a few clicks, said, "Oh my!" He turned back to face the two law officers, appearing distraught.

"I was away all of last week. Before I left, I instructed my assistant ..." here he paused as a look of pain flashed across his face. "As you probably know, Rodney Blakely was my assistant. Well, I collected all of the documentation from the students involved in the project and told Rodney to send it to the proper agencies. He must have ..."

"Surely, you have copies of what was sent," Nicky said.

"Yes, of course," Miller replied and tapped the intercom button on his phone. "Ted, can you bring in the file on the Eco-Fair GMO project." Miller appeared genuinely upset. "As you can understand this has been a terrible ordeal for us–for me personally. I just ..."

The intercom buzzed and Miller lifted the receiver. His face clouded over with an expression of alarm. "What do you mean? It has to be there." Miller dropped the phone, got to his feet and rushed through the door to the outer office.

Nick and Nicky exchanged a glance, got up and followed. Ted was standing idly by as Dr. Miller rifled through the file cabinet. Turning to face Nick, he said, "It's missing. The whole file is missing."

"But you've got digital copies," Nick said.

"Yes, of course," Miller replied. "Ted, bring up the computer files."

Ted sat down and tapped the keyboard. His

hands started to shake. He tapped the keyboard again. When he turned to face the three men, his face grew pale. "The file's not here."

73 DISCRETION

Dr. Miller appeared thunderstruck at Ted's pronouncement. "How can that be?" he asked the young man, his tone accusatory.

"I–I don't–I don't know," Ted sputtered.

"You must have backups stored elsewhere," Nicky suggested.

"Yes, yes," Miller quickly agreed. "Ted, contact the IT department and have them locate the file on last week's back-up."

"Let's go back inside while he does that," Dr. Miller said.

Back at his desk, Miller shook his head as he dropped in his chair. "I'm so sorry about this. I just don't–I can't ..."

"Did anyone else know that you asked Rodney to send the documents?" Nick asked.

"Yes," Miller replied. "Professor McNair."

"We'll need to talk to him," Nick said.

"Of course," Miller replied and picked up his phone. "He's not answering. Let me try the department admin. He tapped a few buttons on the phone. "Barbara, is Professor McNair in his office? I see. Well, when his class is over, would you tell him to come to my office. Yes. ASAP."

Miller turned back to face Nick. "His class should be over in ten minutes. I don't know how long it will take to retrieve the back-up files. Shall I send Ted down to the cafeteria to get us some coffees?"

"No, thank you," Nick replied. Nicky just shook his head.

Miller leaned back in his chair, seeming more relaxed than he'd been a few moments ago. "I just can't imagine how something like this could happen. Unless–no."

Nick said nothing, but aimed, what Holly called, his laser stare at Miller and waited.

"Rodney worked for me for over a year now. He has never made a careless error."

"Are you saying he might have purposely deleted the digital files?" Nicky asked.

"And destroyed the hard copies?" Nick added.

"No!" Miller appeared offended on behalf of his departed assistant. "Why would he do that?"

"You tell us." Nick locked eyes with the scientist.

Miller placed his elbows on his desk, steepled

his hands, seeming to struggle with his thoughts as he stared at the ink blotter. After a moment, he looked back up at them. "Lately Rodney has seemed a bit preoccupied. But still, he never made an error and certainly not one this egregious."

Miller's head suddenly snapped back. "Do you think someone murdered him and destroyed the documents?"

"It would have to be someone with access to your computer files," Nick said.

"Oh. You're right." Miller shook his head. "I knew it was a mistake when Professor McNair let it be known that the project files would be turned over to the federal agencies in charge of GMO production."

"Why was that a mistake?" Nick asked.

"The Eco-Fair was supposed to be a triumph for the college. While we had to withdraw the GMO project from the competition, we should have done it more discretely in order to avoid negative publicity for the college. No one needed to know exactly why the project was withdrawn or the specific steps we were taking to handle the matter. You do understand that."

"So, this Professor McNair screwed up," Nick said.

Miller appeared reluctant to reply. After a few moments, he said, "Since the closing ceremonies, we've managed to handle the matter with the utmost discretion." The scientist paused a moment.

"By the way, do you mind my asking what prompted you to check on whether or not our documentation was received by the federal agencies involved?"

When Nick and Nicky just stared blankly in reply, Miller sighed and continued. "We do have a professor here with a personal involvement in the matter. I'm afraid she may be the reason for this inquiry. She may even be spreading misinformation. Has Professor Holly Donnelly spoken to you?"

74 DISINGENUOUS

The intercom buzzed and Miller once again reached for the phone. "Yes. Of course, the finance committee call. I forgot all about it." He cast an uncertain glance at Nick and Nicky. "Ted, perhaps you could walk my guests over to Professor McNair's office while I take that call. Good."

"Gentlemen, I have a very important conference call that I must participate in. Would you mind very much talking to Professor McNair while I do that? If you have any more questions for me, we can resume our meeting after my call."

"Sure," Nick said as he and Nicky got to their feet.

When they reached Ted's desk the young admin started to get up. Nick said, "You don't need to escort us. Just tell us where McNair's office is."

As they made their way down the corridor Nicky asked, "What do you think?"

"You tell me," Nick replied.

"Well, he sure wanted us to believe Blakely was responsible for the disappearance of the files."

"You caught that, eh?" Nick smiled. "There's a word for it. Your stepmother uses it on me when I'm dodging her questions. Dis–disin ..."

"Disingenuous," Nicky laughed.

"Yep, that's it."

"Well, I want to know how you were going to answer Miller's question about Holly if the intercom buzzer hadn't saved you," Nicky said.

"Let's just say that the interruption was fortuitous–another one of her favorite words. It's probably the only time I was glad she didn't change her name when we got married."

When they reached McNair's office, Nicky tapped on the open door.

The owlish professor was on the phone. His eyes grew wide as the two men stepped inside his office. "Yes. I understand," he said into the phone. "I'll get back to you later." He ran his tongue across his lips. "Can I help you?"

Nick and Nicky showed their IDs.

The professor gave his head a nervous nod. "Have a seat."

Nick began. "Professor, we just talked to Dr. Miller. Are you aware that the documentation on the student project on GMOs was never received by APHIS, the EPA or the FDA?"

"I had nothing to do with that," the professor

replied, his eyes darting from Nick to Nicky, unable to maintain eye contact. "Dr. Miller handled it."

"Are you aware that the project files, both digital and hard copy, are missing?" Nicky asked.

At this question, the professor's eyes grew wide behind his round glass frames and locked on Nicky. "No. No, I wasn't aware of that."

"You were the faculty advisor on the project, weren't you?" Nick asked.

"Yes. I was."

"Surely you must have had copies of the files," Nicky said.

"I did." McNair straightened the stack of papers in the center of his desk. "But I turned everything over to Dr. Miller as he requested."

"A project you believed would win awards, and you kept nothing?" Nick didn't try to disguise the incredulity in his voice.

McNair placed his hands flat on his desk, leaned forward, and this time locked eyes with Nick. "I did exactly what I was told to do."

Nick stared back, but the professor didn't waver. After a moment, he reached inside his jacket pocket and pulled out his notepad, flipping the pages until he located what he was looking for.

"Professor, we have a witness who says they heard you having a heated argument with Rodney Blakely the week before he was murdered. You were heard to have said, 'You're going to regret this,

Rodney!' You want to tell us about that?"

The professor's face flushed red. He lowered his eyes focusing on his hands.

"Did you say those words?" Nick prompted. When the professor again failed to answer, Nick said, "Perhaps you'd prefer to come with us to the Pineland Park Police Station to answer our questions."

"Or we could go to FBI headquarters in Newark," Nicky added.

McNair finally looked up. "That day–that was nothing."

"Doesn't sound like nothing. Why did you threaten Mr. Blakely?" Nick asked with more force.

McNair shook his head from side to side. "I didn't threaten him. I didn't."

Nick looked over at Nicky. "Those words sound threatening to me. What do you think, Agent Manelli?"

"Oh yeah." Nicky nodded. "Most definitely threatening."

"Do I need a lawyer?" McNair asked.

"Did you kill Rodney Blakely?"

"No! Why are you even asking me that?" McNair was on the verge of tears. "Didn't you arrest Luis Navarro for the murder?"

"Our investigation is ongoing," Nick replied.

The professor's face and voice both reflected a

sense of panic. "I won't answer any more questions without a lawyer."

75 HOPELESS

Holly sat on a metal bench outside the main entrance to the college. She pulled out her phone and clicked on the Kindle app. Might as well read while she waited for Peppy and Razor. Yes, reading would take her mind off all the unpleasantness of the morning.

The Kindle had to be the greatest invention since the printing press. So much easier to carry around than a book. She actually smiled as she resumed Spencer Quinn's *It's a Wonderful Woof*. She loved this very funny mystery series written from the dog's point of view. And the best part of reading on a Kindle was that no one could see the cover of the book. After all, a professor was expected to be reading literary works, not cozy mysteries.

Holly barely finished a chapter when Peppy and Razor arrived and joined her on the bench.

"So, *Mami*, how'd it go with Miller?"

Holly grimaced. "Not good, I'm afraid. He

was annoyed to see me. All he would tell me was that everything was turned over to the proper authorities. How about you guys? Find anyone who saw Luis the morning of the murder."

"No," Peppy replied.

Razor shook his head. "The murder took place on a Friday. I think if there's any chance of our finding someone who may have seen something, it'll be on Friday morning."

Holly grunted. "But that's three days from now."

"Yeah. What do we do in the meantime?" Peppy asked, not really expecting an answer.

The trio sat silently as a rush of students exited the building indicating the end of another class.

After a few moments, Holly said, "Well, at least you can tell Ariana and Debby that I drafted letters of recommendation for them and asked Dr. Miller to send them on their behalf."

Peppy smirked. "You think he'll do that?"

"I don't know." Holly frowned.

"Uh-oh," Peppy said.

Holly followed her gaze to the door where Nick and Nicky were just exiting.

"What are they doing here?" she asked, starting to get to her feet.

Razor put a hand on her arm preventing her

from getting up. "Hold on." He made eye contact with Nick who had moved off to the side opposite them. With a nearly imperceptible tilt of his head, Nick appeared to be summoning Razor over.

"You two, wait here," Razor said as he rose and sauntered across to where Nick and Nicky were standing.

"I'm not waiting," Holly said, again starting to get up.

This time Peppy held her in place. "*Mami*, stop. There's gotta be a reason he doesn't want to be seen talking to you here."

"Oh." Holly sank back on the bench. "You think that's a good thing?"

"Maybe. Just stop staring at them. Turn and face me."

Holly huffed and turned toward Peppy, her back to the men. "He was gone before I got up this morning. I can't believe he didn't tell me he was coming here."

"You know he couldn't do that."

Holly aimed an annoyed look at Peppy. "You're defending him?"

"Look, I wasn't happy when he suspended me, but after I thought about it, I knew he didn't have a choice. Whatever's going on right now, he's got his reasons. You know he always does the right thing."

Holly let out a loud sigh. "Yes, I do know that," she admitted a tad unwillingly. Scratching the top of her head, she asked, "Do you think he was here to talk to Dr. Miller or Professor McNair?"

"Probably both?" Peppy said. "Don't turn around. They're leaving."

Holly started to turn, but Peppy again restrained her. "*Calmate, Mami.*"

"Well, Razor better have something to tell us. Is he on his way over here?"

"No, he just wants us to wait a few and then meet him in the parking deck."

Holly whipped her head around, her eyes scanning the area, but Nick, Nicky and Razor were gone. "You two telepathic now?" she asked with a tilt of her head.

Peppy's face morphed into a dreamy smile. "You could say that."

Hopeless, Holly thought as she suddenly felt the urge to find a quiet corner somewhere and escape back into her cozy mystery.

76 NDA

"How'd she take it?" Razor asked as Peppy returned to where he'd been waiting near the car.

"She pitched a fit when I told her we'd meet her back at her house after we took care of something. Then when I said you'd explain everything when we got there, she just got in her car and drove off."

"Poor Manelli." Razor shook his head.

"Poor Manelli?" Peppy glared at him. "He handles criminals on a daily basis. I think he can take whatever his wife dishes out."

"One major difference. He doesn't love those criminals."

Peppy was glad when her phone dinged, interrupting their conversation. "Great," she said as she read the message. "Ariana and Debby just got out of class. She said they'll meet us in front of the library. *Vamos.*"

****

"Any good news?" Ariana asked as Peppy and Razor approached the two girls.

Peppy shrugged. "Not sure. Do you girls have copies of your experiment documents?"

"No." Ariana shook her head.

"Professor McNair had us turn everything over to him," Debby said.

"We even had to sign Non-Disclosure Agreements," Ariana added.

"What!?" Peppy's face registered both disgust and dismay.

"Yeah," Debby pursed her lips. "They made it sound like we wouldn't get our diplomas if we talked about the experiment to anyone, but the federal agencies involved."

"Even then, he told us we'd have to have a school lawyer present when they interviewed us," Ariana said.

Peppy waggled her head and turned to Razor. "That doesn't sound suspicious, does it?"

Razor gave a slight nod. "So you didn't keep anything?"

Both girls shook their heads.

"With our scholarships in jeopardy, we couldn't risk not getting our diplomas too," Debby said, her eyes starting to tear up.

"Wait a minute," Ariana said. "Why are you

asking this?"

Peppy slid her tongue across her lower lip and glanced at Razor. After a moment, the big man replied. "The Feds haven't received anything from the school and the school file on the project is missing."

Ariana stared blankly, appearing unable to comprehend the words she'd just heard. Debby let out a sob.

"Don't cry." Razor gave Debby's shoulder a reassuring squeeze. "The police will figure this out."

Ariana's expression grew fierce. "Somebody's out to get us, aren't they?" she asked, her eyes on Peppy.

"No," Peppy replied. "There's something else going on here. Razor's right. Both the local police and the FBI are working on this. They'll get to the bottom of it."

"But how can they if all our work was destroyed?" Ariana asked.

"Wait." Debby sniffled. "What about Luis? I know he was really angry when McNair talked to us. Maybe he kept copies."

Peppy's eyes met Razor's. "*Vamos.*"

****

"Alvarez!" A smiling Officer Tim Sullivan greeted Peppy and Razor as they presented their guest badges. "Enjoying your–uh–vacation?"

"Yeah, Tim. As a matter of fact I am," Peppy

replied. "How's the prisoner?"

Sullivan's smile faded. "I feel for the kid. Seems depressed. Maybe you can cheer him up."

"Maybe," Peppy said as the policeman opened the door to the visitors' room where Luis sat waiting.

The boy gave them a weak smile. He appeared pale and thinner than the last time they visited him.

"How you holding up?" Peppy asked.

Luis just gave a noncommittal shrug.

"Luis, did you keep copies of your experiment documents?" Razor asked.

Luis' eyes darted from Razor to Peppy. Slowly, he shook his head from side to side. "No."

"Nothing?" Peppy asked.

Luis stared at his hands for a moment. When he finally looked up, he said, "Nothing. You must know McNair made us turn everything over to him and sign statements that we wouldn't talk to anyone about the experiment without a school lawyer present. I could probably lose my diploma for talking to you right now."

"Luis, the Feds didn't receive the files, and the school file is missing," Razor said.

Luis blinked, but after a moment his expression hardened. "So?"

"The files are needed to help solve the case," Peppy said.

"I'm in enough trouble as it is, Peppy," the boy said, a look of desperation clouding his face. "I signed an NDA."

"But the files might help clear you, Ariana and Debby," she said, her tone calm, but pleading.

Luis sat back, his expression sour. "So that's why you're here? To clear Ariana and Debby."

"No," Peppy began to protest, "we ..."

"Forget it." The boy's hands slapped the table. "Why should I help them? They haven't once called or come to visit me. Who's helping me?"

"We are," Peppy said.

Once again he stared at his hands. After a moment he stood and said, "Sorry, I can't help you."

77 LAST HOPE

Kate jumped at the sound of the front door slamming. Lucky ran to the entrance hall and Ivy followed.

"Well, it's about time," Ivy said. "I texted you several times. You know it's your turn to cook dinner."

Holly glowered at her sister. "How does ground turkey meatloaf sound?"

"We don't have ground turkey," Kate said.

"I stopped at the grocery store and got some."

"Does Nick even like ground turkey?" Ivy asked.

"No!" Holly replied. "He hates it." Thrusting a paper grocery bag at her sister, she headed upstairs.

"Uh-oh," Ivy said under her breath. She grimaced as she glanced over at Kate.

"Here, I'll put that in the refrigerator," Kate said. "Then we better go upstairs and find out what he did."

****

Holly was changing from slacks to a pair of jeans when they reached the bedroom.

"Care to tell us what happened?" Ivy asked as she plopped down on the bed.

"No!" Holly replied.

Kate walked around to the other side of the bed, punched up the pillows and lay down beside Ivy. The reclining pair just waited as Holly unbuttoned her blouse and pulled on a T-shirt.

Ivy finally broke the silence. "Did you talk to Dr. Miller?"

As Holly sat down to put on her sneakers, she began to speak and didn't stop for ten minutes straight as the story of her day came spilling out.

"Can you believe Nick didn't tell me he was going to the college today?" she said. "And Peppy and Razor! Wait until they get here. Imagine telling me to just go home and wait until they got here to explain whatever Nick was up to!"

"Wow!" Kate said when she finally stopped. "Who do you think Nick and Nicky were there to see?"

"Professor McNair would be my guess," Ivy said.

"Or Dr. Miller." Holly leaned back in the chair and stared up at the ceiling.

Kate propped herself up on her elbows. "You think it's about Rodney's murder?"

"But then why was Nicky with him?" Holly asked.

"It's got to have something to do with the documents they turned over to the federal agencies, don't you think?" Ivy said.

Holly sat forward. "You know, that's got to be it."

"Guess we'll just have to wait for Peppy and Razor to find out."

"Hmpf!" Holly finally put on the sneaker she'd been holding since she started her story. "I'm taking Lucky for a walk." Tail wagging, the dog looked up at her mistress with adoring eyes. "If they get here before I get back, they can wait for me. C'mon, girl!"

Kate turned to Ivy. "Good thing we made that pan of stuffed shells this morning, huh?"

****

When Holly and Lucky returned, Peppy and Razor were sitting on the couch in the living room. Holly shot them a withering glance as she entered the room and sat down in one of the wing chairs near the fireplace.

"*Mami*, we're sorry we couldn't talk to you before," Peppy said.

Holly jutted her chin forward slightly, but said nothing.

Peppy turned to Razor. "You tell her."

"Wait, wait," Kate said as she walked into the room carrying a tray of glasses. Ivy followed with a pitcher of iced tea.

"Yes, we don't want to miss anything," Ivy said as the pair began to fill glasses and pass them around.

When everyone was settled, Razor began. "Nick and Nicky were there to talk to Dr. Miller because the federal agencies have not received anything from the college."

"We were right," Holly said with a nod to her sister and Kate.

Razor continued "When they asked to see copies of what the school had sent, it turned out the hard copy files were missing and the digital files erased."

"Oh no!" Holly's eyes grew wide.

"I'll bet Green Gardyn Foods is behind this," Kate said.

"Kate, please," Holly said, impatience in her voice. "Go on, Razor."

"So your husband asked us to check with Ariana and Debby for their files."

Peppy sat forward. "That's where we were just now."

"So you got their files?" Ivy asked.

Peppy shook her head. "Turns out the girls were required to turn everything over to the college and get this–they had to sign non-disclosure agreements that would allow them to talk to no one except the federal agencies, and then only with a school lawyer present. They were told they might not get their diplomas if they violated the agreement."

"Oh, tell me that doesn't sound like a cover-up and conspiracy to you!" Kate said, a smug expression on her face.

Ignoring her, Holly asked, "What about Luis? Did he keep anything?"

"We went to see him too," Razor replied. "He said no."

"He said no, but I think he does have something," Peppy added. "I can try to talk to him again. He's our last hope."

"Wait a second," Ivy said with a smile. "What about Brittany?"

78 A LOT AT STAKE

Holly gave Razor Nicky's cell phone number. She refused to place the call herself. Besides, Nick and Nicky probably already thought to contact Brittany as soon as Razor and Peppy told them the other three students had turned their documentation over to the college.

As the couple went to the kitchen, Kate said, "I know you're sick of my saying this, Holly, but you have to realize Green Gardyn Foods is behind the whole thing."

"I'm afraid she may be right," Ivy agreed.

Holly didn't respond immediately. Her sister and friend watched as she mulled over what they'd just said. After a few moments, she nodded. "Okay. Green Gardyn Foods has a lot at stake here. I agree they have good reason to want the student experiment discredited, which they accomplished when the project got pulled out of the Eco-Fair competition. But are we saying they coerced

309

Professor McNair into destroying the experiment documentation also?"

"What else could it be?" Kate asked.

Holly puffed out her cheeks, then slowly blew out through her lips. "But what about Rodney? What was his role in all this? Why is he dead?"

Ivy sighed. "I hate to be the one to say this, but isn't it just possible that his murder had nothing to do with any of the rest of this?"

Peppy and Razor returned to the living room just in time to hear the question. Peppy put her balled fists on her hips. "Are you saying that Luis killed him?" she asked, her tone combative.

"No, wait." Holly shook her head. "You're forgetting I witnessed an argument between Rodney and McNair. What was it the professor said?" Holly closed her eyes as she tried to remember the altercation. "I know," she said, snapping her fingers. "McNair said, 'You'll regret this'. What could Rodney have done?"

"Sounds like Rodney had something on the professor," Razor offered.

Holly's mouth formed a perfect "o". "If Rodney knew the professor had some connection to Green Gardyn Foods, maybe he was blackmailing him."

Ivy frowned and shook her head. "That sounds plausible, but why didn't Professor McNair pull the experiment sooner? I mean, he was the faculty advisor on the project. He knew the seeds were Green Gardyn's from the start."

"Oh, yeah," Kate said. "Remember. That's why Brittany walked out the day of the presentations. They had to revise their slides replacing the names of the companies with Company A, B and C."

"Right," Holly sank back in her chair with an air of defeat.

After a few moments, Ivy sat forward. "What about ..." she hesitated as she made eye contact with her sister. "What about Dr. Miller?"

Holly sat up straight. "What about him?" she asked, her tone defensive.

"Maybe he's the one who pulled the project when he found out Company B was Green Gardyn Foods," Ivy replied.

Holly got to her feet. "No way!" She began to pace. "For heaven sakes, Ivy, you were with me when the kids' display booth got vandalized. You saw him get them everything they needed to recreate their exhibit. It was Rodney who was annoyed that he was being asked to help them."

"That's true," Ivy shrugged.

"But, Holly," Kate intervened, "think about it. Remember your friend Barbara said the only calls McNair got the morning the project was pulled were from Miller and Rodney. Maybe McNair was just following Dr. Miller's orders."

Holly continued to pace. "So you're saying Dr. Miller's behind the whole thing?"

"Makes sense," Peppy said. "Maybe Rodney was blackmailing him and that's why he killed him."

Holly stopped pacing and stared bug-eyed at Peppy. After a moment she shook her whole body. "No. That's impossible. First of all, I don't believe Dr. Miller is capable of murder, but he couldn't have killed Rodney. He was in Atlanta."

"Oh, right," Peppy said. Razor leaned close to her and pointed to his wristwatch. "Sorry, but we've got to go," she said. "We're invited to dinner at Juan's, and we said we'd pick up dessert."

Holly dropped back in her chair. "Go. Say hello to Juan for me."

After the couple left, Ivy said, "You know Rodney was a uniquely unlikable guy. It's still possible he was murdered by someone totally unrelated to the Eco-Fair experiment."

"Or," Kate held up her hand, her index finger pointing skyward, "He was foolish enough to blackmail someone at Green Gardyn Foods."

Holly chuckled and shook her head.

"You laugh," Kate said, "but even you said that company is the one with the most at stake here. If it was revealed in the press that their non-GMO claims were a fraud, their sales would plummet. They stand to lose a fortune."

"She's got a point," Ivy said. "Their stock price would go down and they'd face fraud charges in federal court."

Holly leaned back. "You know, if it weren't for the fact that Luis is in jail right now, I wouldn't even care who murdered Rodney." She closed her eyes, but quickly reopened them when her phone signaled Nick's ring tone.

"Here," she said, handing it to Ivy. "You talk to him."

79 SEARCHING THE INTERNET

"Well, your stepmother's not speaking to me," Nick said as he returned to the chair across from his son's desk.

Nicky chuckled. "I don't suppose it's the first time."

"No." Nick smiled. "But this time I know she's really mad. Ivy said she bought ground turkey to make meatloaf for dinner."

Nicky's face morphed into a distasteful grimace. "You hate ground turkey, don't you?"

"Yep." Nick frowned as his son turned back to his computer screen. "What are you doing?"

"Well, I thought I'd take another look at what we have on Green Gardyn Foods while we wait for Brittany's lawyer to get back to us. In spite of the fact that the company was the victim in the case of the explosion, it just feels like they're behind what's going on at the college."

It was Nick's turn to chuckle. "Kate would be

delighted to hear you say that. She's been convinced from the start that they ..."

Nicky's desk phone rang.

"Agent Manelli."

Nick watched his son take some notes as he listened to his caller.

"Okay. That's great," Nicky said, nodding to his father. He jotted down some notes as he listened. "I'll confirm as soon as I receive them."

Placing the phone back in the cradle, Nicky smiled. "Rodney Blakely tried to visit Brittany the day before he was murdered, but she refused to meet with him and told him to contact her lawyer, which he did. The lawyer said Rodney asked for all of the material Brittany had and that she would need to sign an NDA."

"Just like the other three kids."

"Yep." Nicky nodded. "The lawyer, of course, refused to comply. Rodney threatened that she wouldn't get her diploma and the lawyer said 'we'll see you in court.'" Nicky leaned forward. "And listen to this. There was a break-in at the Holzman's house that night. Brittany's room was ransacked, and a laptop was stolen."

"Damn!" Nick shook his head.

"No, listen, Dad." Nicky grinned. "The laptop that was stolen only had some of the documents on it. Brittany got a new laptop midway through the experiment."

"So, she's got all the documents?"

"Yep. The lawyer smelled a rat and right after he hung up with Rodney, he called Brittany. He had her save copies of the documents to two thumb drives, and then he picked up the laptop and put it in a safe at his office."

"Smart guy," Nick grinned as he leaned back in his chair.

"Yeah. He said he didn't understand why the college was going to all this trouble to get their hands on the experiment results, but he knew they had to be important."

"And a potential bargaining chip in his defense of Brittany," Nick added.

Nicky nodded, but after a moment a perplexed expression clouded his face. "Just one thing. The lawyer didn't say that anyone contacted him again after Rodney's call. It seems to me an institution like the college would get their lawyers involved after an initial request was refused."

Nick's mouth curled into a sly smile. "Not if they thought they had all the information on the stolen laptop."

Nicky grinned. "Yeah. If they just checked the computer file menu, they would see files for the experiment and might think they had everything."

"Bingo," said Nick.

Nicky raised his arms over his head, stretching his neck from left to right. "I guess you can call it a night, Dad," Nicky said. "Why don't you go home?"

"To turkey meatloaf?" Nick grimaced.

Nicky chuckled as he turned back to the computer. "You got to face her sooner or later."

"And what are you going to do?" Nick asked.

"I'll spend a little more time searching the internet for anything I can find on Green Gardyn Foods. Then I'll go back to the hotel. Think I'll have a steak tonight," he said, with a taunting grin.

"Wise guy," Nick grumbled as he got up to leave.

Before he reached the door, Nicky said, "Dad, wait." He pointed to a photo on his computer screen. "Look at this."

Nick turned back and glanced over his son's shoulder at the Green Gardyn Foods Facebook page.

"Recognize anyone?" Nicky asked, glancing up at his father.

"I should have known," Nick said under his breath as he looked at the photo on the screen. "Do you have access to Green Gardyn's financial records?" he asked.

"Not legally," Nicky replied, locking eyes with his father. After just a moment, he swiveled back to his computer and began to tap away at the keyboard.

80 A TEXT

Ivy aimed a despairing glance across the dinner table at Kate. With a slight shrug she shifted her eyes to her sister. "Holly, why don't you call Nick?"

Her sister shot back an icy stare in reply. After a moment, she crumpled her napkin, said, "Excuse me," and got up from the table.

When Ivy heard the bedroom door slam, she turned to Kate. "Ugh! I hate it when they're fighting."

****

Up in her room, Holly flopped on the bed and stared at the ceiling. Maybe she should call Nick. But what for? Even if she begged, he wouldn't tell her anything about the case. And worst of all, she knew darn well he couldn't. She rolled over and punched her pillow.

But he did call to let them know that he and Nicky were waiting to hear back from Brittany's lawyer. Maybe she should have taken his call. She regretted making Ivy say dinner would be turkey meatloaf. She envisioned him eating an artery-clogging steak dinner at a restaurant with his son. He'd be home right now if they'd told him about the stuffed shells.

She flipped over on her back, her mind returning to the missing experiment documents. What in the world was going on? Why was all evidence of the experiment deleted, including the backup copies? And who was behind it?

Not just anybody had access to the college's back-up files. But, as Dr. Miller's assistant, could Rodney have somehow gotten access? Did he even have the know-how to erase back-up files? Probably not, but the little weasel certainly could have told IT that Dr. Miller wanted the files deleted. And she knew firsthand he could make things difficult for you if you didn't do what he asked. Surely Nick and Nicky talked to the school's IT department. If she'd taken Nick's call, she could have asked him what they said. But would he have told her?

This time she rolled in the opposite direction and punched Nick's pillow. Dear God, please let Brittany have the experiment documentation! She picked up her phone. 7:02 pm. By now they should have talked to Brittany's lawyer. So where was Nick?

She jumped when the phone in her hand dinged. Finally, she might get some answers.

Sitting up, she looked at the screen, disappointed to see a text from a phone number she didn't recognize.

Professor Donnelly, could you meet me at the Planetarium at 7:30? I'd like to discuss the letters of recommendation you suggested Dr. Miller write on behalf of Ariana Alvarez and Debby Lewandowski. He and I agree that, with some modification, these letters are acceptable. I'd like your input.

Professor McNair

Holly quickly typed her reply.

I'll be there.

Pulling on a blazer, she reached for her handbag and raced downstairs.

Kate and Ivy were eating dessert.

"Care for some chocolate layer cake?" Kate asked. "I baked it this morning."

"No thanks," Holly replied. "Listen, I've got to go over to the college."

"At this hour?" Ivy asked, clearly not happy with the news. "What for?"

"Professor McNair just texted me. He and Dr. Miller have agreed to send the letters of recommendation I drafted this morning. They want to discuss some minor changes."

"But can't that wait until tomorrow?" Ivy asked.

"They asked to meet tonight and I'm not taking any chances they might change their minds," Holly said as she retrieved her car keys from the key rack.

"Wait," Kate said as she got to her feet. "We'll go with you."

"That's not necessary," Holly said in her most determined voice as she headed to the front door.

"But it'll be dark by the time you come home," Ivy objected.

"I won't be that late," Holly said as she opened the door. "I'm meeting Professor McNair at the planetarium and it closes at 8:00. Go eat your cake."

As they watched Holly open the front gate and get in her car, Kate said, "I don't know, but I don't have a good feeling about this."

"C'mon," Ivy said. "Let's call Nick."

81 MCDONALD'S

As Peppy pulled into a parking spot halfway down the block from Juan's apartment building, Razor's phone signaled.

"'Sup?" he answered.

Peppy watched as the big man's face broke into a wide smile.

"Yep. They'll be happy to hear that." He listened for a few more moments, then said, "Guess you can head home." After a moment Razor laughed loudly. "Good luck."

"What?" Peppy asked as he disconnected the call.

"Brittany's got the documents."

Peppy exhaled a deep sigh of relief. "One problem solved," she said, taking the keys out of the ignition. "What was that belly laugh for?"

"Let's just say Manelli's in no hurry to go home."

Peppy shook her head. "I almost feel sorry for him. Holly's–well, all I can say is I can't think of anyone I'd rather have on my side. She's really smart and wants to help, but she doesn't always understand when she's putting herself in danger."

"Well, the good news is she's home nice and safe tonight. C'mon. Let's go. This caramel flan needs to get into a refrigerator."

****

After clearing away empty dinner plates, Ariana wore a huge smile as she carried in the creamy flan and placed it on the table.

"The perfect dessert for celebrating!" she said.

"After this morning, I wasn't sure we'd be celebrating at all," Debby said.

"*Gracias a Dios*," Maria said, looking upward.

Juan took his wife's hand. "*Si*. We need thank God."

When she finished passing slices of the custard dessert around the table, Ariana sat down and let out a sigh. "I know I should be happy about the documents being found, but I'm still so worried about Luis."

"Don't worry," Razor said. "Manelli's got this."

"But we feel so helpless," Debby said, "and there's nothing we can do."

"You know you can go visit him," Peppy said softly.

Both Debby and Ariana appeared stricken at the remark.

"Oh, *Dios Mio*," Ariana cried out. "I thought he wouldn't want to see us–see me." Tears began to spill down her cheeks.

"Do you think he would see us?" Debby asked.

Peppy nodded. "Yeah. I think he would like that."

"Okay then." Debby turned to Ariana. "Tomorrow let's go right after our biology class."

"Okay." Ariana sniffled, using a napkin to wipe away her tears. She barely dried her cheeks when she broke down and began to sob.

"Ariana," Maria said soothingly as she squeezed her daughter's shoulder. "Trust God."

"Trust God? Mama, we did everything right and look what a mess we're in. All we tried to do was show the effects of GMOs on bees. We just looked for the truth. And while we did find some differences in the effects of the GMO seeds on the bees, we didn't find that the seeds we used in our experiment were all that harmful."

"That's right," Debby agreed. "We followed strict scientific procedures. We documented everything religiously. And now our reputations are ruined, and Luis is in jail for a murder he didn't commit. I'm sorry, Mrs. Alvarez, but it looks like God has abandoned us."

"*Madre de Dios!*" Maria made a sign of the

cross, got up and went to the kitchen. Juan cast a look of apology at Peppy and Razor, got to his feet and followed her.

Peppy placed her elbows on the table and leaned toward her cousin. "Ariana, believe me, things look bad now, but the truth will come out."

"When?" Ariana's face reflected her exasperation. "After we miss a year of school?"

"Or two?" Debby appeared equally frustrated. "And how long will Luis be in prison before the real killer is caught?"

"Look, I know Manelli doesn't believe Luis murdered Rodney," Peppy said.

"But I've watched enough cop shows to know you need other suspects," Debby said, "and so far Luis is the only one."

"Seriously, Peppy," Ariana now leaned forward, her tears gone. "Do they have any other suspects?"

"Professor McNair," Peppy replied.

Both girls let out snorts of disbelief.

"What?" Peppy said. "A witness heard a heated argument between the professor and Rodney."

"McNair couldn't hurt a fly," Debby said with an air of disgust.

"What about Dr. Miller?" Razor asked.

The two girls exchanged a quizzical look.

After a moment, Ariana shook her head. "No, I can't see him doing that."

Peppy leaned back. "Anyway, he has an airtight alibi. He was in Atlanta when Rodney was murdered."

"Wait," Debby said sitting up straight. "That was last Friday, right?"

"Right," Peppy replied.

"I was at McDonald's in Clifton last Thursday night. My cousin works there. I saw Dr. Miller picking up an order at the drive-thru."

Peppy's eyes grew wide. "You're sure?"

"Yeah, I remember, because as he drove through I mentioned it to my cousin. She said, 'Don't they have a McD's in Pineland Park?' Then we joked about how somebody with a PhD had to travel to the next town so they wouldn't be seen eating junk food."

Peppy pulled out her phone. "Or they didn't want to be seen–period." She quickly tapped in a number and waited.

82 CRAZY DOUBTS

The sun had set as Holly neared the planetarium. She was feeling pretty darn good about this meeting. All her work on the letters this afternoon paid off. Yes, at least one good thing happened today.

At the traffic light she glanced up at the overcast sky and realized she'd been wrong about one thing. It might actually be totally dark by the time this meeting with Dr. McNair ended. No matter. She'd ask the Professor to walk her to her car.

As she pulled into the parking lot behind the planetarium, she was relieved to find the usually full lot empty. Great. This was way better than parking in the faculty parking deck and walking the two blocks over, especially since raindrops were beginning to splatter the front windshield.

Holly reached for the umbrella in the door pocket and got out of the car. She moved quickly to the street that ran alongside the planetarium. Except for a couple holding hands and a man walking his dog across Memorial Drive, there was no one in sight.

How different the streetscape appeared in the evening. She rarely came to campus at this time and then only for special events that were well attended. It was difficult to believe this desolate setting was the same one that teemed with life during the day.

When she arrived at the front entrance, she paused and peered through the glass front doors into the lobby. Only a few recessed ceiling lights were on. She pulled out her phone to check for messages. Had the Professor changed his mind? Rescheduled? She tapped the screen and saw no new messages had arrived. Maybe she misread his original invitation, so she pulled that up. No, he definitely wanted to meet with her tonight.

She peeked inside again. Why had McNair asked to meet her here? Why not College Hall or the library? Those buildings were open until nine. A slight shiver ran down her spine and she found herself remembering Ivy's question. Why couldn't this wait until tomorrow?

No. She was certain of one thing. The sooner these recommendation letters were finalized and sent the better off everyone would be. She reached for the brass door handle and smiled when the door opened with ease. As she entered the lobby and the door closed behind her, she paused to listen. Silence.

Maybe she was early. She tucked her mini-umbrella in her handbag and glanced at her watch. The light was so dim she had to walk under the recessed lighting and angle her wrist to see the time. 7:30 on the dot.

"Professor McNair," she called out, her voice echoing through the empty building. No reply. After a few seconds, she repeated more loudly, "Professor McNair!"

"Upstairs!" a male voice finally echoed in reply, startling her.

Holly smiled as she boarded the elevator. This shouldn't take long. When she arrived at the mezzanine, she gazed out the soaring glass windows. It was noticeably darker already and the rain had really begun to come down.

She scanned the mezzanine looking for the Professor but saw no one.

"Professor? Where are you?"

"Inside," the disembodied voice replied.

Holly turned in the direction of the voice and saw the auditorium door open. An uneasy feeling caused her shoulders to tense up. Something about the voice.

She gave herself a small shake. What was wrong with her tonight? Doggone Ivy and Kate! It was all their fault. They're the ones who put these crazy doubts in her head.

With a determined step she headed to the

auditorium. Inside only the stage lights were on. She began to walk down the aisle, when, from behind, a hand grasped her upper left arm. Her pulse began to race as she let out a shrill scream.

83 ON OUR WAY

Nick stared at the computer screen bleary-eyed. Nicky had set him up at his personal laptop to help search through Green Gardyn Foods financial records. After two hours, they hadn't found anything linking anyone at the college with the firm.

"How do you do this all day?" he asked his son.

"It's my job," Nicky replied without taking his eyes off the screen.

Nick grunted. Leaning back in the chair, he smirked. "You know, Holly loves watching those detective shows on television."

Nicky chuckled. "Complex crimes solved in 60 minutes."

"Yep and jam-packed full of exciting action scenes. Those shows would go off the air if they showed that real police work, especially investigations, mostly consists of boring, painstaking grunt work."

"And how much of it sometimes leads nowhere." Nicky let out a weary sigh.

"Maybe we should call it a night," Nick suggested.

Nicky glanced at his watch. "Fifteen more minutes."

Nick shook his head and grinned in grudging admiration as his son continued to study the spreadsheets on his computer. He remembered how surprised he was when Nicky said he wanted to leave a lucrative job with a high-tech firm and join the FBI. To think that his son was worried he wouldn't approve. He couldn't be prouder.

Just as Nick returned his gaze to the laptop screen, his phone signaled. He answered quickly when he saw the caller was Razor.

"Detective, we got some news for you. Dr. Miller was back in town last Thursday night."

Nick sat up straight. "How do you know that?"

"Debby Lewandowski saw him at a McDonald's drive-thru in Clifton."

"She's sure?"

Without a moment's hesitation came the reply. "She's sure."

"Dad, I got something," Nicky said over his shoulder.

"Hold on," Nick said, tapping the mute button as he walked over to Nicky's desk and peered at a spot on the screen where his son pointed to a debit entry. Nick's pulse kicked up a beat as he read: "$90,000 - Dr. Landon Miller - Consulting Services."

He smiled as he squeezed his son's shoulder. "You're gonna love this. Razor's on the phone. We have a witness that puts Miller in town last Thursday night."

It was Nicky's turn to smile. "You got him!"

Nick nodded and unmuted the phone. "Razor, thanks. This is a major break in the case. Keep our witness safe."

"Count on it," Razor said and disconnected.

"What are you going to do now?" Nicky asked.

"Go home and get some rest. I'll pick Miller up in the morning."

"You going to tell Holly?"

"Are you kidding?" Nick asked. "I'd like to get some sleep tonight."

Nick's phone signaled again. "Uh-oh," he said when Ivy's name appeared on the screen.

"What's wrong?" he asked without even a "hello".

"Relax. I'm not sure anything is wrong," Ivy began. "Where are you?"

"Newark," Nick replied. "Where's Holly?"

"Well, that's the thing. She got a text from Professor McNair saying he and Dr. Miller agreed to write the letters of recommendation she drafted this morning."

"Where's Holly?" Nick asked again, an impatient edge to his voice.

"McNair asked her to meet him at the planetarium. She left ..."

Nick disconnected before she finished the sentence.

"What's wrong, Dad?" Nicky asked as his father tapped the phone screen.

Nick gritted his teeth as the call went to voice mail. "Holly, if you get this call, don't go to the planetarium. It could be a trap." Grabbing his jacket, he said, "C'mon," and headed to the elevator at a trot.

Nicky shut down his computer. As he ran to catch up, he saw his father already on another call.

"Razor, get over to the planetarium as fast as you can. Holly could be in trouble. We're on our way."

84 UNEASE

"No need to scream," the male voice said calmly.

"Dr. Miller," Holly said, her heart racing. "You scared me."

The scientist released her arm. "Sorry. I didn't mean to."

"I was expecting Professor McNair, not you." Holly flashed him an apologetic smile. "I know how busy your first day back must have been. Sorry to have added to your workload."

"McNair had some sort of emergency." Miller raised his chin in the direction of the stage, where a table and two folding chairs awaited them. "Let's go up there. I have hard copies of the letters you wrote for us to review."

Holly's breathing returned to normal. "Great."

"You're a gifted writer, Professor," Miller said as he started down the aisle. "Have you ever considered grant writing?"

Holly shook her head. "No. I had a career in marketing. I'm done with that. I really love teaching."

"You'd rather correct all those gawd-awful compositions than just write yourself?" Miller scoffed as they mounted the small staircase to the stage.

"Well, I admit that reading and correcting compositions is not a lot of fun. But I get tremendous satisfaction when I see students' writing improve during the semester."

Miller walked over to the table and pulled out a chair for Holly. As they sat down, he waved his arm over the papers on the table. "These letters show a real aptitude for appealing to the heart as well as the mind. You know, an adjunct's salary is quite low compared to what you could earn in our development office. With your background in marketing, I feel you could take our fund-raising efforts to a whole new level."

Holly was beginning to feel uncomfortable, and she wasn't sure why. "I'm flattered, Dr. Miller, but money really isn't an issue for me." She glanced down at the letter drafts. "Now, Professor McNair said the two of you had some changes you'd like me to make."

When she glanced back at Miller, she was taken aback. His expression seemed almost sinister, but it quickly morphed into what she couldn't help feeling was an insincere smile that didn't reach his eyes as they met hers.

"You're the first person I ever heard say money was insignificant."

"Oh, that's not what I meant." Holly felt increasingly ill at ease. "Of course, it's important. It's just that I'm comfortable with what I have." What was going on here, she wondered. Why was he talking about money?

She pulled the letter drafts closer and began to scan the pages. "I don't see any notations," she said, reaching for her bag and searching for a pen. "Do you want to just tell me the changes you'd like me to make? I can jot them down."

This time when she met his gaze, he did not smile.

"Professor Donnelly, did you know that I had a visit from the Pineland Park police and the FBI today?"

Holly's stomach did a somersault. This is exactly why Nick didn't tell her things. Why did she have to run into him and Nicky this morning? If she hadn't seen them, she wouldn't have to lie. Rather than outright lie, yet unwilling to tell the truth, she simply said, "Why do you ask?"

"They came asking questions about the student GMO experiment. Since you have taken such a personal interest in the matter, I suspect that you are the reason law enforcement officials came to question me." The sinister expression returned to his face.

Holly shifted in her chair. "Well, I–uh–I may have suggested to the students that they contact the federal agencies to see if they'd begun reviewing the experiment results. Um–you, yourself, told me that all the documents had been turned over to the proper authorities." Holly lifted her shoulders in an apologetic shrug.

Miller let out a small, scoffing laugh. "You know, anyone else would have taken that to mean that the case was closed as far as the college was concerned. The average person would have understood that I was telling you to stop meddling."

"I'm sorry," Holly said. "It's just that I want to help Ariana, Debby and Luis."

"Luis?" Miller jerked his head back. "He's a murderer."

Holly felt stung by his words. "But surely you don't believe he killed your assistant!"

"My assistant," Miller sneered. "Another one who couldn't mind his own business."

Holly swallowed hard. Razor's words came back to her. *Sounds like Rodney had something on the professor.* He'd been half right. But Rodney had something on Dr. Miller, not Professor McNair.

Holly pulled the papers toward her and clicked her pen. "So, can we just finish up here? I'd like to get home."

"Ha!" Miller said in a mocking tone. "We're going to finish up here alright, but the outcome depends on you."

"What do you mean?" she asked. The alarm bell clanging somewhere in the back of her brain grew louder.

"If I sign these two letters, will you cease this quixotic quest of yours, drop any further inquiries into the matter and convince the students it's in their interest to do the same?"

"Why would you ask me to do that?" Holly felt the earth shifting beneath her.

"That, my dear, is above your pay grade." Miller glared at her. "But as I alluded to before, your pay grade could be increased significantly if you agree to do what I'm asking."

As Holly made eye contact with the professor, she felt his face now took on a Mephistophelian appearance. Was he actually asking her to sell her soul?

85 PUZZLE PIECES

After a brief pause, Holly said, "Sure. Yes. Of course, I can do that." She was babbling and even before she stopped she knew her answer lacked a shred of credibility.

Miller shook his head in disgust. "Even when your life is on the line, you can't manage to lie with a modicum of conviction."

"My life?" Holly squeaked.

"That's right." Miller's mouth curled in an unpleasant grin. "I'm sorry to have to do this, but you leave me no choice. You simply can't let this go, and I can't let you keep digging. Now pick up those papers and put them in your bag."

"Why? What have you done?" Holly demanded.

Miller glared at her. "You're in no position to make demands, Professor." After a moment he let out a nasty laugh. "Well, what does it matter if I tell you now anyway? Very shortly you won't be able to tell anyone anything."

Holly stared, stunned at his smug expression.

"I have been paid a lot of money by Green Gardyn Foods to make sure the results of that student experiment that you've been so concerned about did not reach the EPA, APHIS and FDC and to destroy any evidence of the student experiment as well. And I will continue to get paid as long as the results of that experiment remain undisclosed."

"So, it's true," Holly said, "Green Gardyn's claims that their seeds are non-GMO are fraudulent."

"Duh!" Miller's expression grew increasingly maniacal. "More than 50 percent of the corn seeds they sell are genetically modified. The results of that student experiment could put them out of business."

"What about ..."

"Enough!" Miller shouted. "Pick up those papers. Now!"

Holly collected the letter drafts. She stuffed them inside her bag and noticed the umbrella. It was the closest thing to a weapon she had. Leaving the bag unzipped, she slipped it over her shoulder and asked, "Now what?"

"Now, we're going to go down the back stairs to your car, so get up."

Holly felt something inside her snap tightly at the command. She was not going to make it easy for him. "And if I refuse to get up?" Holly said, her tone taunting.

Miller reached into his jacket pocket, extracted a shiny object and held it up for her to see. Holly recognized it. A scalpel. Most likely taken from one of the biology labs. Suddenly, another piece of the puzzle fell into place.

"You killed Rodney," she said.

Miller simply glowered at her in reply.

Suddenly Holly remembered the first day she'd met Rodney. "The day before the presentations, Rodney was annoyed when you asked him to get Ariana and her team assistance to recreate their exhibit. He appeared annoyed because he wanted you to find a replacement speaker, but that wasn't it, was it? He was annoyed because you were asking him to undo the damage you ordered him to orchestrate. Was he blackmailing you?"

"Yes, and if you hadn't been on the scene that morning I would have walked away and let him handle things. Instead, I had to be oh-so-sorry for the students, and assist them in any way I could," Miller said in a pseudo-saccharine voice. After a moment, his eyes narrowed. "You're pretty smart, Professor. Too bad it took you so long to figure it out."

"You won't get away with this. My sister knows where I am, and that I came to see you."

"Me? No, you came to see Professor McNair," Miller said with a sly grin. "And best of all, after I get you in the car and slash your throat the way I did Rodney's, the police will start to search for a serial killer–the campus slasher or some other clever sobriquet the media gives him. No one will ever connect your murder or Rodney's to the GMO experiment. Now get up." He pointed the scalpel in the direction of the staircase.

Holly slowly got to her feet and headed in the direction he pointed. As she descended the stage stairs, he grasped the back of her collar. She could feel his breath on her neck.

The umbrella was her only defense, but when would she be able to use it? If she tried to reach into her bag, he'd see it and likely slash her from behind. She couldn't risk it.

When they reached the outer hallway, she asked, "So, you did this all just for the money?"

"Just for the money?" Miller mimicked her, his tone mocking. "What are you some kind of a saint? Money means nothing to you?"

"No, it's just ..."

"Shut up!" Miller sneered. "Keep moving."

When she opened the fire doors to the stairwell, he pushed her toward the steps causing her to trip. She grabbed the rail to steady herself.

"Careful," Miller jeered, pulling more tightly on her collar. "You wouldn't want to die from a fall." His malicious laughter echoed throughout the stairwell.

Holly inhaled deeply and started the descent. The staircase was too brightly lit for her to try to grasp the umbrella. Maybe it was best to wait until they got outside. It was totally dark out now. If she slammed him with her bag, she could maybe break his grip. Then she could run with no stairs or doors to slow her down.

Her heart began to race as they reached the bottom floor. She had to be ready as soon as they stepped outside. It would be her only chance.

"Open the door," Miller ordered.

Edging her right arm up toward the top of her bag, she pushed on the metal bar to open the exit door. As she did, she heard a loud clunk behind her. Miller lunged forward causing her to fall to the pavement. She watched the scalpel skid through a puddle and stop a few feet in front of her.

She scrambled to get out from under her stunned abductor. As she got on one knee, someone came up alongside and helped her to her feet.

"Will you never learn?" her sister asked, then threw her arms around her in a bear hug. As she did, she spun Holly slightly sideways to where a smiling Kate stood brandishing a janitor's broom.

86 UBER

"Guess I swept him into submission, huh?" Kate said with an air of self-satisfaction.

Holly extracted herself from Ivy's embrace and threw her arms around Kate. "I'll never make fun of your use of a broom again."

"Oh, yeah," Kate cast a look of admiration as she twirled the broom in her hand. "I have to get one of these. The wood on this thing makes it much heavier than the average kitchen broom."

As Miller started to get up, Kate said, "Oh no you don't," and gave the back of his head another whack.

"We need to call the police," Holly said reaching into her bag in search of her phone.

"They're on their way," Ivy said. "We already called them."

Holly aimed an amazed stare at her sister. "How did you two get here?"

"We Ubered. How else?" Ivy replied. "Next time you'll listen to us when we say we want to come with you."

"Next time!" Holly shook her head. "There will be no next time."

Ivy and Kate greeted the declaration with skeptical guffaws.

A car pulled into the parking lot just as Dr. Miller, still a tad dazed, attempted to get up again. Kate lowered the broom to his back and said, "Uh-uh. Stay right where you are."

The car doors opened and Peppy and Razor jumped out, rushing to where the women were standing over their vanquished foe.

"*Gracia a Dios*," Peppy said as she surveyed the scene. Her relief quickly morphed into annoyance. "*Mami*, when are you gonna learn?" she said, shaking her head and waving her arms.

Holly sighed and gave a weak smile. "Someday."

Two police cruisers arrived, pulling in on either side of Peppy's car, their lights illuminating the parking lot. Razor reached down, pulled Miller to his feet and dragged him over to the policemen.

Officer Tim Sullivan approached the women, focused on Peppy. "So, Officer Alvarez, what happened?"

Peppy turned to Holly. "Care to explain?"

"Well ..." Holly began.

"Wait," Ivy intervened. "Officer, I think you might want to pick up that scalpel," she said pointing toward the shiny object lying on the pavement.

"Oh, yeah," Holly nodded. "I think that's the murder weapon used to kill Rodney Blakely."

The young policeman looked from Ivy to Holly, his eyes settling on Peppy.

Peppy's left brow shot upward. "Best do what she says, Tim."

"Ortega! Get an evidence bag over here," he yelled over his shoulder.

As he walked to where the scalpel lay, everyone turned when another car, lights flashing, siren blaring, entered the parking lot. The front doors flew open almost before the car came to a stop. Nick and Nicky got out of the car, running.

Nick raced over to Holly and grabbed her by the shoulders. "Are you all right?" he asked studying her face.

Her "yes" got muffled as he pulled her to his chest.

"I can't breathe, Nick."

Not letting go, he loosened his grip.

"You were right," she sniffled. "Dr. Miller killed Rodney. He was behind it all."

Nick gave her a sympathetic nod. "We know."

As she buried her face in his chest, he looked

over at Kate and Ivy. "What are you two doing here?"

"If you hadn't hung up on me," Ivy began, her tone clearly resentful, "I'd have told you that we were in an Uber on our way over to the planetarium when I called you to let you know where Holly was."

"And," Kate stepped forward, "instead of looking at us like we did something wrong, you should be thanking us. We got here first, and I saved your wife's life when I disarmed the perp by hitting him over the head with this." She proudly held the janitor's broom forward as if it were Excalibur.

Nick stared blankly at the broom, then glanced over at Razor who had rejoined the group. "Yep, Miller was already on the ground when we got here," he said.

Nick's glance drifted to Peppy. "Hey, don't look at me. I'm on suspension. You might want to consider hiring bodyguards the next time these three get together."

Without raising her head from where it rested on Nick's chest, Holly grumbled, "Not funny."

The scalpel retrieved and bagged, Officer Sullivan approached Nick. "We need to get statements from everybody, sir."

Nick nodded. "Holly, you have to go with the officer."

"You're not leaving, are you?" she asked, not wanting to let go.

"I need to go question Miller after he's booked.

Nicky will take the three of you home."

She frowned and gave a reluctant nod. "Okay." They exchanged a kiss and she finally let go.

As Holly, Ivy and Kate followed Officer Sullivan, Peppy turned to Nick. "You really think you should be questioning the man who just tried to kill your wife?" she asked.

Nick stared at her for a moment, then pulled out his phone and tapped the screen.

"Yolanda. I need you to meet me at the station ASAP."

87 STATEMENTS

"Mrs. Manelli, please come with me," Officer Sullivan said.

"That's Donnelly," Holly corrected. "I didn't change my name when I got married."

The officer appeared surprised at first, but quickly recovered. "Oh, sorry. Ortega, you take Ms. ..." he paused unsure how to address Ivy.

"I'm Ms. Donnelly also," Ivy replied with a smile.

Not taking any chances this time, he turned to Kate. "And your name?"

"Kate Farmer."

"Washington, you take Ms. Farmer's statement."

Sullivan guided Holly to the police car farthest from the others.

"Okay, so here's what happened," she began without any prompting.

****

Officer Jorge Ortega got Ivy settled in the back of his cruiser and got out his notepad. "Okay, Ma'am. Can you tell me what happened?"

Ivy recounted the evening's events, starting with Holly's announcement that she'd gotten a text asking her to come to the planetarium at 7:30. Ortega was patient as he listened to her describe every agonizing detail of the argument she had with her sister about whether or not to go, followed by the discussion that resulted in her and Kate's decision to Uber to the planetarium. She didn't hold back describing her irritation with her brother-in-law for hanging up on her.

"Okay, Ma'am. What happened when you got here?" Ortega asked in an effort to direct her remarks back to the scene of the crime.

"Well, we got dropped off at the front door. I didn't like the fact that it was dark inside. I wanted to call the police, but Kate insisted there was no time to waste and we had to go inside. So, we tried the door and it was open. We walked around the lobby, but when we didn't see anything, we decided to go up to the second level. I wanted to take the elevator, but Kate insisted we take the stairs. You know, so we wouldn't make any noise. She thinks of everything, Kate does."

At this point, Ivy stopped and stared at the ground as if lost in thought.

"And then what?" Ortega prompted.

Ivy gave herself a small shake. "Yes. Well, when we got to the top of the stairs, we saw the auditorium door was open and so we walked in that direction. As we got closer, we could hear voices, so we tiptoed to the door. We saw Holly and Dr. Miller on the stage. It was odd. They were talking about money. Well, I was about to walk right up to that stage, but Kate grabbed my arm and pulled me back out through the door."

Again, she paused, as she seemed to be picturing the scene in her mind.

"Why is that?" Ortega asked.

"Kate's really smart. She said it might be better if we stayed in the shadows. We could be witnesses to whatever Miller said." Ivy looked directly into Ortega's eyes. "Was she ever right!"

"Why is that?"

"Because we heard Miller admit to murdering Rodney Blakely. When he pulled out the scalpel and said he was going to take Holly down the back stairs to the parking lot and–and," Ivy covered her face with her hands, unable to continue.

Ortega gave her a few moments, then asked, "Did he threaten Ms. Donnelly?"

"Yes, he said he was going to slash her throat, just like he did Rodney," Ivy said, her face reflecting her distress.

"And what did you do?"

"Well, Kate said for me to follow Holly and Dr.

Miller from behind, that she would go back down the way we came up."

"Why did she do that?"

"At the time I didn't know why, but I trust her. As it turns out, she went looking for something to use as a weapon."

"The broom?" Ortega said, the corners of his mouth twitching.

"The broom." Ivy brushed away a tear and let out a weak laugh. "It may sound funny, but it did save my sister's life."

"One thing I don't get," Ortega said. "Why'd you split up? Why didn't you go with her?"

"Oh," Ivy's eyes widened. "Because I was recording the conversation between Holly and Miller on my phone. Did I forget to mention that?"

88 SIMPLE SOLUTION

"We didn't wake you, did we?" Ivy asked as Holly appeared in the kitchen doorway.

"No," her sister replied as she headed straight to the coffee pot and poured herself a mugful.

Kate grimaced. "I thought for sure I woke both you and Nick when I dropped a pot lid in the sink."

"I didn't hear it," Holly said, "and I don't think an earthquake could wake Nick this morning,"

"What time did he get in?" Ivy asked.

"I don't even know. I fell dead asleep as soon as my head hit the pillow."

"So, you don't know if Miller confessed?" Kate said.

Holly frowned. "I think that's highly unlikely. I'm sure he wouldn't talk without a lawyer."

"Well, it doesn't matter," Kate said. "There should be no problem convincing a jury he's gulty, what with the three of us as witnesses to his admission of guilt and Ivy's recording of the conversation."

"And don't forget the murder weapon," Ivy added.

Holly let out a weary sigh. "I just can't believe he could be so, so ..."

"Evil?" Ivy suggested.

"Yeah." Kate nodded. "He's a real Jekyll and Hyde character, isn't he?"

Lucky suddenly got up and ran out into the hall to the front door.

"Guess we've got company," Holly said jumping to her feet. She reached the front door just as Peppy had her finger poised inches from the doorbell.

"Shh." Holly put her index finger to her lips. "Nick's asleep," she whispered. Holding the door open, she waved Peppy and Razor inside.

Ivy jumped up as soon as they arrived in the kitchen, "Good morning. Can I get you coffee? Did you eat breakfast?"

"No thanks," Peppy replied. "We already ate."

"What are you doing up and about so early?" Holly asked. "You couldn't have gotten home any earlier than we did."

"We're headed over to the station to pick Luis up and bring him home," Peppy replied.

"I haven't seen you smile like that in several

days," Holly said.

Razor put his arm around Peppy's waist. "Don't forget the invitation."

"Oh, yeah," Peppy said. "Juan and Maria asked us to invite all of you to dinner at their house tonight for a fiesta to celebrate. Maria's already cooking."

"Authentic Mexican food?" Ivy's eyes widened. "What kinds of desserts will there be?"

"Ivy! Really," Holly said with an admonishing glare.

"What?" Ivy replied. "It's just that I saw a recipe for Tres Leches cake in a magazine and I've always wanted to try it."

"Don't worry, little sister," Razor smiled. "We'll make sure there's Tres Leches cake for you,"

"And Margaritas?" Kate asked.

"And Margaritas," Razor nodded with a small laugh.

A cell phone ding made everyone reach for their phones.

"That's me," Peppy said. "We gotta go. Yolanda just texted that Luis' release papers are ready. Don't want to keep that poor boy waiting."

"No, you don't," Holly said. "Will we see him tonight?"

"I hope so," Peppy replied with a shrug. "But it may take time for him to forgive the girls for not visiting him while he was in jail."

"He'll get over that," Razor said.

Peppy gave him a sideways glance. "You think so? What makes you so sure?"

"He's in love with Ariana," he replied.

"Ah, yes," Ivy nodded with a grin. "There's that."

"Yeah, we'll see." Peppy rattled her car keys. "*Vamos.*"

"See you all later," Razor said as he followed her out the door.

When they heard the front door close, Ivy batted her eyes. "What do you think is going to happen with those two?"

"That's a good question," Kate said. "I was wondering the same thing."

"I can't picture Peppy up in Reddington Manor," Holly said.

"And while I can imagine Razor down here," Kate frowned, "I hate to think what that would do to poor Benny."

"Oh, Benny." Holly appeared suddenly mournful. "I forgot about him."

"But surely, he'd want his friend to be happy. Wouldn't he?" Ivy said.

"He would," Kate agreed, her expression anything but happy.

"There's a simple solution." Holly tilted her

head to the side with a sly grin. "We just have to find Benny a soul mate."

89 HAPPY ENDINGS

Everyone cheered as Juan popped the cork on the champagne bottle. Maria held the glasses as he poured the sparkling liquid, then handed them to Ariana and Debby to distribute among the guests.

Sitting on the couch between Nick and Nicky, Holly said, "I'm so happy the nightmare is finally over."

"You're happy?" Nick and Nicky said simultaneously.

Holly laughed. "Ivy and I may look alike, but you two are twin souls."

The cheerful chatter ceased as Juan raised his glass and said, "I like to make a toast. To family ..." His eyes misted as he looked at Maria, Ariana and Peppy. "And ..." his voice cracked. "And to good friends." This time his eyes zeroed in on Holly. "*Salud.*"

"*Salud,*" everyone echoed, and after a few sips the laughter and chatter resumed.

"So, Nicky," Holly said. "How long will you be working from Newark? You know, you haven't been over to the house for a proper meal with us."

"Well, here's the thing, " he began. "We've arrested two Ecolyte members and I've still got to sift through hundreds of additional emails and texts to determine if there are others we need to charge in connection with the warehouse explosion. Unfortunately, I return to Washington tomorrow."

"Oh no," Holly said.

"Nicky! Come here," Peppy called and waved him over to where she and Razor stood with a smiling Ariana and Luis.

"Excuse me," he said as he got up.

Holly smiled. "Looks like Razor was right."

"About what?" Nick asked.

"Well, Peppy wasn't sure if Luis would want to come tonight because he'd been pretty upset that Ariana and Debby hadn't called or visited him while he was in jail. Razor said he'd get over that because he was in love with Ariana."

"By the looks of it, she's in love with him too," Nick said taking another sip of champagne.

Holly's smile faded. "I hate that Nicky has to go back tomorrow."

"Hey, duty calls." Nick shrugged and gave her shoulder a comforting squeeze.

"And what about you, Detective?" Holly asked. "I won't ask about retirement plans, but any chance you can take a few days off now that you caught your killer?"

"Maybe," he replied.

"Really?" Holly said, clearly not expecting the answer she got. "Can we plan a little getaway? Just the two of us?"

"Yeah. Just the two of us. I think I'd like that. It may be the only way I can keep you out of trouble."

As Holly poked him in the ribs, Ivy walked over with a huge slice of Tres Leche cake. "Oh, my goodness. You have got to taste this cake. It's to die for."

Both Holly and Nick stared back at her with deadpan expressions.

"Oops. Bad choice of words, huh?"

The doorbell rang and Juan went to the door. Conversation ceased as Brittany and George Holzman walked in.

After a moment, Luis said, "You have a lot of nerve coming here," his tone anything but welcoming.

Brittany shifted uncomfortably from one foot to the other. "I know," she said. "I've come to apologize for ..."

"We don't want your apology," Luis said even more fiercely. "And why aren't you still in jail?"

Brittany moved forward. "Look, you have every reason to be mad at me, but not my brother. For your information, he's not in jail because he received whistle-blower status. He risked his life and career trying to do the right thing."

"And what about you?" Luis asked.

"Both my brother and I were set up to take the fall for the Green Gardyn explosion. We had nothing to do with it. Green Gardyn hired a guy to infiltrate Ecolyte. He's the one who sent me the email telling me to show up at the warehouse the night of the explosion and sent the fake video to the police. The FBI has cleared both me and my brother." After a moment, she turned to George. "Maybe this was a bad idea."

"No," he said, stepping forward. "No matter what they think of us they need to hear what we have to say."

Luis was about to speak again, but Kate grasped his arm. "Let them talk. It can't hurt to hear them out."

Luis sighed with disgust and stepped back. "Go ahead," Kate said. aiming a sympathetic nod at the sister and brother.

George began. "Our father went to Cornell University. He's friends with the president." He nudged his sister.

Brittany continued. "He talked to the president and they've invited us to come up and do a presentation at the College of Agriculture and Life Sciences."

"What kind of presentation?" Ariana asked.

"They want us to do the same presentation we did at the Eco-Fair, but they also want us to talk about what happened to us," Brittany said.

"You mean we get to tell our side of the story?" Debby asked.

"Yes," Brittany replied, "and I've turned over all of the documentation from our experiment to APHIS, EPA and the Food and Drug Administration. Dad says Cornell intends to invite them to speak as well."

Debby turned to face Ariana and Luis. "We have to do this. Cornell is the best agricultural school in the country. After presenting there, we could apply to the top schools and we'd probably get accepted anywhere we want to go."

"And our scholarships to the schools where we've already been accepted?" Luis asked.

"That's another thing," Brittany said. "My father said he'll speak to whomever he has to. He'll make sure the scholarships you've already been offered are honored."

Ariana and Debby looked to Luis, who nodded his assent.

"We accept," Ariana said.

Juan, who'd remained by the door throughout the conversation, walked over and put his arms around George and Brittany. "Come. Eat," he said, guiding them over to the table still laden with an assortment of Maria's specialties.

"Well, this night just can't get any better, can it?" Holly said nestling closer to Nick.

"I can think of one way it can get better," he said.

"How?"

"Let's go home and I'll show you," he whispered in her ear.

Holly giggled. "We can't leave now. How will Ivy and Kate get home?"

"I already told Nicky to drive them," he said as he got up and reached for her hand.

Holly grinned as she clasped his hand and got to her feet. "Well, I do love a happy ending."

THE END

Dear Reader:

Thank you so very much for reading this lastest book in the Holly and Ivy Mystery Series. If you missed any of the Donnelly Sisters' earlier adventures, the titles and links to where you can find them follow this page.

I'm not sure yet, where the next Holly and Ivy adventure will be set, but wherever that is, you can be sure there will be gardens growing. In the meantime, you can find me writing an occasional post on my blog: "On Writing, Reading and Retirement". Also, check out The Adventures of Trixie on Kindle Vella written by my faithful companion.

I always love hearing from readers, so feel free to contact me at sally@sallyhandley.com. To receive announcements when I publish something new, please follow, friend or connect with me at the following places:

- Follow me on Amazon
- Follow me on Goodreads
- Like me on Facebook
- Subscribe to my Youtube channel

Happy Reading!

Sally Handley

BOOKS IN THIS SERIES

The Holly & Ivy Mystery Series
Holly and Ivy Donnelly are middle-aged sisters and avid gardeners. At the start of the series, they're both at a stage in life when they are feeling vulnerable about the aging process. As a result of being drawn into murder investigations, both sisters find inner strength, renewed purpose and romance, experiencing a renaissance at an age when many choose to accept the limitations of aging. Holly and Ivy may not have superpowers, but their unique life experience helps them to help others.

Second Bloom

Frost On The Bloom

Full Bloom

Murder Under Tuscan Blooms

The Blooming Treasure Murder

The Mystery Of The Bogus Blooms

ACKNOWLEDGEMENT

Writing a book is a lonely endeavor, but throughout the process a writer needs the help of others in order to complete the project and get it ready to publish.

With me from the very start has been my good friend and alpha reader, Nina Augello. Without her pep talks, I would probably have abandoned writing long ago. She keeps me on track and moving forward every step of the way. Also, I confess that some of the best lines in my books have rolled off her silver tongue.

Also, with me from book one has been Steven Miller. Steve is both my beta reader and proofreader. But he's so much more. Steve provides valuable insights and comments, as well as words of encouragement,

A more recent addition to my team is Joanne Scuderi. Her editing expertise (https://www.joannemanse.com/) and her pointed comments and constructive criticism are greatly appreciated.

As always, Carol Monahan, graphic artist extraordinaire, has designed a gorgeous cover. As I've said before, no one can consistently translate my ideas into images better than Carol. (www.carolmonahandesign.com)

This 6th book in the Holly & Ivy series required a special addition to my team. I owe a world of gratitude to Lauren Tereshko, a science teacher, SNHS moderator, the St. Gianna Molla Life Sciences Schola academic coordinator, and moderator of the Go Green Club at Immaculate Heart Academy in Bergen County, NJ. Early on when I realized I didn't know as much about GMOs as I thought I did, Lauren spent time helping me get some key concepts straight. She also was instrumental in coming up with the science fair project worked on by the students in my story. I couldn't have written this book without her help.

I also owe a special debt of gratitude to my Cozy Mystery critique partners whose genuinely constructive critiques and suggestions make me a better writer.

- Judy Buch (www.judybuch.com/)
- Cindy Blackburn (cueballmysteries.com)
- Wayne Cameron, author of the Melvin Motorhead Series

Finally, thanks to Sisters in Crime (Sistersincrime.org) and Malice Domestic. I appreciate the many kindred souls these organizations have linked me with, both published and unpublished writers, who constantly amaze me with their generosity of spirit and willingness to share their knowledge and experience.

ABOUT THE AUTHOR

Sally Handley

A member of Sisters in Crime and the Public Safety Writers Association, Sally Handley is author of the Holly & Ivy cozy mystery series and the stand-alone suspense novel, Stop the Threat.

Additionally, Sally also writes a series on Kindle Vella entitled The Adventures of Trixie, written from her faithful companion's point of view. She also writes a blog entitled "On Writing, Reading and Retirement" at www.sallyhandley.com.

Sally hosts a monthly, on-line Mystery Book Club. Recordings of Mystery Book Club discussions can be viewed on her Youtube Channel at https://www.youtube.com/ @sallyhandley.